Pull

By Kevin Waltman

Cinco Puntos Press
El Paso ✸ Texas

FIRST EDITION
10 9 8 7 6 5 4 3 2 1

LIBRARY OF CONGRESS CATALOGING-IN-PUBLICATION DATA

Names: Waltman, Kevin.
Title: Pull / by Kevin Waltman.
Description: El Paso, Texas : Cinco Puntos Press, 2015. | Series: D-Bow's high school hoops ; [3] | Summary: "Junior year. Derrick 'D-Bow' Bowen has worked hard for two years getting ready for this season. He earned his coach's trust and his role as the starting point guard for Marion East. But dissension and selfishness are threatening to tear the team apart." —Provided by publisher.
Identifiers: LCCN 2015024953| ISBN 9781941026274 (paperback) | ISBN 9781941026267 (hardback) ISBN 9781941026281 (e-Book)
Subjects: | CYAC: Basketball—Fiction. | High schools—Fiction. | Schools—Fiction. | African Americans—Fiction. | BISAC: JUVENILE FICTION / Sports & Recreation / Basketball. | JUVENILE FICTION / Boys & Men. | JUVENILE FICTION / People & Places / United States / African American. | JUVENILE FICTION / Social Issues / General (see also headings under Family). Classification: LCC PZ7.W1728 Pu 2015 | DDC [Fic]—dc23
LC record available at http://lccn.loc.gov/2015024953

Book and cover design by Anne M. Giangiulio.
Bubba always has his opinions, right, Anne?

Special thanks to Rick Ray and John Kitch for their advice and consultation. You are both good men and good friends. And thank you, of course, to the good people at Cinco Puntos Press for giving my work a shot. —Kevin Waltman

For Holling Fordham Waltman

PART I

1.

It's a crime to make us go back to school this early. August 2? *Crazy*.
I bet some sadistic guy sitting behind a desk just hating on people
thought that one up. Probably hasn't been outside in months, gets no
female attentions, gets cracked on from his boss, then thinks—*Yeah, I'll
show everyone. Kick kids back to school on August 2.*

So it's the last night of freedom for me and Wes. We just cruise.
It's a sweaty, still night. The a/c in this old Nova handed down to me
from Uncle Kid can barely keep up.

"Wanna hit 38th?" I ask. "Get our feed on?"

"Nah. Ain't hungry."

The summer ripped past us like a driver barreling baseline. Just
gone. I tore it up in AAU again, making all the scouts' eyes bug. But it
meant the same old—less time at home, less time with Wes, chasing
Jasmine with no good luck. At least I found time to get my license this
time around.

"What about the mall? See what's up there?"

"Nah," Wes snorts. "What are we, twelve? No mall, D."

Kevin Waltman

Wes sags down in the passenger's side, sneering at the night like it's insulted him somehow. He doesn't mean it with me, I don't think, but he's just always sour. He's barely got fifteen more pounds on that frame from when we started high school, but it's like everything he's added has been attitude.

"Well, what then?" I ask. I sound a little snippy, I know, but hanging with Wes isn't supposed to be some chore. It's supposed to be easy. Fun.

He points to his phone, which just thrummed with a text. "JaQuentin's got something happening," he says.

Now he's really killing me. JaQuentin Peggs? I wish I'd never heard his name. It's like he's re-shaped my boy Wes into some wannabe banger. And I know what it'll be at that place—a half-dozen guys blazing up until some worse idea makes its way into one of their thick skulls. I smell it on Wes again, too—weed. Not that anyone gets themselves worked up over that, but I'm tired of picking up Wes and seeing his eyelids at half-mast, tired of that sweet-sick dope smell on his clothes.

We cruise up College, making one side of our square that goes up to 38th and then back down to 22nd. I know where JaQuentin's is—just a couple blocks over on 32nd if I hang a left, but I've got no interest. Then we're past 33rd—a right there and we'd be at Moose's place, right at Carrolton. But no more. He's packed off to Ball State, trying to walk on to the team. His absence just makes the night feel heavier, more oppressive. Every block we pass seems desolate, maybe just one or two people out, sweating on their porches and giving menacing looks as we cruise. It's the kind of night where one wrong word would be like gasoline on a fire.

"D, if you gonna punk out on JaQuentin's, then just drop me there," Wes says.

"What the hell, Wes?" I snap. "Last night of summer and you want to spend it in a bad mood?"

He leans back just a little further in his seat. It takes an effort, but he manages to lodge his foot up on the dash, just to piss me off. I know this car's a bucket, but it's still mine. I smack him on the shoulder. "Get your foot down. Have some respect."

Wes just grumbles and then, the seat squeaking under him, gets his left foot up there too. It's a crazy uncomfortable position, and I have to almost respect him for going to those lengths just to get under my skin. Still.

This time I reach over and grab his ankle, lift it off the dash and throw it down where it belongs. We swerve to a stop at the Fairfield light. Wes unbuckles and makes like he's going to get out. "You gonna be that way?" he says. "I'm out."

Before he can open the door, I mash it. In the Nova, that only means we lurch ahead and then almost stall out when the transmission shudders under the strain. It's enough to send Wes flopping back in his seat though. Point made.

"I'm not trying to cause static," I say. "I just thought we could hang like we used to."

"Used to ain't..." But then Wes trails off. He was going to keep after me, but maybe he's thought better of it. Maybe I can get the old Wes back after all. He sighs. Out of the corner of my eye, I see him grin. "Used to be you didn't get yourself in a hissy fit just for a brother propping his feet up."

Kevin Waltman

He makes a big show of it now, bending his knees and plopping those Timberlands on my dash with two successive thuds. This time it's all play. I do my part, acting like I'm going to rip his feet right back where they belong again, but he swats at my hand. I try again, shouting at him that he better get those boots off my dash if he wants to keep his feet attached to his body, but I'm laughing as I say it.

It's all good, until I hear it: that quick *whup-whoop* behind me. Then the interior of my car gets lit in flashing red and blue. I know what's up, but I check the rear view just in case, hoping that the cop is after someone else, maybe responding to a call from 38th. No luck. He's right on my tail. We weren't doing anything wrong, but both Wes and I instinctively straighten in our seats. As I ease to the side of the road, I feel my heart pound. My tongue gets thick in my mouth.

Wes fidgets in his seat, getting more nervous with each second. I know the officer's just checking tags, biding his time. But Wes keeps whipping his head around to look, squinting into the glare of lights. "You weren't doing shit," he says. "This is profiling, man. This is bullshit." There's a jangling anxiety in his voice, and it infects me—like the more he claims we're the ones being wronged the more I think I might be in real trouble.

"Just be cool," I say. I really don't want Wes to go all thug mode on a policeman. The way he's been acting lately, you never know.

The officer approaches. I roll down the window and look up at him hopefully. Here I am, all 6'3" of me crammed into this Nova. If I stepped out, I'd tower over that officer. But as is, I feel like a child, impossibly small under his gaze. He gets close—he's thick through the body, some dough on his gut but a big broad chest that says you don't want to mess with him—and leans down. He flashes his light into the car. Wes and I both look away.

"Been drinking tonight?" he asks.

"No, sir," I say.

"Then what were those swerves back there?" He tilts his head back toward the blocks behind us. He must have seen us veering all over the place. My shoulders relax a little. *That's it.* Just those swerves and the sudden start. Hell, maybe it means I get a ticket, but if that's all he's after then I can relax. It's not like we even *did* anything, but you get that police cruiser on your tail and you start imagining crimes—like somehow you robbed a bank and just forgot about it.

"I'm sorry, sir, we were messing around." I start to explain what had happened, but I realize the officer isn't even listening to me. Instead, he's locked in on Wes.

Wes won't look up. He's got his hands in his lap now, nervously picking at one of his nails.

"You have some marijuana in there?" the officer asks. It's more a statement than a question. I start to stammer out a *no*, but he asks to search the vehicle before I can get out word one. Wes tries to tell me something under his breath, but I can't hear it. I just tell the officer *okay.* As soon as that's out of my mouth, Wes lets loose a big, disappointed sigh, like I'm the stupidest guy on the planet.

He makes us wait until a second cruiser arrives for backup. It makes it look like some big bust, so everyone passing slows to a crawl and stares. I hope like crazy nobody recognizes me. That's all it would take to get Twitter popping in the worst way. Then the second officer—he's not as muscular as the first, but he's got a military stare in

Kevin Waltman

his eyes—instructs us to sit on the curb while the first one searches my car. Sure enough, once he's been rummaging around the passenger side for a minute he gives this real pleased shout to his partner—"Well, look here!"—and holds up a cellophane bag.

I've never touched weed in my life, but any fool knows what it is. And any fool knows where it came from. I steal a glance at Wes. He looks away. He better not believe for a second that I'm taking the fall for him.

The police finish with the car and then start on us. We get the full treatment—hands laced behind our heads while they frisk us top to bottom. You hear about things like this—how humiliating a pat-down is—but it's just noise on the news until it's happening to you. The first officer does me, and he's not exactly gentle about it. He just gets all up into me. But I'm clean. And so is Wes—probably since he deposited whatever he was holding in my passenger seat.

Finally the first officer addresses us both. He holds up the weed. "This belong to both of you or just one?" he asks. I don't want to rat Wes out, but he doesn't seem too eager to step up. The officer must see me glance Wes' way, because he takes a step in his direction. "This yours, little man?" he asks.

Wes looks down at his shoes. I can see his shoulders tense on that *little man*. I'm afraid he's going to say something stupid. He shakes his head a couple times in disgust. Then, at last, he mutters something. The officer asks him to repeat himself and speak up. Wes lifts his chin about an inch and mumbles, "I don't know where that came from."

Wes doing me dirty like that is the biggest disappointment of all. He must know it, because he won't even turn his head my way.

"Fine," the officer snorts. "We'll sort this out at the station."

There's no excuse in the world that will work on my parents. I mean, I could have documented proof that the CIA planted the drugs on Kid two decades ago and it was still in the car through none of my own doing, but Thomas and Kaylene Bowen aren't gonna hear it.

Back at the station, Mom waited in the car. Dad came in and was about to bust. To anyone in uniform he was all *yes, sir*, but he turned that gaze at me and it looked like he'd been stung by a wasp. And he's the easy parent.

We got out of the station without much more hassle. I didn't see Wes again, but he finally manned up before I had to turn on him. All I got was a charge of Unsafe Lane Movement, plus a couple lectures. As we walked out of that station, Dad practically shook with anger. "Derrick, your mother," he seethed at me, "is about—." And he trailed off, unable to even finish the sentence.

I climbed in the backseat, right behind my mom. Squeezing in back there pushes my knees up near my chest, but I knew that ride wasn't designed for my comfort. We cruised a couple blocks in silence. Then my mom slowly turned in her seat to look at me. Even in the dark, I could tell she'd been crying—but I could also tell she was ready to kill.

Now it's super late. Last I looked at my watch it was 1:00, but even that glance got Mom mad. "Pay attention, Derrick," she said. So I don't dare look again. We're at the kitchen table, still hashing it out. There's a single lamp on. My parents pace through the shadows.

"What were you *thinking?*" Mom asks. It's now about the fifth time she's hit me with it. She stares at me intently, her face like a sphinx.

Again, I try to explain. "It wasn't *mine*. Wes even told the police."

"Oh, I *know* that," Mom snaps. "Believe me, if it was yours, you'd be in for a lot rougher night than this one. But there were drugs in your car, Derrick. That's on you."

I've had about enough. My shoulders get tighter and tighter each time we go around the same conversation. Finally, I just put my head down on the table. I turn it to the side, staring across the kitchen at the refrigerator. It used to be decorated with drawings from Jayson or report cards from me. "How is it on me?" I ask. "I can't be in charge of what Wes does."

Mom *flips*. "You're in charge of who gets in your car!" she shouts. "You've been raised to have enough sense to know what your friends are up to! And you should know that if Wes is fooling around with drugs then he's not your friend."

"Mom," I say, "Wes is the best friend I've got."

"Not anymore!" she shouts.

This draws Jayson out from his room. He rubs his eyes to give the impression that he just woke up, but I bet he's been eavesdropping for a while. It's not like our house holds back sound that well. He doesn't say anything, but when he sits on the recliner there's a little squeak from the springs.

Both our parents turn. Dad points toward the hallway. "You've got about three seconds to get back down to your room," he says.

Jayson's eyes widen. He looks genuinely worried. He's usually one to aggravate things further, but this time he does as he's told. He pops off that chair and slinks back toward his room. Now both Mom and Dad shake their heads. I realize the look instantly—they're sorry for having jumped Jayson when he didn't really do anything wrong.

"I'll go talk to him," Dad says to Mom. They both cut their eyes at me, like this is my fault too. At this point, I'm pretty sure that if a tornado ripped through downtown Indy, my parents would blame it on the fact that I let Wes into my car with pot.

"Get to bed," Mom snaps at me. As I stand, she gives me a parting shot. "This isn't over," she says.

Kevin Waltman

2.

First, no car. Not until Christmas. Mom slapped that one on me first thing this morning. So I'm back to bumming rides or hoofing it, like I'm a freshman again.

Second, no Wes. That was my dad's order. He didn't give a timetable, but it's not like I'm in some hurry to kick it with Wes anyway.

But now, it's Coach Bolden's turn. On the first day of school, I'm already in his office. Getting called in is starting to seem like an annual ritual. He doesn't waste any time. "I've already heard about what happened last night," he says. "I just want to see if you have any explanation."

It's the kind of opening my parents never gave me—some room to tell my side of things. Then again, this is Coach Bolden we're talking about. There's no easy road here. He listens patiently while I tell him that I had no idea that Wes had weed on him. Then he even nods along while I explain that the only thing I did wrong was swerve a little bit while a cop was watching. But when I'm done, he leans forward and jabs his index finger down on his desktop. "One game," he says. He raises that finger and points it at me. "You sit."

I flop back in my chair and turn my palms up. "What?" I ask. "I didn't even *do* anything." I know that tone will work about as well on Coach Bolden as it did on my parents, but at this point I don't care. I really can't believe people are crashing down on me this hard for something someone else got busted for.

To my surprise, Bolden doesn't lose it on me. Instead, he shakes his head patiently. He runs his hand across his bald dome and then squeezes the back of his neck, like he's trying to rein himself in. Then he leans forward again. No finger jabs. No raising his voice. "Derrick," he starts, "there are a bunch of coaches in this state who wouldn't care that you wound up in jail last night. They wouldn't care if the drugs *were* yours. Hell, they'd barely care if you were selling. They'd only care about getting you in uniform for the season." I cross my arms and look away. I want to say, *Well, yeah. That's what a good coach does.* But instead I just take what's coming. "I care more about this school, about the way we want to do things, than I care about that first game," he says. Then he narrows his eyes, digging into me just a little. "And I sure as hell care about those things more than I care if your feelings get hurt."

I scan the wall behind him. Bare. Most coaches would have plaques or trophies or some kind of mementos from their best seasons. For Bolden the reminder of his best seasons is right in front of him. I'm the one that gave him two straight sectional titles and a regional title. And I'm the one who can get him a big, fat state championship ring this year. Still, I had my chance to get out from under his wing. I could have transferred, but I didn't. So now getting mad at Coach Bolden's discipline would be like getting mad at the winter for being cold. "Okay, Coach," I say. "I'm sorry." Really, what else can I say at this point?

Bolden flashes a brief smile and then yanks open a desk drawer. "I want you to understand something," he says. Out comes a folder. He slaps it on the desk and opens it. Inside are a few pages with my name at the top. I can tell right away they're game logs—full stats for every game I played my first two years at Marion East. Bolden drags his finger across the page like he's reading a medical chart. "There's so much to like here," he says. "Probably why you've got a big stack of mail from schools all over the country. But you know what it tells me?"

He eyeballs me, but I don't answer. He keeps looking at me now, even though his finger is still trailing across the page.

"It tells me your high school career is halfway over," he says. "That means two things, Derrick. The first is that now you're an upperclassmen and a leader. I can't take it easy on you. I have to come down on you or every other player on the team will test me. But the second is more important to you. Being a junior means the word *potential* no longer applies. As a freshman, everyone looked past it when you had a bad night. Last year, when you struggled for a month, nobody recruiting you blinked. Get a technical? Cough up six turnovers? Didn't matter—because you had *potential*. Well, you hit junior year and nobody talks about potential anymore. They want to see results. So listen." He leans forward a few inches further, like he's going to reach across the desk and grab me by the collar if I don't pay attention. "None of those schools will stop recruiting you for what happened last night. They sure didn't cool on you even after you got outplayed in State last year by the Kernantz kid at Evansville Harrison. But if you keep screwing up—you're the one with weed on you next time or you start a fight on the court or you have a string of bad games—a few of them are gonna stop coming after you. They'll start thinking you're just one more guy who never lived up to his potential."

With that, he points to his door. Conversation over. As I leave, though, he gives me one parting shot. "You're a big boy now, Derrick. That means you have to be on it all the time."

Damn. Welcome to junior year.

Of course Uncle Kid's waiting for me outside school. He's styling, sporting a button-down with a flashy pattern. It's a little oversized, its short sleeves rippling in the breeze. It hangs down over his freshly purchased khakis. He's leaning against his new ride—a bright red Chrysler 300—and the sun reflects off his shades. He looks like a million bucks. He can't be raking in all *that much* at his bartending gig.

"D-Bow!" he shouts, loud enough for everyone filing out of Marion East to hear. "Let's take a ride, man." He gazes up into the cloudless sky. "I know you're in school, but the weather says it's still summer." Like a chauffeur, he opens the passenger door and motions for me to get in.

Any fool would know Kid's not just here to take his nephew on a quick cruise. Everyone's got a point to make to me today. But his smile's infectious, so I hop in. Kid trots around to the other side, climbs in and fires up that engine. He gives it a good rev, then pulls out with some velocity. All along the street, heads turn. He's not rocking some Benz, but it's a sweet ride and people notice.

Kevin Waltman

Kid takes a left on 36th and then another on Meridian, taking us south into the city. He smoothes his hand across the dash as delicately as if he were petting a cat. "What do you think?" he asks.

"Not bad," I say.

"Not *bad*?" he sneers.

"All right, Kid," I tell him. "You're killin' it in this ride."

Kid nods, pleased with himself. He lowers his window and loops his arm out along the side. Ever since he started working, he's been all puffed up—both in terms of ego and body. In less than a year's time, he's packed some thickness on his frame. He's not fat, but to see a belly starting to poke out on a guy once as rail-thin as Kid is a surprise. We give him never-ending grief about it, but he just laughs it off. He'll just pat his stomach and tell us some extra poundage is proof he's living right.

We zip downtown. The buildings seem to rise up around us, all those windows reflecting the sun. It makes me wonder sometimes what's going on inside them—people making high finance deals or having late afternoon drinks or scheming white-collar crimes? I don't know—the life inside of them is a total mystery to me.

Kid takes us straight down to the city center, circling around the monument, before kicking us a couple blocks east—right smack at the entrance to Banker's Life Fieldhouse. He points as we roll past. "There's the dream, D-Bow," he says. "Suiting up in that Pacer uni someday. Ballin' out on the biggest stage."

I nod, pretend like I'm into it. Sure, I have my NBA dreams. And, yeah, I fantasize about getting drafted by the Pacers. But I've been on enough of these drives around town with Kid to know that he's up to something else.

Pull   21

"You think about where you'll go in between now and then?" he asks.

"College?"

"What else?" he says. While we're idling at a light, he leans over like he's letting me in on a secret. "And, man, you know your mom is gonna get all up in that decision. You *know* she's not gonna let you go somewhere you can just skip classes for a year before bolting."

I have to laugh a little at that. It's as true as anything Kid's ever said. Then I tell him what I'm thinking—namely, I have no idea about where I want to play in college. Indiana's pushing hard, and I'm most definitely interested. They've got the history, they've got Big Ten competition, they've got an energetic coach who knows his stuff. It's where about 80 percent of Indiana high school players dream of going—but I can't shake the feeling that maybe I should do something *different*. Like maybe I should see some other part of the country and play where I won't get compared to every other point guard in Indiana history. I don't get into all the details with Kid, but he feels me.

"It's a tough call," he says. "I remember when I was your age— had everyone begging me to come to their campus. But, man, they all say the same things. Gets to the point where you can't tell West Lafayette from West Virginia after a while."

It's strange to hear Kid talk about this. Now, he'll talk your ear off about what a baller he was way back when. But he usually doesn't get into what happened at the end of his high school career. In fact, I only know the basics—run-ins with Coach Bolden, suspensions, more trouble, until all that heavy recruiting he's talking about dried up.

We turn left on Delaware, but Kid gets into the far right lane and

Kevin Waltman

creeps. "Problem is I spent more time there—" he jabs his index finger violently toward my window—"than I did at any college." I look and see the county courthouse. Damn. He got me talking about hoops and I almost forgot what was going on—it's another lecture. Maybe Kid senses my disappointment, because he steps on the gas and raises his voice. "Listen, D. Nobody's ever scored a bucket while they're sitting in lock-up."

With Kid, I know I can fight back a little. "Man, everyone's acting like I killed somebody. It was *weed*. The stuff's legal most places. And it wasn't even *my* weed. All I got in the end was a traffic citation. People need to chill the hell out."

Kid nods. He changes lanes and picks up more speed, racing to beat a light. "I know it, D," he says. "But that's how it starts, how it was with me."

"What you mean?" I ask. Everyone still talks around what happened with Kid, always stopping short of coming out with the details.

He holds up his hand to cut me off. "Ah, I'm not getting into all that again. Not twenty years later. All I'm saying is that I might not know as much as I let on about basketball—but I know a thing or two about derailing a career. So listen. You might think Wes is your boy, but you try dragging him along with you, it's gonna be like trying to dunk with sandbags tied to your ankles. If that kid's dead weight, you got to cut him loose."

This—more than the fear the cops tried to put in me, more than my mom's righteous anger, more than Coach's warnings—sinks in. I still don't think I did anything that wrong, but I realize Kid's got a point. At the same time, I don't see how I can drop Wes without tearing off a part of myself. We ride for a while in silence, all that static filling the air. Finally, we cross over Michigan and Kid's had enough serious time. He puts down the windows and starts some beats on his crack sound system. No more old CDs like he used to roll with—now he's got an iPod in the jack, like he's finally joined life in the twenty-first century.

Kevin Waltman

3.

The only event that shook things up was when the calendar hit September 9. Open season for recruiting a junior. And, man, the phone flat *blew up*. I didn't even think that many people in the world had our number. But it rang off the hook. And then it shifted to my cell phone.

Everyone warned me, but I didn't realize how relentless coaches can be. The big names are putting their assistants after me, so I haven't talked to guys like Calipari or Pitino or Krzyzewski yet. Maybe they think they're above it all. But at places like Clemson and VCU and Iowa State, the head man himself has been on with me. And Indiana—Coach Crean called me personally, but I bet that's just because I'm in-state.

For now, I'm just hearing them all out, telling them I'm a long way off from making a decision. And that's the truth. I'm taking everything slow. When I have news for schools, it's coming through Coach or my folks. That's the way we set it up in the summer. I even squashed my Twitter and Facebook so I wouldn't send out something that got taken the wrong way. Besides, like my mom said, when's the last time something good came out of a young athlete being on Twitter? And we decided—all of us together—that we're playing things the right way. No freebies, no payouts, no kickbacks. I know that's not how the game's played these days, but that's how it gets played when your parents are Tom and Kaylene Bowen.

But tonight's the first practice, so I'm that's all that's on my mind when I hit the cafeteria. Then I see Wes. It's not that he's just a friend. That makes it sound like we hang sometimes on weekends, catch each other at parties, and say 'sup when we pass in the halls. He is *the* friend in my life. I mean, I can't remember a time when Wes and I weren't tight. Mom tells me that even before we could walk, we were hanging together. Wes' mom would drop him off at our place and we'd crawl around the living room getting into trouble. To me, Wes is more blood than friend.

So it kills me—just kills me—to see him catch my eye in the lunch room and then look away. He spins on his heel and makes tracks for a far table. Watching him do that makes me feel like a bone is breaking. It hurts worse than when he didn't own up to the weed. Around me, Marion East churns on—students shuffle through the lunch line with their trays in their hands, teachers hover around the edges of the cafeteria on the lookout for trouble, and the whole room swells with the fast chatter of people spreading gossip. Meanwhile, I'm standing there like my feet are made of stone while I watch Wes bail on me.

"D-Bow!" Someone shouts, calling me by my nickname. "Over here," another voice calls. I turn and see our two bigs—Chris Jones and Tyler Stanford—waving to me. They're all amped for tonight. They've got some space cleared out for me at a table with a few cheerleaders.

Kevin Waltman

That's where I belong. I head that way. But then something stops me, like there's a hook lodged in the fabric of my shirt. My parents have banned me from hanging with Wes on our own time. If I walk away now, maybe that's it. If he doesn't want to hash it out, then I've got to be the man in the situation. Otherwise, what? Wes and I are through? No deal.

I stride across the cafeteria, confident as if I'm walking to the stripe to ice a game. I get to Wes and stand over him. Below me, he looks smaller than usual. He's hunched over his tray, trying to just ignore everything and everyone. So I sit down next to him, putting us closer to an even level. "Wes," I say, "man, we got to talk. It's been a month."

He drops his fork on his tray with a clatter. He pushes back from the table. "Talk about what?" he asks. He looks down at his watch, like he's late to some important meeting. All I notice is that it's a pretty heavy piece—way out of Wes' price range.

"What is *up* with you?" I ask. I raise my voice more than I intended, and I can feel the attention of the cafeteria settle on us. So I try to act chill. I lean back in my chair and shrug. "I mean, seriously, why you getting all worked up on *me?*"

Finally, Wes relents. His shoulders slump down and he sighs. "Man, I'm just pissed at the world these days," he says. "It's got nothin' to do with you."

I don't jump on him right away. Dealing with Wes these days is like handling a lit firecracker. "I feel you," I say. "But, man—and I'm not trying to get all up on you—if you put weed in my car, then it has a *lot* to do with me."

Wes stiffens. For a second, I think he's going to bolt and that will

Pull   27

be that. But at last he nods. "I'm sorry, D," he says. "I just panicked when you got pulled over. I knew better, but I thought maybe they wouldn't find it." He pauses, squints his eyes like he's thinking of the answer to some riddle. When he does, his face fills with tension. I get an image of what he'll look like when he's older. "I just didn't want to get run in again."

I nod, silently pleased that he at least apologized. Then it hits me. "Again?" I ask.

Wes juts his chin out. Now that his secret's out, he puts on a tough face. Like getting into more trouble makes him cool or something. "Yeah," he drawls. "I got busted back in June too. Got pinched lifting from Ty's Tower when you were off playing AAU."

Maybe that jab about me being at AAU is a guilt trip—like I'm supposed to be here to take care of him 24-7. Well, it works a little. It kills me that I didn't even *know*. And it kills me more that maybe Wes is in real trouble. I think again about how he hangs with guys like JaQuentin Peggs. I think again about that watch he's rocking. I also think about Kid's warning. There's a time to just cut out on someone. But not yet. Not with my boy. "Wes, man, I'm right here now. If you need—"

He cuts me off. Just holds up his hand like he's heard it all before. "It's nothing," he says. "Home detention's no big thing. Besides, JaQuentin says he's got a guy who can get it dropped in another week. No sweat."

We sit there in silence while Wes takes a few bites. Then he sets his fork down and waves his hand at his tray like he's disgusted by his food. He crumples his napkin and throws it on his tray. He gives a nod to me, scoops up his mess, and he's on his way—to where, I don't know.

Wes was the one who got home detention, but it feels like I got it too. No wheels, no Wes, no Jasmine—it's meant I'm pretty much just hoofing it to school and back, and only getting a sweat up when the weather's been nice enough to hit the Fall Creek court. Well, *no Jasmine* isn't quite right. I still see her. We even fooled around some last weekend when her parents were out. But it's not like it was a year ago. In the middle of a conversation, her attention will wander. It's like sitting with someone who's got a plane to catch—they're right next to you, but part of them is already leaving you behind.

But right now that doesn't matter. Let every coach in the country call. Let Jasmine move halfway across the world. Let Wes waste all his time with losers like JaQuentin. I've got something else at last—finally, *ball*.

Already Coach Bolden's put us through our sprints. And already a few freshmen have damn near bowed out. And already Coach Bolden's gotten so mad at our lack of hustle that he's kicked a ball into the third row, sending his assistant Coach Murphy sprinting after it. But that's all show to get the new guys up to speed. Now the real practice starts—we're going through offensive sets with the first team.

I've got a good lather worked up. I'd love to just run five-on-five. Let it rip up and down the floor. Instead, I obediently listen to Coach. "The whole focus changes this year," he says. "We don't have Moose around, so we can't just work through him in the post. We want to spread teams out and look to drive."

That's my game right there—go to the *hole*. The next thing he says I don't like so much.

"Usually, we'll have Derrick at point, but he'll be sitting the first game. If you don't walk the line off the court, you don't play for Marion East," he barks. Coach Murphy nods up and down in agreement, both of them making a point for the younger players. Then Coach Bolden points at me. "Flip that jersey, Bowen," he says. "Run with the twos until you earn that starting spot back."

That hurts. Everyone in the gym—hell, everyone in the state— knows I'm the engine for this team. Bolden's doing me dirty on the first practice. But what can I do? He's in charge, so I peel off my jersey, and flip it from red to green—the color of back-ups.

That means I get to watch while the coaches work through the sets. They're sizing up our horses for the season, and so am I.

At the bigs we've got Tyler Stanford and Chris Jones. Neither one's a true center, but they've got some bulk. Stanford in particular. He must have spent all summer in the weight room, because he's cut up pretty good. He's a senior now, and he finally looks it—his face has lost that boyish innocence. Now if he sneers when he's grabbing a board, people know they best step back. He's honed his shot some too. I hit him when he's facing from fifteen and in, he'll knock it down. Jones, I don't know about. He's there by default after paying his dues for a couple years on the bench. He's got size, but that's about it. Only way he's getting buckets are point blank—then again, Murphy and Bolden can work wonders, so maybe Jones will develop.

J. J. Fuller's at the three. He's been through the grind with me last year. I can't say we're tight, but I trust him on the floor. He's shaved off his old flat top, which made him look like he was straight out of the 80s, down to a close buzz. But he still looks rigid. His face always has a serious expression, like he's trying to figure out a calculus problem. His moves on the court are the same way—forceful but methodical, always in straight lines with no flow. Even his shot is a line drive, but it finds bottom if he's within sixteen or seventeen feet. And the kid hustles. Even as Coach has them walking through the set, Fuller carries out his fakes like it's game-time.

Then there's Josh Reynolds at the two. A sophomore. Last year, he was a mess. If he can get some confidence though, the skills are there. He's grown a little in the off-season, up to my height—6'3". And that shot is smooth enough. His challenge will be on the defensive end, where older players will try to overpower him.

With me at the point, it's enough. We've got some weaknesses, but you can say that about any team. The problem is, with me sitting on the sidelines, the point's being run by Malcolm Rider, a scared-witless freshman. Even walking through the sets, he looks confused. Fuller rubs off a baseline screen, and Rider is still looking to the opposite wing.

"No, no," Bolden says. He's taking it easy on the kid, not raising his voice. Coach puts a hand on his shoulder and gently pivots him the other way. "Once the play to the wing is done, you're looking for that baseline cut."

They run through the offense a few more times, and then it's live action. I take the floor with the second team. If the ones think I'm going to take it easy just because they're my boys, I've got a wake-up call in store for them.

First thing I do is dig into Rider. He tries driving right, and I cut him off. He looks to make an entry to Jones, and I deflect it out of bounds. Next time I keep my hands active, scaring off any passes except a bail-out to the wing. Once Rider gives it up, it's pretty obvious he doesn't want the rock back. Scared. Since he's no threat, I sag off him. And since I know where the offense wants to go, I give them fits. Reynolds passes to Fuller on the wing. I peel off Rider and jump the pass. I pick it clean and take a power dribble the other way—then I pull up since we're supposed to give right back to the first team instead of running full. But everyone knows that was an easy throw-down in the other direction. Next time, the ones work it down to Stanford, but he's too slow to make his move. By the time he rises, I've dropped all the way down from the elbow. I spike that thing out of bounds. Give a little holler of authority as I do it. That one draws some reactions all around. It's nice to remind everyone that even if I'm in green I'm the boss on the court.

The ones start again. By this time, they look a little discouraged. Rider most of all. He's extra tentative now, and I take advantage. I flick at the ball once and get a piece. He scrambles to control near mid-court, but then he picks up his dribble. "Dead! Dead!" I yell, and my teammates clamp down behind me. Rider pass-fakes, pass-fakes, pass-fakes. Finally he extends the ball too far. I pop it loose, corral it, and this time I can't help myself—I push it down the court with a couple power dribbles and tomahawk one home.

Murphy's beside me in a heartbeat. He's all smiles, acting like he's amped that I'm bringing it so hard the first day of practice—but then he pulls me aside. He calls down to the other end to tell them to keep running drills, then loops an arm around my shoulder. He walks me toward the side basket. "Easy there, killer," he says.

"What do you mean?" I ask. With the bleachers pushed back, I can see all the dust that collects on the floor—it's a faint line about ten feet away from the court where the shine of the hardwood turns cloudy. Murphy keeps walking with me. We cross into that cloudy area.

"I mean, dial it back," he says. He speaks in a hushed tone, like he's breaking some tragic news to me. "You have to let some of these other guys get their confidence up."

I stiffen my back. Murphy's arm slides off my shoulder. "Since when does it help other players to take it easy on them?"

Murphy takes a step back. He cocks his head and widens his eyes, giving me a look that tells me to cool it. "It's one thing to play hard," he says, "but you're trying to embarrass your teammates. Especially Rider. You think it makes you tough to overpower a freshman in his first practice? You ought to be helping him out whenever you can."

I hang my head. My temple throbs with anger. This is *bullshit*. That's what I want to say. At home, I've got letters from every major college you can name. No other player in my position would be paying this big a price because he swerved in his car at the wrong time. No way. I get bounced from the opener. I get bounced from the first team in practice. And now I'm supposed to, what, be a cheerleader for my replacement? But I take a deep breath and look back up at Murphy. "Okay, Coach," I say.

"It's about what's best for the team every time," he says.

"Okay," I repeat.

Then we turn back toward practice, neither one of us believing things are okay.

He grabs me by the jersey. I turn back to him. "Besides, D-Bow," he says. "Save up some of those plays for when we get our rematch against Kernantz and Evansville Harrison."

It doesn't exactly make me cool with how I'm being treated, but I can't help but smile at the notion of some payback against the guys who bounced us from State.

Kevin Waltman

4.

I never really thought I'd be amped to go to a party at J. J. Fuller's. I mean, "party" doesn't mean the same thing at Fuller's. It's more like the kind of gathering that people used to have in middle school—some chips on the table, some cokes, some music on the stereo but not too loud. And his parents lurking upstairs.

But, hey, fine with me. I'm out of the house after some prolonged pleading with my parents. Who cares if this thing is so tame I could have brought Jayson along and nobody would have blinked? It's not like I'm looking for trouble anyway. What I am looking for is across the room—Jasmine Winters. She's shot me down so many times I should know better, but when I see her it's all over.

When I first saw her she was a sophomore. Even then she was pretty spectacular. But now she's over the top. And it's not just how she looks. Sure, she's put together. Beneath those tight curls, her face has features that make her seem refined. Even wearing something simple—a yellow t-shirt with the sleeves down to her elbows and some tight black pants—she stuns me. But it's more the way she carries herself. Cool. Composed. A step ahead of anyone else. Or at least always a step ahead of me.

The vibe at Fuller's place makes everyone act like they're fourteen again, so the guys are all hanging over by the edge of the kitchen, while the girls hold it down in the living room. But I keep glancing over and catching Jasmine's eye. Every time, she pauses for just a beat in her conversation and bats those eyelids at me. Then she turns back to the person next to her and smiles—but I can't help thinking that smile's for me.

"Anyway, so I'm trying to tell him that he should look for me on the back-cut, and he just keeps saying, 'Coach said you'd flare.'" This is Fuller, griping to Jones about Rider at practice yesterday. Fuller's just like he is on the court—full-steam ahead and not paying attention to the reactions around him. Jones looks around for an escape, his eyes wide like when he forgets the play Coach called.

As much as I love hoops, I didn't come out on a Friday night to talk business with the boys. I walk across the room toward Jasmine. She sees me coming and tries to look busy, leaning in to whisper to one of her friends—a junior named Lia Stone, who's got every guy in the city begging for her attentions. But I just buzz right up. I slide between a fence of females—smooth as weaving through defenders on the court— and come to a stop about two feet from Jasmine.

Everyone hushes. Jasmine keeps whispering to Lia for a few seconds, but her eyes drift toward me. Finally she stops and turns my way. Her lips are still pursed around the last word she said to Lia. She looks me up and down, judging. She cocks her head at me, giving a *What-you-think-you-doing-all-up-on-me* look.

I know she's just messing, so I mess right back. I pivot and turn. "'Sup, Lia," I say.

"Nothing, Derrick," she says. She gives me this smoking little smile. Everyone knows I'm really coming over to chat up Jasmine, but Lia looks like she might call my bluff. Her cocoa face is smooth, flawless. I don't dare check the rest of her, or I'll get caught staring like a creep. "You're looking good tonight," she adds. She smiles again, then looks away from me like there's something more interesting on the wall across the room.

That throws me. I was trying to be all cool, but Lia Stone says *that* to you, and your heart leaps a little. I try to stop the thought, but there it is—if Jasmine keeps dragging on me, I might just jump to Lia for real. But like a chump, I mumble around. "Thanks," I stammer. "I—" I look down at my clothing, like maybe there's something I'm wearing she was talking about.

"Smooth," Jasmine says. She puts her hands on her hips and shakes her head like she's scolding me. "You know, for someone who thinks he's a baller, you sure could use some better game."

Now this—Jasmine cracking on me—I'm used to. I straighten up and smile. I nod at her, like *Okay, you got me on this one.* But I fight back too. "Hang with me tonight," I say. "I'll show you game."

Jasmine tries to keep her face expressionless. She makes it for a second or two, but then a smile creeps up on her and turns into a laugh. Lia shakes her head at both of us and walks away. I'd be lying if I said I wasn't at least interested in Lia. The girl is next-level hot. But I don't dare let my eyes follow her—not with Jasmine standing right in front me.

The two of us wander away from the crowd. We settle on a

Pull   37

couch over by the window. Jasmine leans back and looks out, watching traffic pass. From my spot, I can see up the stairs. Every now and then I see two heavy black shoes thud down on the top step—Fuller's dad eavesdropping on the happenings. Poor Fuller—the kid's nice enough, but everyone in here knows this is about as dead as a party can be. Everyone's trying to think of an excuse to bolt. Doesn't matter to me right now—I got myself some Jasmine time.

"How's the recruiting going?" she asks. Normally she wouldn't talk hoops, but she actually cares about where I end up. To answer, I just show her my phone. In the text history, there's a long scroll of schools—Indiana, Clemson, Michigan, Tennessee, Purdue, Kansas State. On and on. Jasmine follows for a minute, but then her eyes glaze. She looks back up at me. "You keeping your head on straight with all this?"

"Sure," I say. "It's not gonna get serious until I start making visits."

"Where?" she asks. It's a basic question, but she absent-mindedly runs her fingernail up and down my arm. Moments like that, it feels like we're a real couple—but I know what'll happen if I bite on her move. We'll find some place to be alone, mess around just enough to get me to my breaking point. Then she'll cut it off, and I won't hear from her for a week. So I play it straight.

"Indiana's most definitely on the list," I say. "But everyone knows that. I'll just take my time and get a vibe for places."

Jasmine nods, then looks out the window again. There's that distant stare. I try turning things around and give her a playful touch on the knee. She jumps like I'm a snake.

"Easy girl," I say. "Touchy. I was just wondering where your head is. What about school for you?"

She gives a big sigh, her shoulders sagging under the weight of the question. "I don't know," she says. "I thought my ACT score was good enough, but now everything I'm seeing says I need to get a 32 or better." This is the first time I've ever seen her uptight about anything academic, and it's a wake-up call—I'm not the only one with some pressure on me.

"What'd you get so far?" I ask.

Jasmine looks away again. "Not 32," she says. She shakes her head in disgust. "I don't get it. I crank out A after A at Marion East, and somehow that's not good enough? It's not right. Maybe I should take prep classes somewhere else." Her fingernails, just briefly, dig violently into the couch cushion. Then she unclenches and tries to laugh it off. "Can we get out of here?" she says.

I don't know what she has in mind, but I'm down for whatever. I grab Jasmine's coat for her, and we jet.

Like he's pulling a night security shift, my dad's standing watch in the living room when I walk in. A quick double-check on my watch tells me I'm in with fifteen minutes to spare.

"How was the party?" Dad asks.

"Fine," I say.

His eyes narrow, like he's inspecting me for some sign of misbehavior. I've got two inches on him, but he's still my dad. That stare would make me feel guilty even if I'd just come from church. "Who drove you home?" he asks.

"Jasmine," I answer. I really don't want follow-ups. I'm in no position to lie about anything, but I don't want to get into it—driving aimlessly with Jasmine until she pulled into the parking lot of a closed department store, making out with her for a few hot minutes, then getting the stiff-arm—again—when I tried to get busy for real. Then she just got all quiet on the drive home, like I was some stranger all of a sudden. Same story as always. With her, I'm like a big who keeps biting on every shot fake he sees.

Dad nods a couple times, considering more questions. This is usually Mom's job—staying up until I get back and grilling me—and Dad's not quite as tough. I know he's supposed to give me the third-degree, but I see it all over his face—he doesn't *really* want to know what his teenage son has been doing with a girl on a Friday night. He's beat anyway. He's cramming in double shifts working security every chance he gets, like he's trying to make up for all the time he lost last year when he was laid up. His shoulders go slack and he motions me back toward the hall. "Go on to bed," he says.

"Cool," I say, then tell him goodnight.

"Hey, Derrick?" he calls, just before I can make my way out of his sight. I turn, ready for more. "In the morning, tell your mom I grilled you good, okay?"

I smile. It's the first sign from my dad in a while that things are getting back to normal. "Most definitely, Dad," I say.

With that, I'm free to retreat to my room. As soon as I walk in the door, I power off my cell phone. I've decided that this—my room, at least—is going to be a haven from the recruiting path. So I always kill my phone—no calls, no texts, nothing. It lets me actually get some studying done or, like now, just chill.

I've streamlined the room. Every time letters come, I organize them by conference and put them in the closet next to my kicks. No clutter—just one basketball in the corner, the Reggie-Miller-signed rock that Uncle Kid got me when I was a little kid. Gone are the posters of CP, of John Wall, of Derrick Rose. I love each of them, dig their games, but now the walls are stripped back to LeBron, Jordan, and Magic. Just the guys with the rings. That's what I want—championships. Starting at Marion East and ending in the League. Where I want to cut down nets in between is still a mystery, even to me.

I lay back and think about Jasmine, about how I keep falling into her little trap. The thing is, it seems like she falls into it too. No doubt, when she sees me she's not thinking hook-up. She's always dealt better when we've just been friends. But there's this connection neither of us can shake. Maybe she gets distant with me just because she's pulled in two directions, one calling her toward college and away from Indianapolis, and one pulling her right back to me.

My door pushes open a few inches. Jayson peeks his head around the corner. Unsure of whether or not it's cool to come in, he lingers there for a second. He's in eighth grade now and he's starting to sprout. We always thought he got the short and squat genes from Mom's side, but he's stretching out each year and starting to look more like someone from Dad's side. Doesn't matter—only place he's a baller is on the X-Box sticks. But as he hangs there, I realize that in no time he'll be full-grown and ready to back up all that game he talks about with females. He's lost all that softness of boyhood from his face. Now there are some black wisps he's letting grow on his chin. They look like streaks of dirt on his light brown features. A terrible look. But it's one every guy's got to figure out for himself.

Pull

"Get on in here, Jay," I tell him.

He smiles, a little embarrassed for having waited for permission but also relieved to have gotten it. "I can't tell with you anymore," he says. "Sometimes you're locked in your own head, and it's like nobody else is supposed to disturb you."

"You know it's always cool with you," I say. "'Sup, anyway?"

"Just more calls," he says. He digs into his back pocket and unfolds a piece of paper. "Mom and Dad got sick of answering, so they put me on phone duty. Wanna hear the list?"

I nod, and he starts in—assistants at Georgia Tech, Louisville, Ohio State, and head coaches at St. Louis, Dayton, and Temple. I think that's it, but then Jayson flips the paper over and keeps rattling off schools.

"You got 'em all written down?" I ask. Jayson nods. I tell him to just set the paper on my dresser so I can check it in the morning.

Jayson yawns, like he's as exhausted by the process as I am. "Man, that assistant from Ohio State called three times in the last two days," he says. "It was like he was pissed at me when I said you weren't home tonight. Like it was my fault or something. I about told him there wasn't much difference between a Big Ten assistant and a telemarketer." Jayson seems bothered by the recruiter, but the way he says it makes it sound like he holds it against me too. He's all sneer these days.

I laugh. Maybe I should just make Jayson the point person for this whole thing. Let him sense who's cool and who's not, then just let him work whatever deal he wants as payment. He'd be good at it. "Jay," I tell him, "next time that Buckeye assistant calls you tell him whatever the hell you want."

He squints his eyes, skeptical. "For real?"

"Straight," I say. "I don't know where I *do* want to go, but I know I don't want to play for Ohio State. Never liked those guys."

Jayson nods approval, then raises his hand to his chin like he's plotting just how he's going to crack on that coach next time the phone rings.

5.

A day before the season starts, Bolden lets me run with the 1s. Maybe he's tired of seeing Rider butcher our offense. Or maybe, just maybe, he's going to turn me loose in the opener after all.

Doesn't matter the reason—we mash it. I fly past Rider and get to the rack for a deuce. I hit Stanford on a seal for a lay-up. A pick-and-pop for Fuller. Everyone's got new bounce in their step, clicking along at full speed at last. Part of it is just knowing each other—I know right where Reynolds wants the rock for three. I also know when *not* to give it to him. I know the sweet spot for Stanford at the shallow wing, but I also know that expression he gets when he's pushed out too far from the basket. But part of it is the ramp-up in skill from Rider to me—when in doubt, I just rip it to the rim. A lay-in. A jam. A dime to Jones.

Problem is, it's a tease. Just as we're getting a good rhythm, Coach barks, "Bowen back to the 2s." I know better than to react, so I just take a deep breath and flip my jersey. When I line up across from Rider, I'm tempted to flip him inside out too—just show out against him so everyone knows that, with me at the point, the 2s could run the 1s off. But I don't. I stay into Rider enough so it's not obvious I'm slacking, but I let him start the offense. When he cuts through to the wing and catches a pass from Fuller, he lets the rock just linger out there in front of him. I could rip it and run, but I just give it a quick poke—enough to let him know he's got to tighten up his stance. He tries an entry to Stanford, but the ball gets tipped out of bounds.

Murphy gets right in Rider's ear. "You just got to see it earlier," he says. "Stanford likes it quick, before he gets a body on him."

Rider nods in appreciation. "I feel you," he says.

Sure enough, next time through he catches on the wing and pops the orange to Stanford quick. Stanford rises in rhythm and fires front-rim-back-rim-out. While I'm boxing him out, I hear Rider grunt, disgusted that they still couldn't get a deuce. Tough luck, kid.

But as soon as the ball's dead, Rider's getting more encouragement, this time from Bolden. "That's not on you," he says. "All you can do is get the ball where it's supposed to be. The rest is up to your teammates."

Rider still looks a little tight. His eyes stay downcast, like the pressure of filling in for me is bowing his neck. Stanford, who never said word one to me when I was coming up as a freshman, backhands him on the shoulder. "Lighten up, man. My misses don't go on your line in the box score, so you can't drag them around with you on the court."

That coaxes a smile from Rider, at least. It's a quick one though, because Bolden fires the rock at him and blows his whistle to set us back to action.

Amazing. I get nothing but grief from people—Rider gets

Pull

nothing but love. Whatever. You can only control what's right in front
of you, and that's what I do the rest of practice. After Murphy's lecture
the other day, I join in on the Rider pity party and take it easy on him.

At last, Bolden cuts us loose. He makes a line for me—moving at as
close to a sprint as the old man can muster. While the other guys hit the
showers, he stops me at mid-court. "I saw you coddling Rider," he says.

"Yeah?" With Bolden, I'm never quite sure what to expect. Maybe
he's going to get pissed at me for this too.

"Well, that's more like it," he says. He smiles. It's not that a
Bolden smile is rare, but his expression is usually pinched into such
a scowl that the act looks like it hurts him—like his face just isn't
supposed to do that. He gives my shoulder a quick squeeze, then holds
up his index finger. "You're just sitting one game. One. That's just a blip
in the season. But the way you handle it will go a lot further than one
game. Understand?"

"Yes, Coach," I say.

He pops me flat-handed between my shoulder blades, a motion of
approval. Then he saunters off the court, his stride looking stiff with age.

I holler to Murphy, who's retrieving a loose ball from the bleachers.
"Murph! Send that one here. Gotta work on my pull-up some."

He smiles. He always loves it when kids stay late to work. Which
means he loves me most of all. For the next fifteen minutes he works
with me. He stays on the blocks and then flashes at me, hand extended,
when I rise to shoot. Then he tracks down my shots, made or missed,
and pops them back at me to start again. By the end, he's got as good
a lather up as I do, and it all feels good. I bury my last six in a row and
call it a day.

Kevin Waltman

But we know. Murphy knows. Bolden knows. I know. Hell, Rider knows. We're doomed without me running point.

Khakis. The worst. Off the court, I lean toward jeans and a plain t-shirt. Just a chill look. But for church, for dinners at nice restaurants, for anything my Mom decides requires proper dress? Khakis and a checked button-down.

I do get a once-over from Jasmine, who smiles at me and says that I "clean up nice." So there's that. But I still always feel like a phony when I'm in these clothes, especially now. In front of me, my boys are getting warmed up. They glide through the lay-up lines. Fuller and Rider burst toward the rack at game speed, while Reynolds works on his step-back. The red and green of their warm-ups flash past, while behind them the crowd keeps filing in. For a team like Brownsburg, people might not pack the gym, but it's still our opener and the place is buzzing. Then the band kicks in—no Wes anymore, though I don't know if it's because he got booted or he ditched it—and I feel that jump to my pulse. I feel like I should sprint back to the locker room and shed these street clothes for a uniform.

There's no telling what they're saying with the band blasting, but now and then I see people nod or point in my direction. On the court, the team's getting warm, the coaches are out near mid-court helping our bigs stretch their hammies. And over here I stand by the bench, clapping encouragement next to the equipment manager. No wonder I'm getting some stares. I guess word didn't get out that I was sitting, but I'm sure by tip every last man, woman, and child in the Marion East gym will have it figured out that Derrick Bowen's a screw-up who got his ass suspended for the opener.

The stares come from the other end of the floor too. The Brownsburg coaches see me in street clothes and then they huddle-up to talk strategy. One after another, I see the Brownsburg players sneak a peek in my direction. With each one, there's this little shift in their expression—just a slight lift of the eyebrows that says, *Hey, we got a chance to come in here and steal one.*

The buzzer sounds. The crowd settles. The starting lineups trot out. Lord, I can barely watch. I've heard players talk about having to sit and play cheerleader while they're injured. They all say that's the worst part of the injury—not the pain, not the re-hab, but just sitting there without helping their teammates. That ball goes up. I've got Oxfords on my feet instead of my new D Rose 5s. It feels like going over to Jasmine's house to watch her make out with another guy.

The game waits for no one. As soon as Stanford controls the tip, they're into it. Not a soul in uniform is thinking about me. They've got a game to play. Kicks chirp against the hardwood. The defensive chatter of *Help here* and *back-screen coming* mixes with the grunts of bigs fighting in the post and claps of open men wanting the rock. Rider does his best. He runs us through our offense. When things break down, he sprints out to get the ball near mid-court and re-set. But on the next time through the offense, he makes the same mistake he'd made in practice—he sees Stanford in the post, but waits an extra beat before making the pass. It gets swiped and Brownsburg pushes the other way.

When Fuller tips a Brownsburg pass out of bounds, Murphy slides down next to me. "Chin up now, D-Bow," he says. It sounds wrong to be called *D-Bow* now. It's like that should be reserved for when I'm on-court. "You still can help us." I nod, but it's not enough of an agreement to please Murphy so he stays after me. "Come on now. Every time-out, you need to be in Rider's ear, telling him what to expect. You got to encourage your teammates out there when things get rough."

"Got it," I say. He's right, but somehow the thought makes me ill.

On the other end, Reynolds gets beat baseline and Brownsburg's up 2-0.

It's gonna be a long night.

We hang. Stanford gets himself rolling in the third, burying a baseline J, a turnaround, a put-back and a little finger-roll in succession. Reynolds knocks in some treys, showing that he's grown up quite a bit from his rocky freshman year.

But we don't have anything on the court that makes Brownsburg get jumpy. After a quick timeout, they start doubling Stanford—and it's not even a hard double, just a guy dropping down a little further to make Stanford think twice. That's the only adjustment they have to make. Aside from that, they stick to the shooters, stay in front of us on D, and box out. Pretty textbook.

On the other end, they hum through their sets. It's basically a flex offense, nothing we haven't seen a million times. But it suits them. Their bigs can shoot, and their guards have some heft to them. So sooner or later, Stanford or Jones get hung on a screen and their men drop in Js. Or Reynolds or Rider gets buried in the paint and either foul or give up an easy deuce. By mid-fourth, Brownsburg's opened up a seven-point lead. Our ball, and we're looking for a spark. So, yeah, we're hanging. But we're not supposed to *hang* with Brownsburg. We're

Pull 49

supposed to slap them with a twenty point beat-down and run their asses back to the suburbs.

I watch Rider on this critical possession. I try to will him to do the right thing. He catches it left wing. His man is slow to challenge. Rider can hit that. *Pull*, I think. *Just pull.* But Rider waits and looks, while his man closes the gap. Then Rider decides to put it on the deck. The kid just does everything a second too late—and a second is an eternity on the court. Rider starts middle, gets cut off, then spins to go back baseline. Right where his man wants to take him. No man's land. He gets pinned on the baseline and picks up his dribble. No shot. No passing lanes. Finally, Fuller sprints all the way cross-court to try to bail Rider out, but Rider is so off-balance he can't get any zip on the pass. It gets picked. Brownsburg runs. And *bang*—a transition three for the kill shot.

When the players filed off the court, our crowd gave them a solid ovation. It's not the kind of thing Marion East fans do after a loss—we're not into moral victories. But they knew the guys gutted it out the best they could without me on the floor. So, in a way, those cheers felt like an insult to me. I mean, I know they didn't *mean* it that way. But it's like the whole gym was saying, *We know this one wasn't the fault of the guys in uniform.*

In the locker room, Bolden was just as encouraging. "You stayed after it," he said, clapping his hands. "You fought buzzer to buzzer, and that's all I ask." It was like some other coach had slipped into Bolden's skin. He was so cheerful it wouldn't have surprised me if he started handing out gold stars to people, like some kindergarten teacher.

Once the showers are going full blast and Stanford cranks some

Kevin Waltman

Pusha T as loud as the locker room stereo can handle it, Bolden decides he's not so cheerful with me. I'm slouched back in my locker, not knowing what to do—no cause for me to shower up, but it would seem wrong to just split—when Bolden steps to me. He crouches in front of me like he does during time-outs, so at least for anyone checking us it just seems like a normal player-coach chat.

"I have to say, Derrick, I'm a little disappointed in you."

My back stiffens and my jaw tightens. It's sure as hell not my fault we got run at home by Brownsburg. What, the guy didn't like the way I cheered or something?

"I know Murphy told you before the game that you had to help Rider along as much as you could. Hell, I told Murphy to tell you that." Bolden shrugs. He shakes his head. "For a quarter, you did that. And then you went silent. Derrick, when you're part of a team then you're part of a team *all the time*. Not just when you're out at center court in uniform." Now he leans forward, a little rasp rising in his voice. "You're part of a team when you're healthy, when you're hurt, when you're awake, when you're asleep. *Always.* So that means you've always got to be looking for a way to help your teammates." He jabs his index finger about an inch from my chest. "Lift them up, so sometime when you're down they'll lift you. That's what teammates do, Derrick."

Then he stands and is gone.

Shit, I think, *I could lift them a lot easier by being out there on the floor.* But I figure I'll get my crack soon enough.

After that, I've had about enough of the post-game locker room, so I hit it. Only there's no quick escape. Immediately I get stopped by Eddie Whitfield, his phone pointed at me like a weapon. Whitfield's

Pull 51

the high school hoops guy for the *Indianapolis Star*, but he's got an even more important column—a blog that always has the scoop on where any Indiana recruit is leaning. I've got to tread carefully.

"Rough one tonight, Derrick," he says.

"Yeah, but we'll bounce back," I say. It's a throwaway line, pure cliché, but saying it on the record makes me nervous. Last year, it was Moose who handled any player interviews. By seniority, it should fall to Stanford. But even Coach knows that people like Whitfield want to talk to me, so I'm in the crosshairs now.

"Any comment on sitting out a game?"

"Just can't wait to get back," I say.

"You feel like your absence made the difference tonight?"

"Aw, man, we could have run those guys, sure," I say. It's out before I think. But as soon as I say it, I know it's a bad move. I look back to the locker room, and there's Stanford. He's ready to cut out, but he heard it, I know. He sneers at the two of us. I'm sure he probably thinks he's the one that ought to be getting these interviews—not a junior who was suspended for the opener.

After that, Whitfield shifts into recruiting questions. I'm a little more comfortable with these, even though my answers are all dodges. I just tell him that I'm taking my time. No favorites. I want a place I can compete for a championship, I say, but that could happen almost anywhere these days. Once he shuts the phone off and thanks me for my time, I remind him that anything official is going to come through Coach or my parents. He nods real quick like he doesn't really believe it. He's overweight, probably from eating gym food for months at a time. His shirt is so wrinkled it looks like he pulled it out of the locker room laundry basket. That and his pasty complexion make him look tired and jaded. "It's not going to stop me from asking you directly," he says. He sounds a little disgusted by my refusal to answer him straight.

He waves at me to go on, like all of a sudden I'm the one holding *him* up. I see Jayson and Kid waiting for me at mid-court. Jayson looks a little bored, itching to leave, but Kid's styling. He's got on a red silk shirt that pops in the gym lights. It's the kind of thing that gets a body noticed, and Kid knows it. He's got that look in his eye like he could stand there all night letting women look him over.

Instead, what he gets is his nephew coming up for some sympathy. "Now I know how you feel," I say—a reference to Kid's playing days under Bolden, his senior year cut short by all his run-ins.

He pulls back and narrows his eyes. "Boy, you don't know the half."

"Well, tell me the whole story then," I say.

Jayson puts his hands on his hips. "Can we *go*?" he snarls. It shuts down the conversation between me and Kid. It'll be interesting to see who Jayson turns into as he gets older. I know he's a good guy, but what used to be just a little mischief is turning into some serious attitude.

I don't have time to sweat that though. I gaze toward the edge of the gym and see none other than Wes Oakes. He's posing tough—got a Bulls hat cocked sideways and a baggy black jacket on, like he's trying to pass for some old-school banger. The problem is that next to him is the real deal: JaQuentin Peggs. Not that I know for real that Peggs is in a crew, but I know enough. And it kills me that that's where Wes is hanging instead of kicking it with me and my family like he used to. He catches me checking him. Just for a second the old Wes shines through. He smiles, big, and calls out, "'Sup, D?" Then he sags back into his sulk. But he steps away from JaQuentin and his boys a few paces and nods at me, motioning for me to come over. I know the ground Wes walks is forbidden for me, but I figure if I can hang with him away from JaQuentin, then that's just what we need.

I nod to Kid and Jayson. "Go on. I'll hoof it home later."

They both know I'm going over to Wes. Jayson raises his eyebrows. "You know Mom's not cool with that," he says.

"She doesn't have to know," I say. That came out a little sharp, so I shrug at them. "Wes is my boy. I can't just ditch him forever."

Jayson doesn't look convinced, but Kid understands. He nods at me and gives a half-smile. He might have lectured me about cutting dead weight, but Kid knows that you have to stay true to your people.

6.

This isn't at all what I had in mind. It's like with hoops—sometimes you play out a whole game in your head, how things will break your way, how you'll put the clamps on the other squad, how you'll get a run-out early to get things rolling. Then that orange goes up and everything switches up on you. The other team's changed offenses. Your first shot rattles out. You get a cheap foul. It all goes to pieces.

That's about how it's gone with Wes tonight. The idea was to get him away from JaQuentin, just let him ease back into being the same old Wes—easygoing, ready to chill, no stupid stuff. Instead, he dropped it on me that he skated on home detention because JaQuentin "had the hook up." Then he told me we could head back to the block together. I figured that meant just me and Wes kicking it on foot like old times, but what that really meant was piling into JaQuentin's black Tahoe, the last place on earth I want to be. I'm in back next to Wes, and there's some thugged-out guy riding shotgun. That guy's about as tatted as Kid Ink. He's got his neck marked, some detailed designs on his forearms. Even his fingers sport tats—a 3 and a 7 on his right hand with a symbol I can't make sense of between them.

And of course JaQuentin isn't rolling straight back to Patton. No, he tells me he's got to make a pit stop, and soon enough we're cruising slow through the streets behind the Marott Apartments. Peggs keeps eyeing his phone like he's waiting on a text. I give the death stare to Wes, but he just shrugs. Then he mouths *It's cool* to me. I just shake my head and turn back toward my window. I don't want to get into it now. Lord knows I don't want to distract JaQuentin from his driving any more than he already is with that phone. It's a sure bet he's riding dirty, so I don't want a repeat of this summer with Wes.

"Can you believe this motherfucker?" JaQuentin asks his buddy in the front. Peggs holds up his phone. "I texted him ten minutes ago and he said he'd be here. *Shiiit.*"

His inked-up friend just grunts. JaQuentin steps on the gas and roars around the corner to start another lap. He loops his arm around the passenger side's headrest and cranes back toward us. He shifts his lazy gaze back and forth between me and Wes. Meanwhile, he's still cruising a few miles an hour, his car drifting across the center lines. "After this we gonna hit up a place on 30th. My boy Hutch is throwing down tonight. You two invited."

When I clear my throat, Peggs doesn't even flinch. "You got a problem, Bowen?" he asks.

"I got to get back," I say. I try to put a little oomph behind it. After all, I've got four inches on the guy. But I can't hide the fact that I'm way out of my comfort zone.

"What? You ball a little and you think you're too good for us?

Shit. You in my car now, D-Bow." Then he hits the brakes and jack-knifes into an open space, the back end hanging out a good two feet. He points out the passenger side's window. "There he is. Let's roll."

He and his friend get out. A gust of night wind comes into JaQuentin's ride. I'm no fool. I know what they're doing. They move beneath dim streetlights down to the corner where a man—older, bulkier—waits. He keeps his body still, but his head swivels slowly, like a security camera. The street's so quiet you can hear the roar of engines racing on nearby blocks. When the man finally sees JaQuentin, his *There you are* cuts clean through the air. After that, they talk more quietly. All you can hear are rises in inflection, bursts of laughter now and then.

"You got to be kidding me," I seethe at Wes.

He's pinched himself all the way back into the opposite corner, as far away from me as he can be. "It's not a thing," he says. "Be cool."

"Be cool," I spit back. It's like someone who's just committed three straight turnovers and been beaten for three straight buckets turning to you and saying *My bad.*

When we were runts, they'd hit us with all these talks at school. They'd bring police officers in to lecture us about every single danger out there. Nobody took it seriously. It was like the more they tried to scare us, the tougher we had to act. They did this one exercise, though, I thought was over the top. They'd have a person stand on the teacher's desk and try to pull up another kid who was sitting on the floor. Nobody could do it. Not even the strongest guy. Then they'd have the person on the floor tug on the person on the desk. Most of the time, the person on the desk would come tumbling down in a heap. They told us that was what it was like trying to help someone who was messed up with the wrong people or on drugs or something. All they did was drag you down.

I guess I always thought that was stupid—like the moral was to never try helping anyone. Until now.

"You didn't have to come," Wes says.

"I wanted to try to help you."

Now Wes gets his back up. "Help me? You think I need *your* help? Just accept that I got my own thing going and deal."

"This is your thing?" I gesture out the window to where JaQuentin slaps hands with the guy they met. They hug it out and then Peggs and his boy start back for the car. Right then the chirp from a police car pierces the night. Everyone freezes. In that pause I feel it all—my season, my career, my dreams—drifting away like so much smoke.

But it's just a noise from another block, signaling trouble for someone else. It's like a warning shot though. JaQuentin hustles back to his ride. He and his boy pile in. He smiles at us in the back seat. "Business is over. Play time now. Let's hit up Hutch's."

"I can't do that," I say.

JaQuentin's smile vanishes. He turns to his boy riding shotgun. "D-Bow *does* think he's too good for us. I guess if you don't have scholarship offers from the ACC then you don't rate in the great D-Bow's book."

"It's not about that, it's—"

"What?" JaQuentin shouts at me.

"I just got to get home."

JaQuentin stares at me for a few seconds. He looks at his friend.

Then at Wes. Then back at me. "Fine," he says. He throws his ride into reverse to back us out, then lays down some tire as he roars down the road. First stop sign we hit, he slows enough that I can hear him mutter to himself—"Some bullshit, Bowen. Straight bullshit."

But at least we're heading back to Patton.

I don't even try to cover it. I'm late, so they'll demand an explanation.

And as soon as the name—*Wes*—is out of my mouth, Mom springs off the couch. "I know!" she hollers. I shake my head, and she can see what I'm thinking. "Don't act like your brother betrayed you. What? You think he's going to lie to me to protect you? Would *you* do that for him?"

I mutter out a *no*, the only acceptable answer. Besides, it's probably the truth. I fear nothing on the hardwood, but, man, *nobody* has the brass to lie to my mom when she gets heated up. I take a quick look at Dad. He's sitting in his chair, hands gripping the armrests. He reaches up slowly, removes his glasses, and wipes his tired eyes. Then he shakes his head. "If you're looking to me for sympathy, you're not going to find it. Come on, son. On the same night you were suspended? You have to be smarter than that."

Still, at least his tone is one of worn-out disapproval. My mom's still on full-tilt. "Every detail," she snaps. "I want to know every single thing that happened tonight." She levels her index finger at me, all business.

I go through it. JaQuentin Peggs. His friend. The noise they got up to. All of it.

"Derrick," my dad says at the end, "what on earth are you thinking?"

"Look. I got out of it as best I could. I didn't go the party with them. I just got home."

"I understand that." He sighs. "But, Derrick, you're not some prep school kid who keeps getting chances. People will give you a little rope because you can play, but not as much as you think. You screw up too many more times and everyone will think you're just another thug." His gaze hardens as he stares past me, thinking about me but something else at the same time. "And you'll be shocked at how cold the world gets when they decide that about you."

I accept the mini-lecture and then take a step toward my room. Mom's not having it. "Where you think you're going?" she asks. "Wait here."

She storms out of the living room, her feet pounding the floor so hard I'm sure that Jayson's wide awake now and listening in. She comes storming back down the hall with a city map in her hands, unfolding it angrily as she walks. Ripping right past without even looking at me, she heads to the kitchen. She spreads the map on the table, then turns around to me and Dad. "Come here," she commands.

As we walk over, she yanks a kitchen drawer open and unsnaps a red Sharpie. A quick wave of her hand indicates that we best sit, and we obey. In red so thick you'd think it would bleed through onto the table, she marks a big red loop on 465, circling the city. Then she scrawls a 144 inside of it. "You know what that means?" she asks me.

I just shake my head.

"That's how many people got killed here last year," she says. She's not shouting now. Instead, her voice has settled into an urgent whisper. "Yeah, when the news covers it, they make it sound like it's the whole area's problem, but"—she takes that Sharpie and presses a big red dot up in Carmel—"they're not talking about people up here. No. It's us. These streets." She motions toward the walls, lingering just an extra millisecond when she's gesturing up the street toward Wes' direction.

She sits now, like she's exhausted from the effort. She buries her head in her hands. Then she looks up again. "You want more? Sixteen white people got killed. Twenty women. I'm not saying they don't count, Derrick. I'm saying that most of the people who got killed"— she jabs her index finger at my chest, emphasizing every word—"look just like you. And it's not just from people in gangs. You don't think a policeman can lose his mind here just like they do in other cities? Think again. All it takes is for you to be with Wes when he runs into a cop on a power trip."

"How do you know all those numbers anyway?" I ask her, trying to hide my skepticism. I mean, I know how things break in the city, but it seems like my mom's putting it on a little heavy.

Dad's the one that answers. "We're parents of a black teenager," he says. "It's our job to pay attention even if nobody else does."

7.

Stanford controls to Fuller. He kicks it to me. First touch all year, and I know what to do with it—rip it right to the rack. I duck under a challenging big for a reverse off the glass. Quick as that, we're up 2-0 on Warren Central.

That's all it takes for the blood to get flowing again. The crowd's jumping too. The season's *on*.

One thing's for sure—Warren Central isn't going to sit back and let me soak in the moment. They rip it back at us. Right off the bat, coach has me on Rory Upchurch. He's their senior scorer, the guy who lit up everybody last year. A two-guard, he's not my natural match-up. And it means I've got to locate him every time down, since he's guarding Reynolds on our end. Right away, I see the problem—since I drove to the hole, he's got about a twenty-foot headstart on me. They kick it ahead before I can catch up. Reynolds races over to help, but Upchurch shakes him fast. Next up, Fuller flies at him. It slows Upchurch down just a tick, enough for me to close some ground. He gets past Fuller to the baseline side, opening up a clean look from fifteen. He lets it fly.

And—*whap!*—I arrive just in time to put that thing in the fifth row.

Upchurch is a legit Mr. Basketball candidate, and he just got punked. Our crowd lets him have it, hooting and jeering and rising to their feet. Upchurch is too good to sweat it, but I check some of his younger teammates. Their eyes go wide. For a couple of them, this is their first road start and they're realizing that we don't set out the welcome mat at Marion East.

Their coach barks the in-bounds play to them. All I know is that I need to stay glued to Upchurch. Everything they run involves him. I fight over a screen and stay on his hip. Then I hear Jones warning me about a back-screen. I turn to locate, keeping watch on Upchurch at the same time. Jones gives me room to make it through, and I've got Upchurch locked down again. That leaves Jones' man with a pop-out to fifteen. He catches the in-bounds, shot-fakes, then fires—way out of rhythm and way off line.

I can't get a clean rip, but I tap it to Stanford. He grips it, then pivots and outlets to Reynolds. That's when I see my opening. Warren Central has to switch just like we do. Upchurch is supposed to check Reynolds, but now he's trailing. While he sprints to catch up, my man tries to slow down Reynolds—and I'm *off*. Reynolds crosses mid-court and fans out to the right wing. That gives Upchurch time to catch up, but when my man tries to recover it's too late. Reynolds sees me and lobs one to the rim. With a free run, I sprint, gather, and rise. I catch that thing a good foot above the rack and muscle it home.

I've been there before. So instead of getting all swole about it, I just give a single fist pump and race back on D. But, baby, inside my chest the fireworks are going off. The crowd on its feet, the rim rocking, the opponents shell-shocked—this is *it*. This is what I live for.

After the grind of last year, I'm locked in with Fuller, Stanford and Reynolds. Jones is the only one who didn't get meaningful minutes last year, so we have to coax him along a little—remind him where to go on some offensive sets, encourage him when he gets beat on the boards a few times.

That togetherness is the difference. Upchurch is a load, but Warren Central doesn't have any backup for him. And the only time he really gets loose is when Bolden gives me a breather for Rider. Man, I hit the bench, and you can see Upchurch's eyes light up. First time he gets a touch, he attacks—shot fake to get Rider off his feet, then a dribble to his favorite pull-up spot. Deuce. Next time he loses Rider on a screen and launches a trey. The kid's shot is butter when he gets a look like that.

Bolden tells Reynolds to switch onto Upchurch, but that's only a little bit better. Reynolds had a brief go at Upchurch last year, so he knows what he's in for—but that doesn't mean he can stop it. Upchurch has to work harder. He rubs off screen after screen, then has to shake Reynolds with a nasty crossover—but in the end, Reynolds is still beat. Upchurch buries another trey. The lead we've spent all game building is suddenly down to three.

"Don't get too comfortable there," Bolden growls at me. "Next dead ball you're back in."

That's what I want to hear. I know he's just trying to keep my legs fresh, but truth is I want to go all 32 minutes every time out. The only time I want to rest is when we've got the game iced.

On our end, Fuller goes flying baseline and gets bailed out with a reach. The whistle's my cue. As soon as I stand, there's a ripple of applause in our crowd. People know what's up. When I jog onto the court, I point at Rider and he hangs his head in dejection. And Upchurch just smiles and claps. I know what he's thinking—he's loose now. He feels like he can keep it rolling, even against me.

Before the game, I eyed all the scouts checking us. Purdue, Michigan State, Louisville, Cincinnati. I know what they're thinking too—showdown in crunch-time between two big-time guards. And, yeah, Upchurch is a senior so it's not like an offer to him means they'll miss a shot at me, but everyone's always trying to figure out the pecking order. Time to prove to them whose name should be on top.

We run an in-bounds play for Stanford, but he doesn't come free so Fuller lobs it way out top to me. And wouldn't you know it—Warren Central's coach has Upchurch switch onto me. Showdown time for real. I know better than to just force it. We run offense. A kick to Reynolds on the wing. A look to Jones in the post. Then a reversal through Fuller out top. Back to me on the left wing. I power past Upchurch, but their bigs jump to the action quick. There's a look at a tough pull-up, but we can do better. Back out to Reynolds on top again. I glide on through the paint, getting a rub off of Stanford. It's just enough to get Upchurch trailing by a step. Reynolds hits me right on time on the opposite wing. Just the slightest pump fake gets Upchurch leaning—and I'm gone. I knife into the paint, getting deep into the teeth of the defense before

Pull

they pick me up. Their center rises to challenge my look. Quick as a whip, I duck under him and feed Stanford. Easy deuce.

Our crowd jumps back into full throat. Stanford pounds his chest and points in my direction—the points are his, but he knows who made that bucket happen. No time to celebrate though. I clap my hands and holler at my boys. "Stop now! Let's get a stop!"

Even as I yell, Warren Central's pushing for Upchurch. I find him on the wing. When he catches, I challenge with my hand but keep my feet balanced. He's smart too. Doesn't force. They run offense instead, which means I get pinballed off screen after screen. I keep contact, helped by my teammates hedging into passing lanes.

Finally I get a face full of shoulder from their center. Probably a moving screen, but not a call you get down the stretch. It gives Upchurch room on the right baseline, a place he likes to work. I close fast, and he passes on a catch-and-shoot. Maybe that swat from early in the game is still on his mind. Instead, he tries driving baseline. When I cut him off, he backs out to the wing to solo me up—and makes one bad mistake. He turns his back. Maybe he's trying to set me up, but it gives me a clean look at the orange. Just a tap is all it takes. The rock ricochets off his knee and bounces toward open court. Their other guard dives after it, but I get there first. I tap it again, pushing it out toward mid-court. I leap over their sprawling guard. Then I'm all alone.

Corral. Push. Feel the energy of the crowd swell as I race to the rack. And then when I rise up, it's all blocked out for the briefest of moments. There's no crowd, no scouts, no coaches. Hell, there's not even a game on. Just me attacking the rim. I break out a big tomahawk, throwing the thing down as hard as I can.

Kevin Waltman

When I land, it all comes rushing back. The crowd is a mob, a rocking sea of red and green. My teammates are howling as our coaches urge us to race back on D. Upchurch turns to the ref and signals for time, his squad down seven again, chances dashed. And all those scouts from the blue chip schools have their answer: Derrick Bowen's the king on this court.

Fuller just wants to talk hoops. Perfect. That's why I hit him up after the game to go get some grub—I know Fuller is the one guy who won't get up to any nonsense.

"We got to get Jones involved," he says. "I'm not saying take shots away from you or Stanford, but we make him into a threat and teams won't know what to do with us."

"I hear it. Right now the only looks he gets are put-backs. But in practice he buries that J from the elbow."

Fuller's chuckles and shakes his head. He looks away like a wistful old man. "There's no greater distance than the one between practice shots and game shots," he says.

"Preach it," I say. My agreement makes Fuller smile. All the kid wants, really, is to belong. He transferred here last year. As much as he's found his fit on the court, he's a tough fit off it. He's so eager it kills him, so sincere he makes people roll their eyes. He falls in love with any girl who looks his way and—even worse—professes it to them right off the bat. And then there was his "party" the other weekend, which made everyone feel like they were back in sixth grade. But the kid's steady. And right now, I can use steady.

So here we are, at Sure Burger on 38th. It's a new place, opened last month, but it doesn't look it. The booths look so old and grimy, it's like they pre-date the building. In the hall to the bathroom there's a small mountain of wreckage—old aprons, a broken space heater, busted crates—and in the men's room the window is clapped shut with plywood. And then there's the grease—everything within 50 feet of the kitchen has a slick coat on it, like someone busted in one night and just doused the place in the oil from the fryer. But, hey, it's got the good eats. That's all we care.

I make the mistake of checking my phone. The scroll of texts is longer than the Constitution. On one hand, it makes me feel good. I mean, that's part of the point, right? Ball out and get a ride to college. Then own it there and make it to the L. But already the voices are blurring. *Good game!* and *Way to tear it up!* and *Saw your line, D. Way to be!* and *We need a scorer like that at Creighton!* They all start to look the same after a while. The names of the schools change, but it's all the same. I need to narrow them down. Fast.

Fuller points at me with his fork, a mess of stabbed fries on the end—I mean, the guy eats his fries *with a fork!* "More questions from Whitfield?" he asks. It's a loaded comment. More snark than usual from a guy like Fuller. But I know I deserve it. The interview with Whitfield did *not* go over well in the locker room. Nobody was truly falling out, but Stanford and Reynolds both made sure to give me some static on it. Then again, I basically proved myself right on the court tonight. Maybe that's why Fuller backs off when I don't answer right away. "Probably schools, huh?" he says. "Where you thinking?"

I sigh. "I wish I knew. Indiana, maybe," I tell him, but even that I can't say with conviction. It's just my default response.

"Playing it close to the vest," Fuller says. He says it like we're conspiring on something. Then he nods in approval, like he's been down that road before.

"I'm just telling you how it is," I say. "I'm not trying to hold back some secret."

"Oh, I hear you." But he has that look like he *knows* I mean something else. Whatever. Let him think what he wants to think. "But if you need to hash it out with someone," he says, "I'm here." On *that* I've got to fight back the urge to roll my eyes. It's like he *wants* to sound like a pathetic guidance counselor. He must read my thoughts because he puts his fork down and bugs his eyes. "What? What'd I say?"

I shake my head. "Nothing, man. Just take it easy. It's cool." But when I look past him, now I'm the one bugging. What I see up at the front is the very last thing I'd expect late-night at a grimy place like Sure Burger: Jasmine Winters, a stack of books clutched under her arm. Her eyes look a little bleary, and she's got her hair bunched up under a baseball cap, but she still looks *good*.

I don't want to just rush up on her. But Fuller sees me looking and wheels around so hard that his chair scrapes on the floor. Jasmine turns, sees us gawking. She smiles and shrugs her shoulders. "Hey, Derrick," she says. "What can I say? I needed to re-fuel."

I figured Jasmine would head downtown, hit up some dimly lit coffee shop, instead of cracking her books next to a pile of chili-cheese fries.

"Come sit with us," Fuller blurts before I can respond. Makes me cringe. If the guy had any subtlety, he'd wait to see what Jasmine wanted. Or, even better, hit the pavement so she and I could kick it alone. But that doesn't seem to bother Jasmine—she jumps at the offer.

Pull   69

She comes over and slings her stack of books down to the floor. I know she came here with the intention of more studies, but she thuds those things down like they weigh five-hundred pounds each. There's an ACT prep book, a thick novel for her English class, and then a little pamphlet. It's got pictures of kids of all races, their eyes eager, all of them looking forward like they're listening to some lecture. It's got the IUPUI logo on it, but I know Jasmine hasn't studied herself crazy for four years to go there. Jasmine catches me looking at it. She kicks the novel over to cover the pamphlet.

"Heard you won tonight," she says.

"Ah, we put it *down*," Fuller says. "Dropped Warren Central." If I didn't know better, I'd swear Fuller was trying to act the big man for Jasmine. Crazy move. She might not be my girl, but she's not exactly *nothing* to me.

"Well, that's good, I guess," she says, a little ice in her voice. Fuller sits back, realizing just how unimpressed Jasmine Winters is by a high school basketball game.

Fuller checks his phone. It's probably just a way of pretending like he doesn't care that Jasmine dogged him out, but then he purses his lips. "Three missed calls from Mom," he says. "I better bolt."

He wads his napkins and wrappers on his tray and then hits it, giving me a clumsy fist bump across his tray before he leaves. That leaves me and Jasmine. For a few seconds we stare at each other in awkward silence. It gets broken by a guy calling her order number out, so Jasmine stands to go get it. As soon as she walks away, I kick myself for not having better manners—I should have got it for her. But before that thought's even done, I do something else rude. I toe that top book a couple times until I can get a good look at the pamphlet she brought in. It's from IUPUI all right, and it's got some application materials. But it's not for college exactly. Instead, it's for dual enrollment classes. I've heard about that stuff, but it's not the kind of thing kids from Marion East do, so I don't know exactly what it means.

Before I can pry further though, Jasmine sets her tray down on the table. "Snoop much?" she says. Busted as can be, I start to stammer out an apology. For once, Jasmine lets me off the hook. "It's okay, Derrick," she says. "You're digging, but I've been holding back. So it's okay."

"So what's that about?" I ask, pointing to the pamphlet.

"It's so I can take college courses next semester," she says. "Get some basic credits out of the way before I get to college next year." She sees some confusion on my face. She explains more. She's not going to IUPUI for college, she tells me. She's still holding out for a better ACT score. But the stuff she takes at IUPUI in the spring will transfer to college.

I nod and start chowing down on my last few bites of burger. Then it hits me. If she's at the IUPUI campus next semester, then that means she's not at Marion East. "So you're gone?" I ask. I try not to sound hurt, but I think I do anyway.

She nods. "I've got everything I need to take at Marion East out of the way," she says. "There's not much more there for me." She winces on that last sentence. It stung me and she knows it. "I didn't mean it that way, Derrick," she says. "I've been waiting to tell you because—I don't know. Because you and I have always had this *thing*. But I guess I just realized it's a high school thing. One way or another, we're going separate ways soon enough."

I feel blindsided. Coach Bolden could walk in the door and tell me that I just dreamt the Warren Central win, that Upchurch lit me up for 30 and we got run out, and it wouldn't be a smack upside the head like what Jasmine just put on me. I can't let it show though. I take a second to gather myself, and then point at her tray. She's made a tragic mistake—she's tried to go sensible at Sure Burger. Plain fries. A burger with no cheese or mayo, but extra lettuce and tomato. "Damn, girl," I say. "Even when you're trying to indulge, you don't know how."

She smiles. She offers a polite little laugh. Both of us know it doesn't erase what she just told me, but it lets her breathe easy about it.

Besides, she'll still be in the city even if she's on a different campus. As long as we're in the same state, it's never really over. Both of us know that much.

8.

Indiana. Michigan State. Florida. These schools aren't going anywhere. Neither is anyone else texting and calling and peeping my lines. They might be in a rush to sign me, but it's not like they're gonna stop playing college basketball if I don't give them an answer.

But junior year at Marion East? That's disappearing with each second. So I best make it count. And if Jasmine's bailing on me, and Wes has his head all fogged up with smoke, fine. That just means it's me and my boys.

So come the next Friday, I'm not checking the stands to catch a smile from Jasmine or a fist pump from Wes or to take inventory on the recruiters. Sure, I give a nod to my people, but all my attention's on the other end of the floor. Louisville Ballard. Stacked. All five starters are going Division I, and they have a freshman coming off the bench—LeGarrett May—who's going to be better than any of them. It's the first game of a four-team tourney in Louisville, the kind of thing Marion East never got invites to before I hit the scene.

I make the rounds during warm-ups, pumping my boys up.

They're all juiced for the chance to take on a big-time team from another state. I just want to make sure they've got confidence in themselves, so I talk each of them up. But with a minute left in warm-ups, Coach Bolden grabs me by the elbow and pulls me toward the bench. "What do you think you're doing?" he asks.

"Getting guys amped," I answer.

"Amped," he repeats, like I've said some dirty word. "Why not *focused* instead? Derrick, I know you can go toe-to-toe with any player on Ballard, but that's *you*. We don't want Josh Reynolds thinking he needs to put up 20 tonight. We don't need J.J. Fuller thinking he's a three-point threat. What we need is for them to know we want to make them work on defense. That we've got to give up crashing the offensive glass so we can get back in transition."

"I hear you, Coach," I say. The man's the man, and there's no changing that. I jog back out to get a few more Js in before game-time. A pure three from the corner. A pull-up from the right wing. And then one rip to the hole for an up-and-under. Ready.

In the huddle, Coach runs through our game plan, shouting at us like we've already messed it up. Then it's time—starting line-ups and tip. Just before I hit the boards though, Coach Murphy gets in my ear. "Hey, don't sweat Bolden," he says. "The old man gets amped too, and that's how it comes out. Help rein the other guys in, but you attack when you get the chance."

That's the message I want to hear. As I put my D Rose 5s on the hardwood, I just know—feel it in my bones—I'm about to drop the truth on this gym.

As soon as I get out to center court, I see what Coach means.

Ballard's the real deal. They've got size across the board, especially down low with a 6'10" beast named James Lacy. And I know from watching game film that everyone but Lacy can stretch the D out to the arc.

Lacy controls the tip over Stanford, and they come at us. I know they can rip it and run in transition, but in the half-court they're pretty methodical. They reverse and look for Lacy. We sink down to scare off the entry, so they zip it back around the perimeter. Not a lot of cuts. Hardly any screens. But all it takes is one slow rotation. And they get it from Reynolds, who keeps his kicks in the paint a split second too long. He can't get back out to challenge his man at the arc, and—zip— Ballard's got a 3-0 lead.

Jones kicks the in-bounds to me, and Ballard offers some pressure. It's just to slow me down a beat. As soon as I get my shoulders past the first man, they all retreat. On our end, we're the polar opposite of them. Sure, we look inside, but our O is built on cuts and screens. I kick to Reynolds on the wing and cross-screen for Fuller. Reynolds looks post, then fakes to me flashing at the elbow. Soon as that's done, he runs a dribble exchange with Fuller. By then I'm coming all the way to the opposite baseline with a little breathing room. Fuller puts it in my mitts. Right away I see two coming at me. That leaves Jones alone on the block. I hit him. Lacy helps, but even Jones is quick enough to shuttle a pass around him to Stanford. An easy bucket.

I decide to give a little pressure right back. I hound my man for the first few dribbles up the floor. Then I hear Bolden thump his foot on the sideline. "Just get back, Bowen!" he shouts. I obey, but I saw enough. Their point guard has size and a sweet stroke—but his handles are shaky. He wanted no part of my pressure.

Pull   75

The game's like a boxing match between a heavyweight and a featherweight. They want to stand there and slug it out—pound, pound, pound down low—and when we get a chance we want to make them chase us until they drop. It pretty much evens out. They've got a 12-11 lead with about three minutes to go in the first.

And then it all changes—May checks in. You can hear the energy ripple through their crowd. He doesn't start, but he's second on their team in scoring behind Lacy. And he'll be running the hardwood the rest of the night. He's a load. He's 6'5" and rangy. He doesn't have any bulk on him yet, but he's strong enough to post. And the kid has hops like nobody's business. Even I can't rise inch-for-inch with May. His natural position is the three-spot, so Fuller gets first crack at him.

Right away you can see where they're going. Straight to May in the post. Fuller's face is all creased with concentration. He tries to root May out of the post. It's enough to make May catch it shallow wing instead, but he doesn't seem to mind. He faces, then jab-steps baseline to make Fuller move. As soon as he's got a little space, he rises—even fading away just a touch. All Fuller can do is stand and watch. While it's in mid-air, I hear May holler *Bucket!* It's no lie.

It's just a deuce in the first, but Ballard's crowd reacts like May just dropped a three at the buzzer. They know we don't have anyone who can check him. I mean, they might not play anyone this year who can. And we can't double both him *and* Lacy. There's almost a little laughter in their cheers, like they're saying *You can't do anything about it, boys.*

Well, maybe not on the defensive end. But as soon as I get the rock, I go to work. I'm not going to just freelance, but I'm looking for a crease every time I touch it. Finally, I get some room on a reversal and attack. I rip it past my man. I have a pull-up available, but that's not what I want. Time to challenge that big man in the middle.

I take a power dribble into the lane. I muscle past a few reaches. Then I'm squared up on Lacy. Only I've got some momentum and he's flat-footed. He waits until I leave my feet, then rises to challenge. I try to go right through him to the rim. And he does what 6'10" guys do— sends my shot into the second row. But I get the whistle I was looking for. So instead of Lacy woofing at me, I head to the stripe for two. Lacy's saddled with his first—it's just one, but it's a start. And everyone knows there's no difference between a 6'10" guy and a 5'10" guy when they're sitting on the pine.

It kills Bolden to see us struggle on defense like this. Sometimes I think the old man would rather we lose 22-21 than win a game in the 80s. So each timeout he's switching someone new onto May. Then, at halftime, he draws up a triangle-and-two scheme—three guys playing zone with one each tagging May and Lacy.

No dice. Nothing works.

By mid-fourth, May's got 26, and he's made it look easy. By now we've gone back to the original plan of checking him with Fuller. But even my boy Fuller—as gung ho as any player's ever been—is starting to hang his head in discouragement. Bolden claps his hands on the sideline and tells him to stay after it. We can also hear people shouting advice from the stands—*Body him up!* and *Make him go left!*—like nobody else has thought of that.

And it's not like Lacy's struggling. He had a double-double by mid-third, and now he's just wearing Jones and Stanford out. It's

Pull   77

Ballard's ball under their basket, with them up 76-70, and both our bigs are gasping for air.

Now I hear another voice cutting through the buzz of the crowd. It's Kid's. "Star time now," he shouts. "Be the star, D-Bow!"

Problem is, I don't have the size to check either Lacy or May. There's only so much I can do from the point. I've dropped 20 on them with 8 dimes to boot, but that doesn't get us stops. And, simple as can be, they lob an in-bounds over a worn-out Stanford. Lacy reels it in with his left and gathers with a big slap of his right. He's too deep for anyone to even challenge. He thunders it home. Eight-point game.

Bolden calls time. When we get into the huddle though, he doesn't say anything. He pulls out his whiteboard and uncaps his marker, but then he stops. His marker hovers over that board. It alights for an instant, leaving a tiny mark, and then comes back up. He caps it again. "Just get your breath," he tells us. "Get your legs back."

We each slump back on the bench, chests heaving. We take swigs of water. We wait for Bolden to say something more. When he sees that expression on our faces, he shakes his head. "That's it. Look, we've thrown every scheme at them. There's nothing more to try. Just take the rest of the timeout and suck it up. Dig down for one more run."

We do as we're told. When the buzzer sounds, we rise for more. Coach reminds us that we can't get all eight points back at once. "Just get a bucket and a stop," he says. "Then go from there."

I'm two steps onto the court when I feel that old, wiry grip at my elbow again. "What's up, Coach?" I ask.

Bolden squints up at me, just the hint of a smile on his old owl face. "You always want to get the guys *amped*, right?" he says.

Kevin Waltman

"Yeah," I say.

"Well, now would be the time, Derrick."

And there it is. For two years and change, Coach has held me back. He made me ride pine as a freshman. Made me play at a snail's pace as a soph. But right here, in a hot gym in Louisville, he's handing me the reins. "I got this, Coach," I say.

I don't have time to bark at my teammates before the ball's live again. I'll have to change their attitudes with my play. Fuller throws the in-bounds to Reynolds in the corner. Right away, it's clear we're dead if I don't do something. Reynolds just looks around, lost, and lets a trap clamp down on him. He tries a weak pass to Stanford, but it gets tipped away. I scramble to the right wing to scoop up the loose ball. I don't even bother re-setting. Just attack. I explode past my man into the paint. Lacy drops down to challenge, but this time he's late. I power one through before he can get there, and his momentum carries him into me. A late whistle, and I've got a chance for more at the stripe.

Plus, that's Lacy's fourth. While the Ballard coaches bellyache to the ref about the call, I sink the freebie. Down five. Our crowd buzzes with hope. That prompts some enthusiastic chatter from Stanford and Fuller, but for all their *Dig in on D now* and *We're still in this* noise, I know I've still got to shoulder the load.

Ballard brings it up. They're not in any hurry. They just want to eat some clock, then find Lacy or May on the blocks. *Bury these guys* is what they're thinking.

I position myself just between the circles, waiting. I even turn my head to shout at Reynolds to not double too early on the post. But that's just show. I'm a snake coiled for the strike. And as soon as that point—the same one who had the jitters early from my mock pressure—crosses mid-court, I cut him off from going right. A quick stab at the rock when he crosses. A deflection off his ankle. It trickles back between his legs, and he's dead. Before he has time to turn, I've already pinched the pill from him. As I race ahead, I can hear our crowd rising, hoping for some fireworks—a tomahawk, a reverse throw-down, *something*—but now's not the time for showboating. I get to the rim fast as I can, offer a vanilla dunk. It's a deuce all the same. Enough to prompt a timeout from the Ballard bench, their lead sliced to three in a matter of seconds.

"That's what I'm *talking* about," Stanford shouts as we head back to the huddle. "Get these boys *rattled*."

He's hollering like he's the one balling out. But let him. Thirty seconds ago, half the team didn't even believe. So if he has some swagger back, let him woof.

This time, Bolden's got more of a plan too. He gets that whiteboard out and starts diagramming feverishly. "All game long we've been doubling from the top," he says. "Let's change it up one time. As soon as Lacy or May gets it, we're doubling from the backside." He stops and draws it on the board, so we can visualize. "That means the rotations are going the other way, and"—he makes a quick jag on the board, showing the off-play perimeter player diving down to the paint—"the most important part is this one. You've got to cut off that other post before they see it."

Back on the floor, Ballard's point brings it up really carefully against me. At the first sign of real pressure, he just dumps it off to their two guard. When they cross mid-court, the plan's obvious. They want

Lacy deep. May's been the man, but I guess when it's crunch time, they want their senior to get the rock. They plod, waiting to get the right look. At last, Lacy gets position on Stanford. They get it to him, but Stanford works hard to nudge Lacy about a foot off the block. That's when we react. Jones comes on a hard double from the baseline. I dive down to take away the easy look to the other post. Reynolds floats out top, playing safety between the perimeter guys.

But Lacy's not looking to pass. He feels Stanford shading him middle. He spins hard for what he thinks is a free run at the rim. Instead, he barrels smack into Jones. The two of them spill in a hulking heap at the baseline. The trill of the ref's whistle splits the air. The whole gym inhales, waiting to see which way it will go. The ref hesitates for a second, like he's caving to the hopes of the home crowd. But then he cups his hand behind his head and punches the air with the other. Charge. Lacy's fifth. Our ball.

The Ballard coaches lose it. Their senior center called for a charge late? For his fifth? Their head coach storms almost out to mid-court, eyes bulging in rage. I can't hear over the boos of the crowd, but I'm pretty sure I lip-read a couple f-bombs. The ref spins toward him, ready to jack the coach up with a T, but his assistants drag him back to the bench before things get worse.

While Ballard regroups and finds a sub for Lacy, Coach Bolden huddles us on the sideline. "Listen up!" he shouts. "That play means nothing if we don't keep pushing. We're still down three. Let's get a good look here. And when they get the ball back, we're doubling May everywhere. I don't care if he catches it 40 feet out. Double." Then he snaps his fingers angrily at Coach Murphy, who fetches the whiteboard.

I peek at Stanford, who smiles. He's been around long enough to know that when Bolden starts ordering Murphy around like that, the old man's feeling salty. Bolden thinks we've got 'em. He quickly draws up a set. It's a cross-screen to free Stanford, since Lacy's sub will be checking him. "Don't force it," he snaps. "If it's not there, iso Derrick on the wing and then space around him." Then he looks at me. "Don't you force it either. If the defense jumps at you, find a shooter."

One of the refs intrudes on our huddle, tells us we have to move. Ballard's sub checks in, and it's back on. We run Coach's set. Fuller looks to Stanford low. He gets it to him, but Stanford mishandles the pass and has to leave the block to reel it in. He's fifteen feet out now, back to the basket. It's not there. He squints in concentration and starts to back his man down. Forcing it. I race to the wing and call for the rock. Stanford takes one more dribble, but then relents. He kicks to me and I back it out. I eye the scoreboard—two and change left—but as I do, my man motions toward May for a switch. So now I've got a freshman on me—only it's the best freshman in the land, and at 6'5" one I can't just shake and shoot over. *Fine.* Bring him. Best on best.

I size May up. A couple jabs left. A quick cross to my right. He barely moves. His range means he can challenge my pull-up or try to flick the ball away on a drive, without reacting to every little fake. So I just *go*. I shudder to my left, then rip right—leaving May guarding air and wondering why he never saw moves like that in middle school. I jump-stop in the paint. Draw the D. Rise. But at the last instant, I do the right thing. Reynolds is all alone in the corner. I put it on the money to him, and he's got a sweet look at a three.

Money. Ballard's crowd sits. Their players hang their heads. The only noise in the gym is the ruckus of our small crowd and Bolden stomping his feet and screaming: "Back! Get back on D!"

We do, but I've got one more surprise left for Ballard's point. As soon as he nears mid-court, I sprint at him. He picks it up, wanting no piece of my pressure. And as soon as he does, I jump back into the passing lane. He's stranded. The ten-count keeps ticking, and now Reynolds and Fuller dig into their men. I can read the thought process on that point's face. He stares at May, thinking his best out is to lob it to him. I bail hard toward May. I arrive with the pass. Since I've got some momentum and May is standing still, I outleap him for it.

Fuller and Reynolds fill the wings. I push the other way. This time though, I'm not giving it up. I race it right up on that point. He just raises his hands, hoping for a cheap charge. I'm around him easily. This time I add a little sugar—cocking that rock behind my ear before throwing it down.

Another Ballard timeout, but everyone knows they're dead. When they break, they try to work through May, but we follow Coach's plan—double, double, double. They miss a trey. May forces and misses. Then forces again. And we ice it at the stripe.

That's a serious win. A comeback on the road against some big-time talent. And, yeah, I made some plays when we needed it, but Reynolds and Jones stepped up too. Those were the question marks coming in— could Reynolds step up? Could Jones replace Moose's bulk in the post? Things are coming together.

I speed through my shower, pack my gear and hit the bus. When I climb those steps, Coach Bolden is waiting on me. He's always there,

Pull 83

win or lose, to throw a few words at each player, even if it's just a quick *Good game*. But when he sees me, he points at the seat behind him. Always obedient, I slide in and wait for Coach as he says his few words to all the other guys filing on. But the whole time I'm anxious. Can he really be mad at me now? It's like no matter how hard I try, the guy just demands more.

Finally the whole team's on. Coach signals the driver. The engine roars to life and we start the drive to the hotel. Coach doesn't waste any time. He digs the stat sheet out of his pocket and hands it back to me. He points to my line. "Tell me what you think," he says.

What I think is that it's pretty impressive—3 steals, 8 rips, 9 assists, and 27 points on only 14 shots. That's a killer line, really. But I know Coach. He wants me to dig out the negative, even now. "Too many turnovers," I say. It's only four, which isn't a nightmare, but I have to give him something.

To my amazement, Coach shrugs. "Well, you can always cut down on turnovers. But I'd have to be one mean S.O.B. to gripe after that."

Bolden takes the stats back from me. As the lights from the Ballard gymnasium fade behind us, Coach wads up the stat sheet. He flicks it in the air. I follow its arc to see it just miss Murphy in the seat across from him. Behind us, the whole team's in celebration mode. Stanford, I can tell, is in the middle of an exaggerated boast, Reynolds and Fuller are cracking up beside him. Jones keeps trying to shout Stanford down. The younger guys are soaking it all in, basking in the afterglow of a big win. Bolden leans over to me. "I've never been much of a numbers guy," he says. "But when I see that"—he points to the players, everyone living it up—"I know my point guard's done his job."

9.

Mid-December and things are cranking. After beating Ballard, we just went ahead and won the championship of that tourney, then ripped into Cathedral last night. So just as the temps are dipping lower and lower, the boys at Marion East are heating up. Later tonight we've got St. Joseph all the way down from South Bend in our gym. I can feel it. We're gonna wreck them.

Right now, it's like old times at my house. Jayson's got the afternoon game on, a Big Ten-ACC showdown between Minnesota and Clemson. Used to be I'd just settle in and check it for the sake of the game. Now I picture the mailers from both squads, think about the texts I've got from the coaches on those benches. Minnesota I don't feel, even though they're a Big Ten squad. I mean, I walk out my front door and it's cold enough. I don't need it any colder. Clemson? I never thought much about them until I started getting contacted, but they're intriguing. It's a long way from home. They're not exactly the big boys of the ACC. But then that's part of the appeal. Start fresh, go someplace where I could knock off Carolina and Duke. Because if you go to those places or to someplace like Syracuse, there's nothing special in winning the ACC. It's been done. But, man, suit up for Clemson and lead them to glory? They'd probably name the arena after you. Anyway, it's not like I'm making up my mind any time soon. Just thinking.

But there's not much space for thinking in this house. Jayson's got the set blasting, but the real noise is coming from Uncle Kid. And it's not because he's up to no good. Nope. Like always, he's over on a Saturday before a game, but this time he brought company. In the past, that's meant shady friends who set my dad on edge, but this time Kid's got himself a woman. Not just any woman. She sits, legs crossed, at our kitchen table, one heel dangling off her foot just an inch. Her pants are tight but not too much—just enough to turn heads without seeming sleazy—and she's got a bright red sweater hugging her curves. When she smiles—which she does all the time—her eyes light up and her face turns girlish. She's got to be a good ten years younger than Kid. Her name's April, and it fits. She's pouring pure sunshine into our house on a bitter day.

At the table, my parents pepper April with questions. "So what do you do?" Mom asks.

April smiles again. More sunshine. Even my mom, always skeptical, is taken in by her. "I'm a nurse at Methodist. In oncology." She sees my mom's face tighten at that last word, but she just smiles again. "It's no picnic some days. We see people that are really hurting. And some who aren't going to make it. But that's why I figure it's so important to show up every day in good spirits. I feel like I have to be in a good mood for them. And then sometimes we see people on the days when the doctor has good news for them. That makes it all worth it."

Impressed, Mom leans back. Then she glances at Kid and folds her arms. I can see her wheels spinning. She's not sure what, but she's pretty sure Kid's been selling April some lies.

"How did you two meet?" Dad asks. There's a catch in his throat as he says it, an uncomfortable sound. Anyone could tell what he's really wanting to know is not how they *met* but how two people like them could get *together*.

"Thanks for the vote of confidence, big brother," Kid says. Then he laughs, easy with the whole thing. April reaches over and puts her hand on Kid's knee. It's a little gesture. Not like some big passionate embrace. But it's one of those things people do when they're comfortable with each other. And that's the thing—this is the first we've met April, but already she and Kid seem like they're a couple through and through. I mean, as far as I knew, Kid was just still scouting for easies on the weekends. "Back when you"—he points to Dad—"were in the hospital, we kept bumping into each other in the cafeteria. Then we met a month ago at St. Elmo's. We were both there with some friends and were getting a drink afterwards."

Now we're all skeptical. St. Elmo's? That place takes coin. Uncle Kid is making decent money bartending, but no way is he affording that place. Then there's his new ride. All the new threads he's been sporting. I see my dad give a half-smile that fades into a look of concern. *Same old Kid*, he seems to be thinking.

Kid must sense it, because he pops up from the table. "Anyway, that was the beginning." He winks at April. "All good since then."

April smiles back, but then looks away real quick like she's slightly embarrassed. That move—the smile then lookaway—reminds me for a flash of Lia Stone. The thought of her sets my pulse racing

Pull 87

the way Jasmine used to. "Babe," April coos, "would you mind getting me a glass of something cold to drink? I feel a little hot with this third degree." She says it like syrup though. That, way more than Kid bouncing nervously from the table, defuses everything. My parents lean back and laugh. They apologize for grilling April. She just smiles like it's not a thing at all.

And Kid, happy to be off the hook, cracks the fridge like he owns it. "We've got Coke and orange juice and"—he rifles around for a second—"some lemonade it looks like."

April's eyes brighten. "Lemonade, babe."

"You got it, girl." Kid pours her a tall glass with ice. He does it with a little flourish, raising the pitcher high over the glass so the lemonade cascades down. Then he serves it to her, along with a little brush of his hand along her shoulders. We all just watch. They're on their own planet right now, like this has been their kitchen and their house all along, while we're just guests intruding on their leisurely lovers' Saturday.

I'm watching all this from the couch, my attention cycling between that and the game. Jayson's pulling for Minnesota, but as I watch Clemson I'm intrigued. They don't get out and go as much as I'd like, but they play their offense way up high. Lots of room for their perimeter guys to slash. They don't have the horses right now, but a few times in a row Minnesota gets lost and Clemson just carves them up. *I could turn some ankles in that offense,* I think.

As I'm imagining that, something else intrudes on my concentration. It's the *thuuzzz thuuzzz thuuzzz* of a thumping bass in a passing car. It's not like it's some big deal. Happens about a dozen times

Kevin Waltman

a day. But something—maybe how it's creeping extra slow—makes me get up and check. I go to the window and sure enough, it's JaQuentin's ride oozing down Patton. It makes me shake my head. Only one place he's headed—a couple doors up the street to Wes' place.

I've tried with Wes. I have. As much as I can with my parents watching every move. But more and more it's clear Wes wants no part of me. Or that he's changed into someone else entirely. I mean, last time he texted me he signed off with a dollar sign in his name instead of an S: *We$*. Ridiculous. But if he wants to turn himself into a joke, I guess it's his business. I just hope he doesn't get killed doing it.

The craziest thing is, Wes should *hate* JaQuentin. This whole thing started last year when JaQuentin stole Wes' girl Iesha. And as far as I know she and JaQuentin are still at it. So, what, Wes wants a front-row seat? I don't get it. Not at all.

"*Hoooo!*" Jayson explodes. I turn back to the living room, figuring Minnesota's on a run. No—on the replay, I see Clemson caught them napping for an alley-oop that even Jayson had to respect. Jayson's exuberance draws Kid and April into the living room too—though maybe they just want a break from my folks. Whatever. All I know is that noise out on the street isn't mine to deal with. I got what I need here.

"Clemson's gonna pull away," I say. "They're tight."

Jayson starts ripping on them, partly because he wants Minnesota to win, but mostly just to disagree with me.

Kid gives April's knee a quick squeeze then jumps in on Jayson's side. "You watch, D. Gophers are tough at home. Besides, things get jumpy late. You know they'll get some home whistles."

"Nah, Kid. The refs can't guard people for them. They're all turned around on D."

Kid smiles, leans over to me. "Okay, big man. You so sure, put some action on it." I beg off, telling him that not everyone has money to burn. But he keeps on. "Don't have to be money. Tell you what. Clemson wins, I'll clean your room for you. Organize all that recruiting mess. Hell, I'll even text the bad news to all the schools you want off your back. But if the Gophers win you gotta clean my ride."

It's a sucker bet. I know Kid's never gonna clean my room. Not even if Clemson wins by 40. I peep at Dad, who's been eyeing us as he picks up the kitchen. He shakes his head at me, telling me *no*. But I can't back punk out, or I'll never hear the end. So I reach over and shake on it. I even give April, who's just been laughing at all of us, a quick wink—working up the confidence I'll need to turn that on Lia first chance I get.

"Hey, I want a piece of this," Jayson chimes. He thinks for a second. Then he lands on it. "Dishes for a week," he says.

I pause. Take a glance at the screen. Clemson's up six with five and change to go. Got the ball too. "Make it two weeks," I say.

"Deal."

And, just as soon as the word's spoken, Minnesota gets a cheap charge call on the baseline. It wipes out a bucket and sends Clemson's bench into protest.

"There it is," Kid says. "Like clockwork, D. You gotta listen to your uncle. People been getting the screws put to 'em in Minnesota since before you were born."

St. Joseph probably regrets the trip. It's a good three hours down here, but after the beat down we're giving them, the trip home will seem like 20.

It's early fourth and we're up 19. Everyone's got theirs—Reynolds dropping smooth treys, Fuller working the mid-range game, Stanford busting out an array of post moves, and Jones cleaning up around the rim. Me? I'm flirting with a triple-double—14 points, 8 rips, 8 dimes. A handful of steals and blocks to boot. Only thing stopping me is Coach. With six and change to go, the buzzer sounds at a dead ball and in comes Rider.

It's cool. A triple-double *would* be nice. But I get the logic. Break in the back-up with a safe lead. Save the mileage on my legs. I hit the sidelines and get a big ovation from the crowd. They know. Lots of fans just get hung up on points. It's not like my 14 is melting the scoreboard. But as they whistle and stomp, it's clear they get that I've controlled every inch of the hardwood tonight. I give them a little acknowledgement back—raise one finger real quick to let them know I feel the love.

I hit the pine and Murphy gets in my ear immediately. "That's how you ball, D," he says. "You keep it rolling like that and *nobody* gonna come in here and take us down." He thumps me on the back, then moves down the bench again to talk to other players.

The ovation's nice. The hype from Murphy is appreciated. But at this point, I'm like a well-trained dog. All I want is the approval of the man with the leash. I gaze down the bench toward Bolden, but he's leaning forward to follow every play like the game's hanging in the balance. Finally, he turns his head a few inches and sees me staring. Then he nods his head ever-so-slightly and gives me a knowing wink. It doesn't even take a second before he's back to the game, but, man, that wink is worth a hundred standing ovations. I hate to admit how much it swells me up with pride. Forget waiting another week for a game, I want back on that court *now*.

Trouble is, it doesn't take long for me to get my wish. Rider's a mess. He gets beat baseline the first trip down. Deuce for St. Joseph. Then he drags his pivot foot to give the ball back. They cash it in with another bucket, Jones getting pinned in the paint. Then Rider throws a long, lazy cross-court pass toward Reynolds. It's the kind of thing that would get pinched in a middle-school game. St. Joseph races down on a break. Rider makes matters even worse by taking a late hack at a guy who's already at the rim. And-one. Just like that the lead's back to 13, with a free throw coming to make it 12.

Bolden doesn't even speak. He just points in my direction and snaps three times. When I check in, Rider hangs his head. He sulks off, looking for pity. But what am I supposed to tell him? What I want to say is *A man gives you the keys to the car, don't wreck it first time around the block*. I figure better just say nothing and let him figure it out himself. When he hits the bench, Murphy and Bolden are both in his ear. They don't jump him exactly, but they're trying to teach pretty urgently.

St. Joseph knocks in the freebie. I get the in-bounds from Reynolds and they pick up with some soft pressure. It's not like things are tight yet, but with five minutes to go they've at least got some life again. I take my time. I cross mid-court and then kick it to Fuller—waiting until he's far enough out that he won't get any wild notions about trying to score. Then we just run our set. Any time I see someone get a look in their eyes like they might force, I clap my hands and sprint over to get the ball. After about 30 seconds though, Jones catches shallow wing. He's dropped in 10 tonight, his career best. That's all good, but it's given him a false sense of confidence. Before I can sprint over to get it from him, he fires one up.

Right away, I see it's off. I dart into the lane. My man peels off, leaking for a run-out if they get the board. No such luck for St. Joseph. With a free run, I time it up. I plant my feet and rise between their bigs. Pluck the orange as it pops off the rim. Then power it back home. The rim snaps back up with a *pop* and the backboard shudders like there's been an earthquake. The crowd? They take a collective gasp—not every day you see a follow-up jam from a point guard—and then they let it rip. I mean, *howl.* My teammates are hyped too. Stanford gives me a shove of approval and shouts, "That's the real deal, right there."

St. Joseph's done. They knew it was a long-shot anyway, but that jam was the final nail in the coffin if there ever was one.

The only challenge left is to navigate another interview with Whitfield. He's waiting for me outside the locker room, drinking a Coke from a paper cup. As soon as he sees me, out comes that phone. "You were right about running things when you got back," he says. It's not a question. He says it like he's a buddy trying to liven me up. But I know better.

"We're playing better as a team," I say. "Things are starting to click." I hate talking in clichés. But it's better than the alternative of giving straight answers.

He nods, takes one last sip of Coke. He shakes a little ice out and then talks to me while it's still in his mouth. "I have to ask. Any news on colleges?"

"No news," I say. "They're all hitting me up pretty regular, but I don't know step one yet."

"There was a rumor trending last night that Indiana might have an inside track," he says.

He's fishing, I'm almost sure of it. "No," I say. But that draws a startled reaction from him, like I've just ruled the Hoosiers out. "I mean, I'm not saying anyone's out either. I just...look, man, I don't know yet. Indiana's in the running, I guess. But so are about a million other schools."

He frowns again, like I'm lying to him. So he shifts gears. "Big revenge game coming up," he says. "Any thoughts on Evansville Harrison?"

Yes, I think, *I could fill a book with my thoughts on Evansville Harrison.* He's talking about our December rematch in Banker's Life Fieldhouse. Our chance to avenge our loss in the playoffs from last year. But I catch myself. "My only thought is that we've got to win the opener if we want a crack at Evansville Harrison."

He presses on. "But you've got to want that rematch against the state champions. And any thoughts on squaring off with Dexter Kernantz? Do you think you two are the top point guards in the state?"

This time I can't help myself. "There's only one top point guard," I say. Then I point to the court. "He was running those boards tonight. And he most definitely wasn't wearing an Evansville Harrison jersey. The D-Bow Show only plays at Marion East."

That draws a smile from Whitfield. He shakes out a few more

ice cubes and crunches them as he thanks me. Immediately I regret it. That will absolutely make the paper. It'll be bulletin board material for Evansville Harrison. And it will make it all about me again, just the thing that burned my boys last time around.

You get told all your life to tell the truth. But I'm learning that there are plenty of benefits to holding a little truth back sometimes.

10.

"I don't see the big deal. Just go to Indiana." This is Jayson's take. I'm chilling with him and Uncle Kid at Sure Burger, chowing down and soaking up the St. Joseph win.

"Not as simple as that, little man," Kid says. Now that he's got himself cleaned up, he's taken on this knowing air. He even made a face when we walked in the place, sneering at the greasy, dingy atmosphere. It's like he's suddenly trying to be the big man around everyone. I'm not buying it. "Your brother's got a lot to weigh," he goes on. "What system will fit? What coach will stay? Where can he get some hardware?"

I wave them both off. "I only care about two things," I say. "Beating Evansville Harrison next weekend and getting into this grub." With that, I dig in, and they follow suit.

We eat in satisfied silence for a while, people-watching while we chow down. There's a guy in the corner, hood pulled up, so wrecked he can barely sit up to eat. A couple older guys two tables over, already fat as houses, shoveling cheese fries like there's no tomorrow. Then random

Kevin Waltman

kids my age, all acting the fool on a Saturday night—yapping and laughing, the guys bumping fists and the girls hugging everyone they see, all of them making an impossible mess of discarded straws and lids and burger wrappers. Some of the older guys have that low-lidded look like they've added a little something extra to their drinks.

After a few minutes, Jayson and Kid go back to arguing over where I should go. Jayson gets a little worked up, more than I'd expect. That just lets Kid play his new role. He talks in this patient, relaxed voice to Jayson. And that just sets Jayson off more. "I'm *thirteen*," he snaps. "I can think for myself. You act like everything I say is stupid." It's *loud*. Angry. An outburst even for Jayson.

It pops the whole place to attention. Even the derelict in the corner rouses a little, eyeing our table for a second before sinking back down into his fog. Kid eases off. He raises his hands and pushes back from the table. "Easy," he says. "Nobody's saying you're stupid. You're entitled to your opinion." Then he gives this chuckle. It's not Kid's natural laugh—more like something more mature he's imitating. I'm with Jayson. Not about making a snap decision to go to Indiana, but that this new version of Kid is a drag. I want my Uncle Kid back. Easy, funny, down to hang. Not this guy stuffed into a button-down, checking his smartphone every two minutes to text April.

Then again, the old Kid would have been running some game. He'd have been playing Kentucky for a car and Louisville for a load of cash, probably ten other schools for some other kind of mess. So maybe the "new Kid" isn't that bad a deal.

And then—Lia Stone. She comes through that door, looking *fiine*, a few friends tagging along. Her friends aren't bad either, but they're not the reason Sure Burger goes still. When Lia Stone comes in a room, people notice. Every guy in the place swells up—chin out, chest puffed, acting all big. And their girls cut their eyes over at Lia in jealousy. The only person that doesn't seem fazed at all is Lia herself. Composed as can be, she just walks to the counter and checks the menu. Even the guy at the register—stringy-armed and pint-sized, not a chance in the world—eyes Lia, checking her from her tight black jeans to her dope gray sweater with the black trim. His jaw hangs open like Beyoncé just walked in.

My heart's still with Jasmine. But my body's here in the same place as Lia.

"Easy on the stare, D," Uncle Kid says. "Creeping never helped a brother."

It's the first good advice I've had from Kid in a while, so I go back to my burger and fries. But I still check her. Lia orders, waits on her friends, then goes to find an open table. And then—yep—*she* checks *me*. I don't turn to look straight at her, just keep her in my peripheral vision. She hesitates, like she's not sure she should step over. Then she slings her purse down in her chair and comes our way. "Derrick?" she says.

I do my gentleman thing, stand to greet her and introduce her to my brother and uncle. Then we kind of stand there, wondering what to say. Leave it to Jayson to break that silence. "I already know who she is, D," he cracks. Then he turns to her. "You know, I'll be at Marion East next year. Ain't no rule says a freshman can't hook up with a senior girl."

That knocks even Lia off-balance a bit. It takes her a second to recover. She shakes her head real quick like she's dazed. Then that smile comes soft and easy and all is good. "You're gonna get big and break hearts, aren't you?" she says to Jayson.

And with that Lia does something nobody in our family's been able to do for years—she renders Jayson speechless. A goofy grin spreads across his face. He even has to look away, all bashful. He's been bristling pretty good at everyone lately, but I know she just made his world.

Then Lia turns her gaze back to me. I try not to buckle under it. "You guys balled out pretty strong tonight," she says.

Immediate relief—she's going to talk hoops. "We got after it pretty good," I say. "But the real test is next week. Gotta get revenge on Evansville Harrison."

"You'll get it," she says. "The way you're playing, you'll get everything you want."

I glance down at Kid. The guy trying to be all-wise and above it all is gone. Just the old Kid now. He leans forward a tad, eyes bugged, silently urging me to take Lia Stone up on her word. If I don't do something soon, Kid's going to ask her out for me. "How about after that game you and I kick it?" I say. Then, afraid that *kick it* makes it sound too much like we're friends, I clarify. I look her in the eye, say, "Just us. Someplace a lot nicer than this."

"You're on," she says. Then she's out.

I sit back down, as amped from that little exchange as I was at any point during tonight's game. When I finally check Kid and Jayson, they're just shaking their heads at me.

"Man," Kid says, "you got quicks on the court, but you are *sloooow* around women."

"What?" I say.

Jayson jumps in now. "Staring at a gimme and you almost couldn't pull the trigger."

They laugh, and I take it. Because when they're done laughing, I'm the one heading out with Lia Stone next weekend.

I explain why. No Wes. No nonsense. No trouble. Just a real, honest-to-goodness date. I mean, a *date* in 2015. It's so quaint my parents should be thrilled. But you'd think asking them for the car and some extra cash is as big a deal as getting them to change their will.

"Where are you taking her?" Mom asks.

"I don't know. Some place decent downtown. I haven't figured out every move yet."

"What kind of girl is she?" Dad asks.

"She's nice," I say. "It's not like last year." And that's about as much as I'll say to them on that subject. I know I got myself tangled up with Daniella Cole last year, but I've learned my lesson. I don't want to re-hash it.

"Fine," Mom says at last. "Figure out where you're taking her so I know how much money to give you. Text me when you get there. Text me when you drop her off at home. And be back in this door by 11:30. Or you will never drive a car again until you're 40."

Again, I just take it. All I want is the car, a decent time with Lia. If that means they're going to treat me like I'm some liar and criminal, fine. It's humiliating. But whatever.

Dad can still see me seething. So when Mom's finished her little lecture and gone to bed, leaving me and Dad alone to check a West Coast game, he picks at that thread. "Don't sulk. You're getting what you want."

"I know," I say. "But you two act like I shot someone this summer. Can't you finally let it go?"

It's a risk. Dad could get offended and rescind the permission I just got. But he nods, actually acknowledging that I have a point. Then he rubs his jaw and neck, pondering something. He looks at me, thinks some more, and then he starts in. "Your Uncle Kid had a chance. He was something to behold back in the day. People in the family were the only ones who used to call him Kid. That's because he was my kid brother, no other younger cousins. So it was all *Kid, Kid, Kid.* But outside the house he was Sidney. He was Sidney to his teachers, who loved him. He was Sidney to his youth coaches, who saw all his potential. Then he hit high school and started wanting everyone to call him Kid. It became like this persona he had—reckless, nonchalant, impulsive. It wasn't the Sidney I'd known, and it was hard to watch."

"Dad, I'm not—" but he just holds his hand up. Not my time to talk. So I just settle back on the couch and listen to Dad's story.

He looks away sometimes while he's talking, either because the memories are too hazy or, maybe, too fresh. "Still, he wasn't in any real trouble. He'd piss off his coaches, sure. Just had to do things his way. But that story's as old as sports. Nothing bad. And when Bolden took over Kid's senior year, it was clear right away there was going to be friction. That your eighteen-year-old uncle and Joe Bolden somehow landed in the same locker room is a sign that God most certainly plays tricks on us." He smiles then, amused at the idea. Then he's back to it. "Anyway, even then there was nothing bad until a few weeks into his senior season. He came home one day and was off the team. Just like that. I remember being at college and asking my parents why, but they didn't have any answers. Well, come Christmas break when I was back home, they finally explained it to me."

Now he stares at me, a long and serious look across our living room. I see the lights from the T.V. flicker on his face, but otherwise his expression is dark and foreboding. "Bolden found a few grams of cocaine in your uncle's locker." Dad sighs, still pained. "Kid swore and swore, and would swear today, that he was just holding it for a friend. Maybe that was true. He'd gotten in with some bad people. But it didn't matter either way. Bolden suspended him. Then Kid kept screwing up every chance he had to come back. He was late to every bus. He got in a fight at practice. And then, late in the season, he got arrested. Same thing—more coke. He told Mom and Dad he was just holding it for someone again, but even they didn't believe him this time."

I didn't know any of this. I imagined some of it—Kid missing buses, acting like a fool under Bolden's watch. But I never knew about the drugs. I mean, I suspected it sometimes. It's not a complete shock. To hear Dad say it makes it real though.

As he talked, Dad fell into a kind of trance. His eyes fixed on some random place on the wall behind me. Now he snaps out of it and looks at me. "So. It's not just your Mom and I being paranoid. We had just started dating when Kid got into that trouble. And, son, we don't think you're going to do stupid things like that, but you get in with the wrong people and—"

Now I'm the one interrupting him. "Wes isn't one of those people, Dad." I don't know if I fully believe that myself anymore—but it's not okay for anyone else to badmouth him. "He's just going through some stuff, and he needs some help."

Dad nods, trying to be understanding. "I hear you, Derrick," he says, "but I've spent almost two decades trying to pull Kid up. It wouldn't take so much effort if I could have just kept him away from the wrong people in high school."

"That's not gonna happen with me and Wes," I say. But again, I don't half believe my own words.

Finally, Dad waves his hand in the air like he's trying to shoo a fly. "Fine. Let's leave it. You want cash and the car for a date and we're giving it to you. Good?"

"Good," I say. That's that, but I know the conversation isn't really over.

11.

Two weeks before Christmas, and it's the showdown in Banker's Life Fieldhouse. They've got the four schools that made State last year all together for a two-day tourney. We squeaked by Muncie Central last night, so the Saturday night showcase is us and Evansville Harrison. The two of us are a combined 14-1, and that only loss is from when I sat out the opener. But I don't care about the venue. I don't care about the crowd. I don't care about any games this season that are in the rear view mirror.

I care about what's on the other end of the floor. Evansville Harrison stole our season last year. They caught us fresh from upsetting the Hamilton Academy powerhouse and clipped us before we knew what had happened. And then there's Dexter Kernantz. I seethe every time I see someone rank him higher than me, but here's the dirty truth—he outplayed me last year. He controlled the game from wire to wire. I got mine, but he got more.

As we warm up, I check him on the other end. He's in constant motion. Darting to the rim, chasing down a loose ball, flitting from teammate to teammate to talk them up. He's got this ashy look, one of those guys who seems to be any number of races depending on the light. He's got a tattoo of a Chinese character on one shoulder. When he talks with his boys, he jukes around. But none of that matters. What matters is he's got the quicks and he's got the smarts. I better bring it tonight.

After a few more minutes getting loose, we huddle up. Coach goes over our sets. He doesn't mention last year's loss specifically, but he sends us off with a little dig. "Remember," he says, "just because these guys don't run every chance doesn't mean they're not getting after it. Don't get lulled. Not again."

That's all the pep talk I need. We hit those boards, and there's a fire in my belly. I do my quick checks of the stands. Family. Jasmine, who gives me a quick wave. Then Lia, five rows behind Jasmine. Can't look at her long, or I *will* get distracted. Then over to the band, my head turning out of some kind of muscle memory, even though I know there's just some anonymous kid where Wes used to sit.

"Derrick!" I hear. "*Derrick!*" I turn back to the bench and see Bolden, waving me in for one last word. "You okay?" he asks. His eyebrows are pinched down, like I've done something to get him worked up.

"I'm good," I say.

He gestures toward the floor. "Usually you're trying to get everyone all wound up. You're quiet. That's not like you."

I nod. "I'm done *talking* about getting amped, Coach. Tonight I just want to *play*."

That brings a rarity—a big ol' wide smile on Coach Bolden's

leathery face. He claps his hands once in approval. Then he's back to the bench and I'm back to the hardwood.

The refs get us set, the crowd simmering in anticipation. Harrison's big man, Scotty Sims, isn't terribly skilled, but he's got several inches on Stanford, so when the ball goes up they control easily. Right away they get it in the hands of Kernantz. He's a waterbug. Driving. Backing it out. Changing directions. He hits me with a killer crossover to get a crease, but I recover in the lane. I have some size on him, so he can't rise up clean. He kicks it to the wing instead, and their offense hums along.

Everyone gets a touch. No looks though. So it's back to Kernantz. He circles out top, resetting, and everyone else flattens to the baseline. First possession, first time soloed up with Kernantz. I clap my hands and dig into my defensive stance. I keep my feet light so I'm ready to move. I know he's too quick to just clamp down, but the key is not to let him get all the way past. Then someone will have to help, and that's when Kernantz just carves folks up. He takes his time, using a few rhythm dribbles to his left. Then, quick as a whip, he spins right and attacks. I stay on his hip as he rips into the paint. He gives a deft little bump, planting his left shoulder in my chest, then hops back to create space. I jump with him, but I'm just taking the bait. He leans back toward me as he rises. He's got no chance at the shot, but when we make contact he gets what he wants—a whistle, first foul on me, two quick free throws.

The guy's good. Crafty.

He buries them both, so we get the rock down a deuce. We're in no huge hurry on our end either. We run through our offense multiple times. On a few occasions, I know I could attack, but I don't want to show off all my moves yet. I want to hold back some go-to stuff Kernantz has never seen. On a quick reversal, I spot Stanford short baseline. I put the leather in his paws. He can drain that, so Harrison's big lunges at the shot fake. A quick duck under and dribble to the rim and Stanford ties it.

It's like that the whole first, then into the second. Long possessions, but good ones. It's not like every shot falls, but nobody starts chucking up cheap ones. And I swear there's maybe three turnovers between the teams.

Every player who's hit the boards has brought their best, but I know what's up—this is really a game between me and Kernantz. No, we don't score every bucket. But those possessions run through us. The team that wins the point guard match-up is going to be the team that wins the game. Even Bolden knows it. "You're doing a good job out there," he tells me at a dead ball. "Keep distributing. Keep staying into Kernantz." That's about as thick as Bolden lays on the praise in the middle of a game.

We're tied at 19, our ball out on the side. I bring it into the front-court and start into our offense. Again, there's nothing easy. When I give it up, Kernantz follows me through some screens, always between me and the ball. Textbook. On my baseline cut, I stop short at the post. "Ball!" I shout to Reynolds. It takes him a second. By the time I squeeze the orange, Kernantz has me bodied up best he can. Still, with my size some help comes from the high post. *Zip.* I put that thing on a cutting Jones. He fights through some traffic for a shot, but as soon as it leaves his hands I see it's off. I put a swim move on Kernantz to get position. I time it up. Then I rise for another throwdown off the rebound. Plus a whistle.

That gets the crowd pumping again. And it's just a little sign that no matter how skilled Kernantz is, there are things I can bring to the court that he just can't.

One problem. The official's pointing the other way. Evansville Harrison ball. Nobody can even figure out why. Bolden just puts his hands palms-up on the sidelines and stomps his feet. "What's the call?" he shouts. Then I see Kernantz down on the baseline. He's sprawled there like he's been shot. At last the ref points to me and makes a hook motion with his elbow. Un*real*. He's calling me for that swim move. I look at Kernantz, see him crack a little smile while his teammates help him up—all of it was an act.

Our crowd throws an absolute fit. Two seconds ago they were celebrating my jam. Now they're about to storm down and murder that ref. It doesn't matter. They can yell all they want, it's not going to change the call.

Evansville Harrison gets ready to in-bound the ball, but not before a buzzer at the scorer's table—it's Rider, coming in for me. That draws a fresh round of *boos* from our crowd. Not because they're on Bolden's back—he's just protecting me from a third first-half foul, hoping we can hang until halftime—but because it makes that call seem like even more of an injustice.

I hit the bench in disgust. I towel some sweat off my face, hear all my teammates tell me it was a garbage call. Coach Murphy clears a seat next to me and gets in my ear. "Don't let it get to you," he says. "Get back out there in the second half for winning time. We'll hang until then."

So he says. But when he looks at the court, I see the expression on his face change. Murphy takes a deep breath, then rubs his jaw like he just got punched. Rider against Kernantz. That's death.

Kernantz lets the offense run for a little while, just sizing Rider up. Then *bam*—he catches it off a cut and sees Rider leaning. Crossover. Dip into the lane. Deuce.

We can't answer. We've got no zip to our offense now and Fuller takes the game's first truly bad shot—a leaner in heavy traffic. Sims clears for Evansville, hits Kernantz at the hash, and that kid is gone so fast he leaves vapor trails. Rider makes a desperate stab at the ball as Kernantz leaves him, and then it's a free run-out for another deuce.

I check the clock. Three minutes until half. The way this is going, we'll be down twenty by then.

It's not twenty. But it's bad. They put a seven-point run on us before Stanford stopped it with a bucket. Then they closed out the half with another six-point run, to make it 32-21 at the half. That's a tough climb against any team, but against Evansville Harrison it's Mount Everest.

"You can't get all this back at once," Bolden tells us in the locker room. The other starters are slumped down in their chairs, catching their breath. I'm the only one at attention, so it feels like Coach is talking directly at me. "If we get impatient, they'll carve us up. We just have to take it one possession at a time. But we can't just wait around either. Soon as that clock starts ticking we've got to be sharp."

The locker room is pretty dead though. My first two years when we'd get run by Hamilton Academy, we knew it was just because they were so deep and talented. But it just made us want to take another crack at them the way little brothers keep itching to take on their big brother. Against Evansville Harrison it's not so much that they're more talented, but they're so in control of everything. They're so assured of themselves, it's like they've filled us with doubt.

"We got this," I say. "Heads up, boys."

That lifts spirits a little bit, but it's mostly show. Time to take my own advice—lead on the floor.

We get the ball first, and right off I'm itchy to make my mark. But I know Kernantz is just waiting for me to lower my shoulder so he can flop again. Instead, I run the offense. This time I'm not holding anything back though. When I run a dribble exchange with Reynolds out top, I break our set and cut straight down the lane. Jones and Stanford widen out to the baselines, giving me space. I open up in the paint. Reynolds is quick enough to see it. Gets me the rock before help can come. I use my size to just rise over Kernantz. Bucket.

Poof—doubt's gone. Nothing like seeing that rock find bottom to get people's minds right.

I pick Kernantz up full-court. I've got no fantasies about turning him. I just want to show my teammates that it's time to get after it. Kernantz barely notices. He brings it up and sets their offense humming. They're in no hurry with a nine-point lead. But it's *way* too early to try icing things, even for them. When they dump it to their center Sims in the post, I can see he wants to take Stanford. But he's slow with his move. He dribbles, dribbles, dribbles, trying to back down. I'm at the foul line, waiting. When he picks up his dribble, I dive down hard. Hands straight up so I don't draw a whistle. He's off-balance, but he forces one up anyway. Front rim and off. Fuller rips.

I sprint to the hash for the outlet, but Kernantz and the off-guard are back, so I hold up. I widen to the wing, but I see Stanford busting it hard. Sims is trailing a good three steps behind him. I wave Fuller out of the middle to give Stanford space and then hit the big man right in stride. He gathers, takes a late hack from Sims, and muscles one in with the whistle. Just like that, we're right back in it. Our crowd knows it. They're on their feet and *loud*, feeding our fire. And Kernantz knows it too. He calls his boys into a quick huddle before the free throw and rips into them pretty good—I can't hear everything, but he gets up into everyone's face, jabbing his index finger at their chests. This thing's back on.

We chip and chip. These guys are too good to just let us chew through their whole lead with one big run, but the closer we get the more they press. Even Kernantz forces a few. He misses an impossible runner. The next trip he tries to fool me with the same move he threw at me in the semis last year—he points behind me like he's calling for a ball-screen and then snaps back for a three. Only this time I'm not fooled. Instead of turning my head, I get all up into him. He fires anyway. An easy swat. Then it's a footrace to the ball, one I win. I feel the crowd rising, ready for me to throw one down, but Kernantz makes a late play—knifing across my path and swiping at the ball—so they have to settle for the lay-in. It still cuts their lead to a single point with a little over two minutes left.

Now they're really sweating it. Except for Kernatnz, they all look tight. And I know that means one thing—he's going to try taking over. Sure enough, when he crosses mid-court their coach makes the signal—his right index finger up with his other hand flat. Iso Kernantz. The two of us on an island up top. My calves are burning from checking him all game, but I know I just need one more stop. First Upchurch. Then May. This is the third time now I'm locked up with another elite, game on the line. Two out of three won't be good enough.

While he dribbles, I can hear my teammates behind me, shouting *Stick him, D* and *You on this now.* The crowd is one massive roar. Behind Kernantz, I can see our bench. The players are all up pumping fists and waving towels. Murphy's crouched on one knee, scowling so severely you'd think he was the one getting ready to check Kernantz. But then there's Bolden. He's standing straight. Arms folded across his chest. A calm expression. *Damn,* I think, *Coach thinks we've got 'em.*

Kernantz takes a couple deep breaths, then starts toward me. The key is to not bite on any fakes, but to be ready to jump when he attacks for real. He crosses left, then between his legs right. Then a step-back. Then it comes. He spins back right and darts into the lane. I'm on his hip the whole way. He comes to a jump-stop at about ten feet. Every nerve in me says *Rise,* but I keep my feet. I body him, straight up, and all of a sudden he's got nowhere to go. "Dead!" I scream. "Ball's dead!" And my boys clamp down. Kernantz pass-fakes, pump-fakes, pass-fakes again. At last there's a whistle. No cheapie on me this time. Steps on him instead. Our ball. Two minutes even.

Now it's my turn. We don't flatten out like they did, but after a few ball reversals I get some space on the wing. Kernantz comes at me a little hot. I blow by. But when he turns his hips, I throw a nasty move on him—just rip it back between my legs and plant my feet behind the stripe. Then I launch a trey that's wet the moment it leaves my hands.

Timeout Evansville Harrison. Their crowd sits, stunned, while

Kevin Waltman

ours goes over the top. I don't showboat, but I take my time walking back to the huddle, soaking in the sound. Every soul in this gym knows who the best point in the state is. As if there's any doubt left, Murphy rushes five steps onto the court to greet me. He stomps his foot for emphasis, yells, "That's the *truth*, D! Nobody gonna check that!"

Bolden hollers for us to quit celebrating and get in the huddle. There's still a lot of time left, he reminds us, and he gets down to business. He draws up the play he thinks they'll run and then gets in our faces. "No let down!" he screams. "Stay focused!" We all put our hands in and he smacks the top of the pile with a little extra *oomph*. "Team!" we all shout.

Evansville Harrison has no chance. It's like Coach is in their heads. Just like he said, they run a double-screen to get the ball in to Kernantz on the wing, then set up a pick-and-roll toward the middle. Fuller's ready. As soon as Kernantz comes his way he gets chest-to-chest. I trail to clamp the double team on him hard. Kernantz does the right thing—he locates his forward rolling toward the hole and zips it to him. But that's where Bolden's got us a step ahead. Reynolds, sagging off his man, steps in and picks the pass clean.

An outlet to Fuller. A throw-ahead to me. Kernantz takes a futile leap at Fuller's pass. And now there's nothing but me and open court. This time the crowd *knows* the kill shot's coming. And I'm not going to disappoint. I take a power dribble to the block, getting ready to cock it back and rip. But as I rise I feel a *pop*. I mean, I can *hear* it, even over the crowd. And then the pain shoots up from my left calf—a violent, immediate agony.

Then I'm down.

Pull   113

PART II

12.

The hospital reminded me of last year. All of it came flooding back. Uncle Kid driving me there. Mom explaining to me and Jayson that my dad had been in a bad wreck. And then seeing Dad in that bed, his leg elevated, monitors beeping and pulsing in the dark.

At least they took me to the Sports Medicine wing this time. Different walls, different nurses, a different doctor. Then, with Dad's help, I made it back to the examination room. "You want me to stay?" he asked. I didn't answer, because the truth is I didn't know. I wanted to man up and face it alone, but if it was *real* bad news I knew I'd need someone. "I'll stay," Dad decided.

It took the doctor an eternity to get there, but once he did the diagnosis didn't take long. I explained to him what I'd heard and felt. He gingerly pressed up and down on my calf. He had me flex my knee and ankle, checking those joints and my Achilles as I did. Then he put it on me. "You've got a torn calf," he said, "which you probably knew the moment it happened. The good news is it's not a complete rupture. The muscle shape is still intact, so you won't need surgery.

We could do an MRI to be sure if you'd really like, but I've seen enough of these to know."

I sighed in relief. Even managed a smile at Dad, who was standing at attention in the corner. Then came the bad news. The only way to heal it was ice and elevation. And rest. Lots of rest. "You try to push it too soon and you'll pull that thing in two," the doctor said.

When we got back to the waiting room, at least Uncle Kid had some more good news. He'd just got off the phone with one of his boys, who said we'd hung on to win. Even as I lay on the baseline I saw Fuller, forever hustling, clean up my miss and get fouled by Kernantz. After that, I was on the way to the locker room and then the hospital.

And so that—as I ride back home with Mom and Dad in the front—is where we stand. I'm squeezed between Kid and Jayson in the back, my leg stretched into the front seat for some relief. As we cross over Central, I try clicking down the schedule in my mind. At least with Christmas coming things ease up a little. But if I'm not back for three weeks, that's six games I'll miss—including real tough match-ups with Lawrence North and Muncie Central. *Just when we were crushing it*, I think, *this has to happen*. It seems a grave injustice. We're 7-1, fresh off a win against the defending state champs. But we're looking straight at a month of whippings unless I can get back on my feet faster than the doctor thought.

When I sigh, Jayson elbows me in irritation. "Come *on*, Derrick," he says. "It's not like you tore your ACL. Don't act like you're dying or something."

Mom whips her head around to give him a look. She's never pinned too much on hoops, but she hangs quite a bit on the expectation that Jayson and I act like civilized and kind people. "Some *sympathy*, Jayson," she says.

He looks out the window and mutters, "I'm just sayin'."

My mom hates that phrase almost as much as she hates a tired *whatever*. "You know," she says, "that attitude isn't getting you anywhere, Jayson. You're getting grown enough it's not cute anymore."

"Ain't about *cute*," he pops back. I see Mom's hands clench on her purse. A chill settles over the car.

"I swear, Jayson," she says, but lets it drop for now.

At least Uncle Kid knows where I'm at. Anyone who's really played knows. He leans over to me as we turn onto Patton, trying to get my head right and change the mood in the car. "Just listen to the doc, D. Get better. These games coming up? They ain't a thing. *Regular season*. Get healed up. Get strong. Get things rolling come playoff time. *That's* what matters."

I nod in agreement. In some ways, he's right. But no baller wants to sit in street clothes.

Dad pulls into the driveway and everyone spills out. It takes me some time, sliding across the seat until Uncle Kid can help me out into the cold night air. It feels like it should be two in the morning, but the sound of Saturday night traffic and the houselights up and down the street tell me that it's really not that late. Around me, the city is still enjoying its weekend.

Kid offers to help me to the house, but I wave him off. He tells me to hang in there, then heads to his car, probably eager to catch April when her shift's over. I limp across the lawn, trailing my family. Mom and Dad stand by the door, waiting, but Jayson just cruises on in like nothing's the matter. I can walk as long as I don't push off that left foot at all. Still, I want to try—just test it. Maybe this has all been a mistake, a bad dream that I need to wake from. Or maybe there's no muscle pull, just the worst cramp ever. Every so slightly, I push up on my left toes. Instant daggers. Mom sees me wince and stumble. She rushes to me like I've been shot.

"I'm okay, Mom," I say.

"No you're not."

I have to tilt down awkwardly so she can wedge her shoulder under my arm. I know she's not letting me do this on my own so I accept her help. We hobble together to the door.

At last I get inside and collapse on the couch. My parents keep offering me things—a chance to talk, something to eat, a pillow to prop my leg on. They keep hovering there like drones, watching my every move. All I want is to be left alone in the dark so I can click on the tube and zone. But I know they're not going away that easy, no more than that throb in my left calf will. Dad gets me a bag of ice and Mom sets me up on the couch, propping my leg on a pillow and covering me up like I'm a baby. Even though I was fighting it, I kind of like the treatment.

As soon as I get settled, there's a ring at the door. I figure it's Kid coming back for something, so I don't even budge. But when I hear Dad get the door, it's a female voice that responds. And before I can react, standing there in front of me is Lia Stone, a couple pizza boxes in hand.

I scramble off that couch in a flash, calf injury be damned. Truth is, I'm embarrassed for her to see me lounging like that. I feel as vulnerable as if she'd walked in on me changing clothes. "What are you doing here?" I ask.

She raises her eyebrows. "That's how you greet me?" Then she laughs. "I figured you could use some company," she says. "Besides, *nobody* stands me up. We're having that date."

Meanwhile Mom and Dad are in action. They pull the old T.V. trays out from the kitchen and set us up with drinks and plates for the pizza. I shove that ice bag and pillow over to the corner of the couch and make room for Lia. As she squeezes in beside me, she reaches over and massages the back of my neck. There's still some chill from the night on her fingers, but I don't care. Feels good. And when I cut my eyes her way, see her smooth cocoa skin and her curves in that sweater, it feels even better. "You okay, D?" she purrs.

"All good," I say. Mom and Dad disappear down the hallway as silent as smoke. Just us now. "I'll be back balling out in no time," I say. I give her my best meaningful look.

Lia tilts her head back and laughs a little. "Whoa. I'm just here to hang and find something to watch with you. I'm gonna need a bigger night than this before you start running game at me." She snatches the remote from my hand and starts clicking, bypassing a few good games as she does. I don't dare protest. Then, when she lands on what she wants—some romantic flick, but I'm so dizzy with Lia fever I can't even figure out what it is—she curls her legs up and then stretches them across my lap. She leans back, slice in hand, and makes herself at home. Instinctively, I drop my hand to her knee, then edge it up an inch or two on those fine legs. She swats at me. "You're injured," she says. "Save your strength."

Talk about *game*. Girl's got it.

I just chill then, trying to pick up the thread of the movie—and trying to ignore that pulsing pain in my calf. Later, Jayson walks in. He stops when he sees Lia. He sneers at me. Shrugs. Then he poaches a couple pieces of pizza and heads back to his room. The kid's getting some serious attitude, but at this point I don't care. Lia doesn't seem to mind, and she's about all I've got going right now.

13.

The texts stream in. It started last night and cranks up again as soon as I turn on my phone in the morning. They're all variations on the same thing, a million different ways of telling me to hang in there. They're from teammates, sure. And friends. Even Wes and Jasmine chime in, though their names on my screen just serve as reminders that they're all but gone from my life. But the flood comes from assistants all over the country. Indiana, Michigan State, Wisconsin. Kentucky, Tennessee, Mississippi State. Clemson, Duke, Virginia. Even schools that haven't been after me that hard, like Kansas and Oklahoma.

In a way, it's nice. I mean, a pulled muscle on Indy's near East side is somehow news now in Lawrence, Kansas. At the same time, it's *crazy*. It's a reminder that, as a recruit, I'm part of a blood supply to them—they *need* me. Or, really, guys *like* me. So the cynical side of me knows this is all show. They're just scrambling to be first in line to text me, to seem like the good guy in case that gives them some slight edge come decision time. Probably some of these guys aren't even mashing out the texts, getting some secretary to do it instead. But if something were really wrong? If I were going under the knife for a surgery that might affect my game? They'd find plenty of other point guards in that supply that wouldn't be damaged goods.

So the only two I text back are Jasmine and Wes. Times like this, it's good to stick to your roots. And Jasmine hits me back pretty quick with a request to hang. I bounce off my bed—as much as I can with a bum leg—and get cleaned up. When I hit the living room, everyone else is already well into their Sunday. No church today, I guess, since last night was rough. Mom and Dad start to stand from the kitchen table, where they're sipping coffee and sharing the newspaper. Jayson is already checking Sportscenter, which is busy hyping a Syracuse-Duke showdown. He nods at me, but he kind of looks annoyed at my presence.

"Can I borrow the car?" I ask.

Even Mom says yes. Maybe they're amazed that I don't want to just mope around the house feeling sorry for myself. As I scoop the keys from the counter, she remembers her duty. "Where you headed?" She tries to sound casual, but she can't quite pull it off.

I don't dare make anything up. "I'm hanging with Jasmine for a while."

"Wait a minute," Dad says. He doesn't have that edgy tone like Mom, but he loops his arm over the back of his chair so he can twist to see me. "Why Jasmine? What about that girl that was here last night?"

"Lia?"

"Yes, Lia. She seemed nice."

Nice is one way to put it, I think. But I know this is still an aftershock from last year. My dad doesn't want me getting my head mixed up with girl trouble again. And he sure doesn't want me doing another girl wrong. So I have to put him at ease about Jasmine like I had to for Mom about Wes. "Dad, Jasmine and I are—" I start, but even I have no idea how to finish that sentence. *Friends* isn't quite right. "Jasmine and I aren't happening," I say at last. "We gave it a shot. Like, twenty shots. But at this point it is what it is."

Dad lets it go at that. Even he isn't up for pressing me about my sex life on a Sunday morning before he's finished his coffee.

With Jasmine, it's push and pull. One moment we're back in our old groove. She's flirting with me, babying me over my injury, touching my arm. The next she folds her arms across her chest and seems a million miles away. She wanted to meet at a bookstore on the far Eastside. It's tucked in a neighborhood that's a weird mix of Mexican groceries and dollar stores and old two-stories getting revamped by young white couples with some scratch. It's an independent place with a sort of thrown-together look. There are magazines spilling out of racks, paperbacks piled high near the register, signs taped to the shelves telling you what section you're in. Basically, it's the kind of place I'd never set foot in if it weren't for Jasmine. It seems like, sometimes, we live in different Indys. But it's cool. I don't mind browsing with her.

"Come here," she says, holding up a book.

The wood floor creaks under me as I limp. I put too much pressure on my left side and have to reach out and grab a shelf for balance. I stop to gauge the pain, and Jasmine comes over by me. She stands real close so I can look over her shoulder. I get a whiff of her perfume. My head reels with it.

"Remember?" she asks.

All I see is the heavy work in Jasmine's hands and a somber-looking author frowning in her photo on the jacket. I have no idea what Jasmine's talking about. My silence clues her in.

"The author!" she says. "Remember? We were flipping channels that night at your place and we saw her being interviewed? She was talking all that radical stuff about the government owing reparations, and we just cracked up. This little white lady getting all fired up over it." Jasmine looks up at me expectantly, but I'm blank. What I remember from all those nights cozied up on the couch with her isn't what was on the tube. Now she cocks her head at me and narrows her eyes, disappointed that I don't have perfect recall about every second we spent together. "Well," she says, "*I* remember." She slaps the book down in my hands. "It's probably an interesting read," she says.

Jasmine walks further down the row and I flip through the pages in front of me. My eyes settle on phrases here and there, but nothing sticks. Ashamed a little that I forgot, I want to get into it now. But it's not happening. Sure, it might be *about* people like me, but that doesn't mean it's *for* me. I gaze around at the endless stacks. All those books and it doesn't seem like any of them are for guys like me. I know that's not true. I can hear my mom's voice in the back of my head—*Derrick Bowen, when you put down a book it says more about you than it does about the person who wrote it.* So I try again, digging through stacks to try to find something that fits. I scoop up a collection of sports writing from a few years ago. It doesn't have any athletes on the cover. It looks like serious literature instead so it won't automatically get dissed by Jasmine.

Outside, we stand by our cars. I parked right behind her on a side street, the houses sitting on a little rise so they seem to tower over us. The wind kicks up, some real bite to it. You can just feel a winter storm on its way. Jasmine shivers in her coat then looks to her car like it's drawing her away. She tells me it was good to see me. She starts to say something else, but a big gust of wind kind of rips her breath away. She smiles, gathers herself.

"I'm not gonna see you much more, am I?" I ask.

That smile vanishes. She hugs her bag of books to her chest. Behind us, I hear the bells on the bookstore door jangle as someone else goes in. Right then I decide that when Jasmine takes off, I'm going back in to buy that book she dropped in my hands. A Christmas present for her. It's not much, but then again it's not like we're a couple who has to hook each other up with something fancy. And it might make her smile and think of me on Christmas morning.

"Not really," Jasmine finally answers. "Not at school. And my new classes are going to be a load. And I've got to keep trying to get a better ACT score. And—" she trails off. She looks around at the houses, the row of stores, the traffic on Washington Street—anything but me. Then she sighs and gives me another half-smile. "This isn't *goodbye*, Derrick."

"I know," I say. Then I say something ridiculous, this thing my grandpa used to say. "See you 'round the campfire."

"What?"

"I don't know," I say, laughing. "It just popped into my head. It just means I'll check you later."

She sets her bag of books down on the ground and steps across the distance between us. She buries her head in my chest and hugs me, squeezing tight. We stay like that for a while, our body warmth shielding us from the cold. I imagine someone looking at us from one of those houses and seeing a glow around us, one bright bubble against the cold December day.

"Take care of yourself," she says when she pulls away. "Take care of that leg."

"It's nothin'," I say, trying to act tough.

Then she's gone and it's not my leg that hurts.

14.

The season stops for no one. That train leaves the station and there's no holding it back. So even though *my* season's on pause doesn't mean the schedule stops.

So here's Park Tudor warming up in our gym, ready to roll. And one look at their squad gives another lesson in how a season is relentless. It doesn't care that you've hit a rough patch. It doesn't give a damn you've got a key player injured. It's not going to offer you some cupcake just so you can click off a win. No. It'll give you Park Tudor. They have things ramped up, sitting at 10-2. They've sent guys to Xavier and Indiana recently, and they've got a couple other high major guys— Travis Bookley and Donte Walker—this time around. Walker's their point, all muscle on his 6'2" frame, with a deadly stroke from deep.

Then I look at our side. Stanford can hang, for sure. Fuller's not crazy skilled, but he'll fight to the death. Reynolds has shown flashes, but his best days are all out in front of him. That leaves Jones, who's really just a big body. And Rider. Even warming up, Rider looks shook. He spins out a lay-up and shakes his head. Fuller goes over to him to

Kevin Waltman

give him some encouragement, but next time through Rider pulls up for a short J and just scrapes front iron.

Give our fans credit. They've still packed the joint out. As the clock ticks toward zeroes, their sound swells in anticipation. Bolden calls everyone in for last instructions before tip, and there's a buzz of energy coming off guys. The fans believe. Why not a win tonight? Why not an early Christmas present for Marion East? And that kind of thinking gets my blood pumping too, so much that when Bolden crouches down in front of the bench I almost, out of habit, grab a spot right in front of him. But then I remember—the constant pain in my calf, the khakis, the street shoes. So it's behind Bolden for me, standing with the back-ups and managers. All this game energy and nothing to do with it but watch.

Murphy stands next to me and squeezes my shoulder. "You still gotta stay into it," he says. "Be another coach for us."

He's right. So when the huddle breaks and they start announcing the starters, I grab a spot next to Rider. His leg's bouncing so hard with nervous energy, he's about to wear himself out before the ball even goes up. "You're okay," I tell him. "Just remember you don't have to be a hero." I gesture out toward the crowd. "Nobody out there expects you to be me."

"I know that," he says. He starts to stand.

"I didn't mean it bad," I say. I stand too, so he has to listen to me. "Just stay within things. Don't force."

"You mean don't screw things up," he sneers.

This has gone all wrong. But just like between the lines, there are no do-overs. Rider's name gets called and he bolts out to mid-court. I wonder if he took anything good from what I said. It doesn't take long for my wondering to get answered. First trip down he catches left wing and drives baseline—head down. He runs straight into the teeth of the D and picks up his dribble. He fakes and fakes, then gets the ball knocked away—off his leg and out of bounds. So much for not forcing it.

Walker brings it up and passes to the wing, then jogs down the lane—Rider on his hip—toward the block. Then Walker heads back out to the wing. And when a screen comes, Rider does the unforgiveable. Instead of staying tight on Walker, he goes under the screen. Walker can read that in his sleep. He pops to the three-point stripe, catches the pass in rhythm, and lets loose that pretty J of his.

Whatever buzz our crowd had diminishes to a murmur just like that. They all sit back down, ready for what looks like a long night.

It wasn't a bloodbath. But that's just because guys like Fuller and Stanford fought like madmen. And Bolden pulled out all the stops. He tried to hide Rider on defense by switching Reynolds onto Walker. He even ran more basic sets on offense so Rider wouldn't have to make snap decisions.

But it didn't matter. Park Tudor's a tough out even if we're at full strength. And without me to deal with, they cruised. They built a nine-point lead by halftime. We dug back to five—even Rider dropped a couple buckets—by the end of the third. But then Park Tudor just pulled away in the fourth, leaving our gym with a 60-48 win that was never really that close.

For Lia, I choose a place I never went with Jasmine. It's downtown, packed late on a Saturday night so Lia and I have to wait for our table. *Way* out of my price range, but Uncle Kid hooked me up with some extra dough on top of what Mom and Dad gave me. "So you can take it next level for once," he said. All of it makes an impression on Lia, I can tell. She checks some of the women walking by in their expensive dresses, some of them with pearls strung around their necks. A lot of the men have that almost-rich look. Not loaded like they're CEOs or anything, but I see some heavy watches, some suits that look like they cost some serious coin. The hostess definitely did a double take on us, but she took my name and told us to have a seat. We're not the only two slumming up the place. There are plenty of guys throwing back at the bar, rocking sweaters and jeans. But I still get the feeling like maybe I've overdone it. When we squeeze into the crowded waiting area, I feel small and insignificant even if I've got a good two inches on every person there.

"You okay, Derrick?" Lia asks. I nod all nonchalant, but she senses something's off. "You know," she says, "we can go somewhere else."

"It's cool," I say. "I got this." For whatever reason, I feel committed to the move. Like if we jumped now people would all stare at us and point, laugh and say we couldn't afford it.

"I know you *got it*," Lia says, "but—" She trails off, interrupted by some middle-aged guy trying to squeeze next to her on the bench. I'm seventeen and have the common decency to let a girl have a seat, but this guy lacks it. Maybe he thinks his big ol' belly makes him deserve some rest. Or maybe Lia's just invisible to him.

"Excuse me," I say. But he just ignores us, mashing out a text with his fat thumb. "Ex*cuse* me!" I snap. This time his head pops back. Full attention. Not just him, but every single person in the waiting area. I try not to laugh. Nothing like a black teenager raising his voice to get the pretty people all stiff. It makes me want to get all swole on him. Give him a good scare. But I cool it. I gesture, gentle as a cat, toward Lia. "You bumped her. I think you owe her an apology."

His face gets all squinched up like he's insulted. But then he senses it. Everyone is watching him. In a heartbeat they've gone from being scared of me to frowning at the guy who had to be taught some manners by a teenager. Splotches of crimson rise on his neck. "Well, I—I didn't—I…"

Lia doesn't give him the chance to finish. She reaches her hand to me. I pull her up. Even that effort causes a little tweak in my calf, but I don't dare show signs of pain now. As if she's casting a spell with a wand, she waves her hand at the bench. "You can have it if you need it that much," she says.

We don't even need to talk it over. We both know it's exit time. And now, instead of feeling like we bailed because we were out of place, we can spin on those people and act like *we're* too good for *them*. Even before we make it to the door, Lia's shaking as she tries to hold in her laughter. Then we're out in the cold December night and she lets it loose. She almost doubles over. She grabs onto my arm for balance. Around us is a swirl of flurries, people hurrying through the cold. The beams in the passing cars all seem to blur as they pass, like the very light is sticking to the air. But it's all good. So good.

When Lia regains her composure she squeezes my arm. "Derrick, there are more ways to impress a girl than dropping forty dollars on a plate that costs ten on Central," she says. She raises onto her toes and gives me a soft kiss by my ear. "You just found one," she whispers to me.

We make it back to my car. As soon as we get in, my impulse is to lean over Lia's way and go as far as I can with her. But I've learned a little patience in these things. So instead we leave downtown and head up toward our neighborhood. Soon, the streets get dimmer and the storefronts grow less inviting. I'm not sure where to take her. She says she doesn't need someplace over the top, but I want somewhere decent at least.

She must know I'm struggling to find the right spot. The car's been too quiet for too long, so she finally offers a suggestion. "Head up Keystone. There's that new place up around 56th."

I tap the gas and we're off. It's a clean, well-lit chain restaurant. Custom made for first dates. And, no, it doesn't have the splash of the place downtown. Or even the gritty character of places closer to our blocks, but I'm not about to gripe.

We park and head for the restaurant. And bump smack into some guy who's trudging along with his head down, hood pulled up so you can't see his face. I immediately tense up. I might get cracked up at white people tripping because of me. But the truth is, you never know. I get between the guy and Lia, but I don't say a word—better to just keep your head down and move along.

"D?"

I wheel around again and see J.J. Fuller, his hood pulled back now, staring at us. First thing I think is that if Lia and I wanted to keep it to ourselves, that's done with. Not that Fuller's racing off to Twitter to spread the news, but all it takes is for him to tell one person and then the word will move through our school like a virus. But that worry fades fast. Instead, I wonder what Fuller's doing hoofing it this far from home.

"Where you headed, Fuller?"

He shrugs. In the parking lot lights, I can see embarrassment wash across his face. "Nowhere," he says, trying to play it off. But Fuller's brow furrows up as deep as Bolden's does sometimes.

"You walk all the way up here?" I ask. "You got a ride?"

He relents now. He sighs, and his breath puffs into a cloud between us. "Yeah, I walked. It's stupid, I know. But after we lose, I just can't take it. I try to sit somewhere and it just gnaws at me. So I started walking, and before I knew it I was almost up at the mall." He looks away again, worried maybe that he's sounding ridiculous. Everyone on the team always cracks on Fuller for being so earnest, so eager. Maybe we've made him self-conscious.

I'm not going to give him some big apology for that—giving each other hell is one of the best parts of being on a squad—but seeing him all torn up over a loss? That's different. I remember my freshman year when I just walked and walked after we got whipped by Hamilton Academy. I know *exactly* how Fuller feels. And I realize that maybe I should stop acting like nobody on the team has as much invested in it as me. It's pretty clear Fuller's all in. "It's gonna be okay," I tell him. "You should know by now nothing comes easy at Marion East. We'll get this thing rolling when I get back."

Fuller nods, but something doesn't sit well with him. "Look, D. I

Kevin Waltman

want you back in the lineup. With you, we're a threat to win the whole thing. I just—" He breaks off and shakes his head.

"Say it, man." Behind him, traffic rips up and down Keystone. The neon light of a tattoo shop buzzes against the night. Down the street a light snaps off in a car repair place—either someone working late or someone raiding the place.

"Fine. It's just that it would be nice if we could get a win without you. Like, let people know we're more than just the Derrick Bowen Show."

Before I can say anything back, I see Lia out of the corner of my eye—her arms are pulled tight to her chest and she's shivering. I tilt my head toward her and tell Fuller we've got to get inside. Then I tell him to stay safe. But when I turn back to Lia to head to the restaurant, she's frowning at me. I just hold my palms up, wondering what I've done wrong now.

"You are *not* gonna let your boy walk home from here," she says. "In this cold? This far from home? Tell me you're not gonna do that."

Damn. She's right, and I know it, but sometimes it would be a whole lot easier if I weren't surrounded by people reminding me to do the right thing.

So, in a minute, we're rumbling back down Keystone, Fuller in the backseat. We're almost back to Fall Creek Parkway when my hunger starts kicking in for real. "We're still getting some food, right?" I ask Lia.

"Absolutely," she says. "Remember—nobody stands me up."

Then Fuller chimes in from the backseat. "I'm kind of starving too," he says. "You two want to hit up Sure Burger?"

I start scheming for excuses, some good reason I've got to drop Fuller at home first. But I come up dry. I look over to Lia for some help.

"Pretty soon it'll be about the only place open," she says. "Let's just do it."

So there it is. Sure Burger with Fuller tagging along. Not exactly what I had in mind. But before I let myself get all tensed up about it, I take stock. Good grub, hanging with a teammate, clocking time with the finest girl at Marion East—I've had myself some worse nights than this one.

15.

For Christmas I get a bag of ice. Well, not really. I get hooked up with some new jeans and some shirts from my folks. Standard stuff. But Kid blows the doors off. He drops a pair of Pacers tickets on me—fifth row for their next game with LeBron and the Cavs. How he collared these things, I don't know. My Dad audibly gasps when he sees them. I can feel him wondering what Kid's got himself mixed up with. But I don't care. I keep rubbing those glossy babies between my thumb and fingers like they're gold.

After that though, it's the ice. I'm kicked back on the couch, leg elevated. Twenty minutes on the ice, then twenty off. Over and over. I haven't done a great job of it up until now, so I figure with Christmas break I've got a chance to really get this thing healed. In a way, it's kind of nice. I can sit back and just take it all in, like instead of a teenager I'm the grandpa who gets to chill and observe.

Mom and Dad are as bleary on Christmas morning as they are any other day. They're run ragged from raising me and Jayson and from trying to make ends meet. But they open each other's gifts and they light up. Ten years younger on the spot. And I can see those looks they give to each other—knowing expressions with almost two decades of marriage behind them. But at the same time they're still flirting, like what they really want for Christmas is for this house to empty out for an hour so they can be alone.

There's Kid, all up on himself because he can throw around his new-found coin. Most Christmases he'd have scrounged up some cheap things for everyone, so this makes him feel good. He's not half knocked out from drinking too much the night before either. In fact, he's looking sharp, which means he's got the hook up later with April.

And then Jayson. He's over at the kitchen table, organizing some Christmas money he got from relatives. But he's quiet. Usually by now he'd have torn down the hall with NBA2K16 and have that X-Box blasting. Not this year. He gave Mom and Dad a pretty cordial *Thanks* and then set it on the kitchen table for later. When he got an authentic Russell Westbrook jersey from Kid, his face brightened, but just for a second. He gave another *Thanks*, only slightly more enthusiastic than the one he gave Mom and Dad, then he folded the jersey back up and set it in its box. Normally Mom and Dad would have jumped him for his lousy manners, but it's Christmas and nobody wants drama.

But when Kid fires up ESPN for the pre-game show and Jayson still doesn't budge, Kid calls out to him. "Jayson, what's up? It's Christmas and you're sitting there like the Grinch."

Jayson turns to Kid and gives him a withering look. "The Grinch?" he asks. "What, you think I'm ten?"

Kid just laughs. "You getting all big on us, huh?"

Jayson squints at Kid like he'd just as soon throw a knife across the room as say word one. Mom and Dad look at each other, the fatigue of two teenage boys taking over from those flirtatious glances of earlier. Dad nods, almost imperceptibly, but it seems to tell Mom that he'll talk to Jayson this time. Mom stands and says she has to make Christmas lunch. It's no big spread anymore. She said years ago that she was through making turkey for four men who were just going to shovel it in their mouths while they grunted at the T.V. But it's an excuse for her to not deal with Jayson.

In fact, when she heads to the kitchen, Jayson makes his exit. He gathers up all his stuff into one box and shuffles through the living room. He refuses to make eye contact with anyone.

"Jayson, come on," Kid says. "The game's coming on."

That tears it for Jayson. He drops the box, creating a small explosion of gifts and wrapping paper at his feet. "So what?" he shouts. "I don't even *care* about that game. There's more to life than *basketball*. Not that anyone in this house knows it."

On that last line he gestures toward me. Jayson's talking crazy. If he thinks *our* family only cares about hoops then he should check out another family—*any family*—with a son who's getting attention from the likes of Michigan State. If anything, Mom and Dad downplay hoops because they want things to stay as normal as they can. But whatever. This is just Jayson being Jayson.

Dad follows Jayson down the hall, calling after him in the most patient voice he can muster. That leaves me and Kid in the living room, kicking it with a game on like old times.

"Thanks for the tickets," I tell him again.

"Nothin'," he says. "Thought maybe you could take your girl Lia."

"True enough," I say. Neither of us look at each other while we talk. We each want to act like nothing's that a big deal—not the tickets and certainly not me clocking time with Lia. Once the game gets rolling we shut it down. Nothing said but some commentary on the plays in front of us. The only thing that breaks it is an alert on my phone. Incoming text. I figure it's a school hassling me on Christmas, but instead I see a note from Jasmine. My pulse races a little more than I'd like it to. It's a thank-you note. And not much of one at that. She even drops into textspeak—*ur a sweetie*—which is something she almost never does. It makes me feel like it was just a quick chore she had to get finished. Nothing any more meaningful than taking out the trash. Fine. I can never quite kill my thing for Jasmine, but the thought of taking Lia out again sure helps.

Dad comes back out from his talk with Jayson. Mom meets him with a plate of food—like it's a reward for going into the lion's den. "How'd it go?" she asks.

Dad slumps his shoulders and shakes his head. Mom's back stiffens. She looks toward the hall. I know that look. She's about to march in there and lay into Jayson. But Dad runs his hand gently along her back, letting it rest just above her hip. "Let it go," he says. "Come sit with me." So they retreat to the kitchen, leaving Kid and me in peace to watch hoops.

First timeout, Kid pops up to get some grub. I start to push myself up, too, but he waves me down. "Ice that thing," he says. "Get healthy. I'll hook you up."

As he heads for the kitchen, I ask him how he scored such choice tickets anyway. I don't mean anything by it. I'm really just curious. But when Kid answers, his voice rises up in that old defensive tone. "I just got 'em, okay? Don't worry about some grand jury inquiry. Just take your girl and have fun." Then he catches himself. That answer let the old Kid shine back through his new polished attitude. He straightens up and puffs out his chest a bit. "Besides, you ought to see what I got for April. Gonna be a very merry Christmas when she unwraps my gift."

Full of himself again, Kid turns to fix our plates. When he moves, I see the kitchen table behind him. And there's Dad, his hand gripped around his fork like he's trying to snap it in two, watching his brother. He *knows* Kid's up to some nonsense again. This time it's Mom's turn to calm Dad. She reaches across the table and rubs his hand. She whispers something to him. And slowly Dad's tight-lipped stare eases into a smile, then finally a laugh.

Family can be an uneasy thing. Even during good times, there's always something about to snap. And yet we hold together. Give each other gentle checks. Call each other out when we have to.

Kid comes back with some food for me. He settles back into his seat. I reposition my leg on my ice. Mom and Dad continue a hushed, easy conversation while they eat. And, finally, from down the hall, comes the sound of Jayson firing up his X-Box. I guess he's digging on his Christmas gift even if he wants people to think he's too old for it, wants to show more attitude than gratitude.

16.

The first practice after Christmas is a mess. Everyone's lugging around that holiday weight—sluggish and slow, unmotivated with the next game still a week away.

I'm still sidelined. The calf's getting better. Pretty quickly, really. I can walk normally. The only time I really have to ease off is if I'm going up stairs. I'm not going to do anything stupid and test it too early, but I've eyed the schedule. The Northwest game this weekend is a lost cause. But there's a chance by the weekend after—Covenant Christian on Friday or Bishop Chatard on Saturday—that I could be back in action.

And not a moment too soon. Rider's *struggling*. Even walking through our sets with no defense he gets turned around. He cuts baseline when he's supposed to widen to the wing. Or he down-screens when he's supposed to cross-screen. The first few mistakes Coach Bolden takes in stride. "Back it up," he says. "We'll get this." He puts his hand on Rider's shoulder and guides him through the right cuts.

But there's only so much a guy like Bolden can take. I mean, the man was probably born impatient. And it's not like age has mellowed him. So after the fourth Rider mistake, Bolden's tone gets a little clipped. After the sixth, he sighs in exasperation and stares at the ceiling. And after one more time, he's finally had it. "Good *Lord*, Rider!" he snaps. "It's a cross-screen after the reversal. A cross-screen! A *cross-screen!*"

As soon as the words are out of his mouth, Bolden regrets it. His stance softens and he says everything's okay, using the soft tone a parent gets when they've just shouted at a kid in the grocery store. Rider tries to shrug it off, but everyone in the gym can tell he's getting more and more rattled with every mistake. Fuller comes over and loops an arm over Rider's shoulder. He turns Rider away from Bolden, walking him toward the far side of the court while he talks a little encouragement.

"Why don't we run fives, Coach?" Murphy offers. He's standing down on the baseline, a basketball tucked into his elbow. He asks the question gently, like someone trying to ease the car keys away from a friend who's had one too many. "Let these guys stretch their legs and burn off some Christmas fat, maybe?"

Coach swivels his head slowly toward Murphy. I know what's going through the old man's head—why on earth should he let them run full court when they can't even get the half-court sets? He thinks about it, then relents. Maybe he knows that if things keep going like they are, he'll really blow a fuse and go off on Rider.

Leg propped on a folding chair, I watch the guys run it back and forth. Every time there's a break in the action, Fuller's right back in Rider's ear. Fuller's eyes are wide and he leans forward and pumps his fist in front of him as he speaks—all pep talk for our freshman. And maybe it works. Each trip down, the worry starts to ease out of Rider's face.

Soon enough, he hits Stanford right in rhythm for a lay-in. Then next trip he rips it past his man and hits Reynolds for a spot-up. "Nice," Fuller hollers. "Atta baby." The rest of the guys clap, starting to get on board.

But on the sideline, I can hear Bolden grumble to Murphy. "He *still* can't figure out the offense," he gripes. "We're not gonna get easy ones like that against any team with a pulse."

Then Bolden whips his attention toward me. On a lot of squads, an injury gives you some kind of special status, immunity from a coach's wrath. No such luck at Marion East. "And *you!*" Bolden yells. "Lounging there like you're on vacation. Why aren't *you* teaching Rider? Why does it have to be Fuller? Or me? Or Murphy? An injured calf doesn't give you laryngitis, does it?"

He stares at me, eyes blazing. I stare back. Two and a half years of this. I get the guy, I do. And I know he's always trying to make me better. But one of these days I'll be the one to snap. "No, Coach," I say.

"Well?" he shouts. Behind him, the team is still in mid-possession, but guys glance over every chance they get. I feel that old anger and embarrassment ride up my neck and into my cheeks. "Get off your ass and *talk to him!*" Bolden screams.

Scolded, I pop up. And the moment I do I feel that old pain in my calf. It pisses me off. I mean, how come everyone else gets slack and I'm the one that always catches hell? It's just like before the season. I didn't do anything wrong then. And now it's not like I *tried* to get hurt. But, for Coach, it's all my fault, I guess—my injury, the blustery post-Christmas weather, the aches in his old bones. All me.

With my good leg, I kick at that folding chair. It's not a full-on kick. I make it so it looks like I'm just trying to get it out of my way.

The problem is, it tips back and clatters down on the hardwood. I can feel every head in the gym turn my way, but I don't even look up. Especially not at Bolden. I just make my way—limping a little extra for show—over to the sideline close to Rider. "You're okay," I tell him. "Just listen to me if you're in doubt."

When the ball goes live again, I call out his cuts for him. Every time I say something, he nods. At first he seems appreciative of the help, but after a couple possessions his nods get a little exaggerated, almost like he's mocking me. Soon as he does that, he screws up again. He down-screens even as I shout *Cross!*—and Fuller's pass bounces off of Rider's back instead of finding Jones for an easy deuce.

It doesn't get much better after that. Rider's feeling surly because he's getting instructed like he's at some pre-school camp. I'm sick of the abuse from Coach. And Coach is just plain angry at the world. After some more slop on both ends, he just decides to run guys for the last 15 minutes of practice. When he calls that out, I stay on the sideline, palms up, like, *You want me to talk Rider through this too.*

"You can sit now, Bowen," he says. Withering.

In the locker room, everyone's just kind of done with it, as if the tension between me and Coach has spilled over. Guys peel off their practice unis and hit the showers in silence. I chill at my locker for a few minutes. I feel like if I just bolt then somehow that will anger Bolden even more.

Only Fuller breaks the silence. He comes over and offers a fist. I wait a second like I'm going to leave him hanging, then go ahead and give him a bump. "It's gonna get good again, D," he says. He scrunches his brows up like he's a concerned parent.

"You base that on what?" I ask.

"Hey, come *on*, man," he pleads. "You know Coach is always gonna rag on you. That's the price of being the star."

"Star, huh?" I say. "Just the other night you were saying how you wanted to win without me." I know the guy's just trying to help, but he can't have it both ways.

Fuller squats down in front of me, so close he almost drips sweat on my street kicks. He looks down at the floor, thinking about what to say. In that pause, I feel myself give in. The guy's trying. Give him that. "I didn't mean it that way," he says. "You know that. I mean, I just want guys to get along."

"Okay," I say. "We're good." I gather up my backpack. Anyone else on the planet knows that means a guy wants to bolt, but Fuller doesn't budge.

"Hey, speaking of getting along," he says, raising his eyebrows like he's in on some dirty secret, "how you getting with Lia?" He even slaps my knee like we're some old friends who swap tales.

"I'd be getting with her a lot better if you didn't crowd our space," I tell him. I deadpan it, like I'm mad. It's worth it just to watch his face drop. Then I stand. "Don't sweat it, Fuller," I tell him. "I wasn't getting anywhere, anyway. We're cool."

I may not have been getting anywhere the other night, but right away this one feels different. Lia got herself decked out for the game—skintight jeans and a bomb leather jacket that still manages to show her curves—and it was all I could do to keep my jaw off the floor when I picked her up.

Now here we are, fifth row. Styling. I've been to plenty of Pacers games before. During the regular season you can score tickets for cheap, especially if you don't mind sitting up in the clouds. But this is a different world. We can hear the players and refs bark back and forth. We're nearer the Cavs' bench, so I can see LeBron up close. I knew the guy was big, but, man, in person he's a true beast. At 6'3" I can lean on some high school guards, but if I'm ever making the leap to the League I won't be banging with King James.

I'm rooting for the Pacers, but I can't stop paying attention to LeBron. He's in control of everything. I can hear him learning up the younger guys. I can see him baiting people. I can even see him turning down shots—things he'd bury in crunch time—just to get other guys involved. It's a lesson in how the game's supposed to be played.

Still, the Pacers hang tight. And down this close, you can really feel the arena. You can see the bright T.V. lights, see the ESPN crew courtside, and when the Pacers go on any kind of run—a trey by Miles and a dunk by George—the crowd roar is deafening. It's like there's a tidal wave of sound pouring down from above. Even Lia's impressed. She gets into the game like everyone else, but she also checks out the scene. At one timeout she grabs my arm, her fingernails digging into my flesh just a touch, and points across the court. "Is that Andrew Luck?" she squeals.

I follow to where she's pointing and, sure enough, there's the Colts quarterback, flanked by a few guys so huge they must be some offensive lineman. It's cool, but I don't really care. Seeing pro athletes doesn't make my heart race. But Lia's nails on my arm? That works. Then she leans over to whisper in my ear. She drops her hand to my leg. "I have to say, Derrick, scoring these seats is a pretty baller move."

The rest of the game? A blur. I know the Pacers had a chance to tie it late, but LeBron rejected a weak runner in the lane, then iced it on the other end. After that we filed out with the masses, squeezed so close with everyone else that we could smell the beer on people's breath. Lia looped her arms around mine like she needed protecting. I played right along. Even through our coats, I could feel that tight body of hers—all I could do not to start plowing people over so I could get alone with her.

And now here we are. At my car. There are still people filing through the parking garage and cars swoop down the ramps, their tires squeaking in the turns, so we can't really get to it. At least that's what I'm thinking. But when I lift the keys to the ignition, Lia grabs my wrist. "No hurry, right?" she says. "We could just hang here."

"Yeah," I say, and I don't really know where to go from there.

But Lia's got it covered. She stretches across the car, her coat making a slow swoosh against the seat. I lean for the kiss, her lips glistening in the lights of a passing car. But she pulls back a few inches. She smiles. Then she places her index finger under my chin and gently tilts my head up. When I let her, she traces kisses—one, two, three, four—from just below my jaw down to my collar bone. She pulls my coat and shirt back so she can kiss a little lower. Then she shifts again, so she can reach across with her other hand. And that one goes first to my knee, then slides on up to rub me. Meanwhile, she keeps kissing on my neck.

I can barely catch my breath. For a minute I think she's going to

Kevin Waltman

keep going on down my body with her mouth. She unzips my coat and unbuttons my first two buttons, but then—like she had in her mind just exactly how far she was willing to go—she raises her head back up, and smiles again. She must see the want in my face, because she shakes her head. "Uh uh," she says. "I'm not that easy."

I itch with lust, but I've been in this kind of spot before with Jasmine. I pushed with her—pleaded, guilted, acted like a whiny little brat. And I'm not going there again. This thing with Lia? I want to make it work. "It's cool," I say. Then, when Lia leans back the other way, she tilts her head as if to say *Come on*, and then it's my turn to get her on high blast. I try to match what she did step for step and kiss for kiss, only I get the arm-bar when I go for the zipper on her coat.

I sit back up, my temples throbbing. At least I can tell Lia's feeling it too. "*Lord,* D," she says. "We got to *go* before I get stupid." I turn back to her for a second, but she shakes her head. "No way. You get this car started."

I do as I'm told. We back out, not saying a word as we go down the first couple levels. We pull out onto Maryland Street. The windows shudder in a gust. People hurry along the sidewalks. The traffic lights change colors. And all up and down the blocks, restaurants and bars teem with lights and life. Simultaneously, we start laughing. It's like we're coming out of some trance. The fact that the world is still just going about its business is hilarious to us.

I turn North on Meridian, heading toward Monument Circle. "You good?" I ask at last.

"Real good," Lia purrs. Then she drums those nails of hers on the dash, like she's still a little wired. She unzips her coat. I have to look away for a second—I can't let my imagination get riled up again or we'll crash right into the Soldiers and Sailors Monument. There's a buzzing beside me. In my peripheral vision, I see Lia's phone lighting up. She scrolls for a second, then rattles off a text. Soon enough her phone vibrates again. "Ooh," she says, but when I look back over she stashes her phone and acts all nonchalant.

"What?" I ask.

"Nothing," she says. "Just my girl Cailyn making some noise at me."

I nod, but there's something that doesn't seem quite right. It's like the atmosphere in the car has changed. My jealousy kicks in—no doubt Lia's got plenty of other guys chasing her. It's not like I have some claim, but I don't want to be lied to. "Come on," I say. "Tell it."

"I don't think you want to hear this," she says. "But Cailyn texted me that your boy Wes got dinged by the cops again."

17.

Public intox. With JaQuentin, of course. Out on the corner at 38th for the world to see, which is how the news travelled to Lia so fast.

I barely hint at it. I don't even make it sound judgmental. I just say, "So, you think you should cool it with JaQuentin?"

That's all it takes for Wes to recoil. "*Shit,* D. I don't need it from you, man." He flings a shirt back at the rack in Ty's Tower and acts like he's going to storm out. "It's gonna get tossed anyway. They won't even hit me with home detention again."

"Wes, come on," I say.

"Come on yourself, Derrick. Like you've never hit up a few drinks."

Now it's my turn to get my back up. I mean, I'm not perfect, but I've never touched a drop and Wes should know it. Even if I weren't into keeping myself in playing shape, I wouldn't dare take a sip of alcohol—I bet I could be in California and the hairs on my mom's neck would stand up the moment the first beer touched my lips. "You know what your problem is, Wes? You think you know every damn thing, but as soon as you open your mouth you prove otherwise."

Wes pops. He charges at me, right there in the store, and shoves me. But it's nothing. Even with all his force he can't make up for our size difference. I rock back about two inches and just stare at him. That makes him even angrier, his eyes blazing up like coals. "What about you, Derrick?" he seethes. "*You're* the one who thinks he knows but doesn't. You've got JaQuentin wrong. I know what people say. He's all up in that GangstaVille Crew. That's just people yappin'. It ain't like that at all." His chest heaves in heavy, furious breaths. Behind him, the owner watches us. He likes me. Offered me some freebies, in fact. But he's not thrilled I brought Wes, since this is where Wes got caught pinching merchandise last summer. So that owner will dial the police in a heartbeat if we give him a reason. "Besides, you ever think that maybe I know what I'm doing with JaQuentin? You ever think that maybe I'm the one running game on him?"

We stare at each other. Truth is, those questions scare me more than anything Wes has done. A public intox? That's nothing. Even that bust for weed isn't that huge a deal. But, man, if he thinks he's gaming JaQuentin, then my boy has flat lost his mind. I don't ask what he means. I don't want to know. So instead I point to the shoes on the nearest wall. "I was thinking about getting these," I say as I walk over. And I intentionally pick out the blandest pair I can find—some white and gray New Balance walking shoes you might see on some 80-year-old doing laps in the mall.

Wes squinches up his face like he drank curdled milk. "D, have you lost your mind?" he says. He starts waving at them. "Put those things back. Put them *back!*"

I act all dumb. "You kidding? These things have swagger!"

He knows I'm putting him on, but it still seems to cause him physical pain. "Stop it, D," he says. He puts his hands on his stomach. "Hearing you talk about swagger makes me ill."

"I got swagger," I say.

Wes laughs. "No, D. You've got game. But swagger has never been your thing." And that's the thing—we might be messing around, but Wes is a friend who can call me on stuff like nobody else can. Parents and coaches I can tune out. And recruiters are never going to tell me anything I don't want to hear. But Wes—when he's being himself—can tell me how it is. That's good for anyone, but a guy in my position *needs* it.

I put the shoes back. The owner, who's still been eyeing us, shakes his head. "Let's bounce," I say.

"Where to?" Wes asks.

"You got the ride," I say.

So Wes leads, but the owner stops me before I hit the door. With Wes standing on the other side of the glass, he offers me a deal. He waves his arm toward the store. "Anything you want, D-Bow," he says. "Say the word. Then you get to the League and you can still come back here to give my store some pub."

I nod, but don't take him up on it. Then I start for the door.

He's not done though. He points at Wes. "Just don't come back in here with trash like that," he says.

This time I don't even nod. I just hit it. And when Wes asks me what was up with the owner, I just shrug. "He wants to know if you need a part-time job," I say.

"Shiiiiit," Wes laughs.

Then we're off, exploring our city in a bleak January. Just like old times.

We end up at Circle Centre. It's mostly an excuse to get out of the car and get inside somewhere, because in truth the place doesn't have much for guys like us. Used to be we could head up to the top of the mall and kick it at Tilt or Glowgolf, but those places are for kids. We haven't been there in years. And most of the stores are filled with either things we don't want or things we can't afford.

All that's left to do is get some pretzels at the food court and people watch the post-church crowd. We sling our winter coats over the backs of our chairs and gaze around. I remember long ago seeing Roy Hibbert strolling through this very spot, but there's no such stargazing today. Instead it's just the anonymous blur of a city shopping—middle-aged men with their bellies straining at their belts or harried-looking shoppers toting bags and checking receipts or people in suits powering past with a cell in one hand and a fresh cup of coffee in the other. Mostly white. Mostly older. Mostly Indiana the way people imagine it. Unless they're looking up stories on crime, and then they'll get the Indianapolis that my mom talked about the other night—guys our age scowling for mug shots.

And, sure, people imagine hoops when they think Indiana too. But even that's pretty white. I mean, the list of Indiana guys in the League is made up of people like Mike Conley and Courtney Lee and Zach Randolph and Jeff Teague—but you mention Hoosier basketball to most people and they still want to go on about old white shooting

Kevin Waltman

guards like Steve Alford and Damon Bailey. Like they count more or something, even though they never made a dent in the NBA.

But that's not my fight to fight. I know where I'm heading. Someday if I sit in the Circle Centre food-court, people will line up for autographs.

"Look at that guy," Wes says, snapping me out of my little daydream. About fifty feet away, there's a security guard, a pudgy guy who probably couldn't catch a shoplifter if they were hopping on one leg. When he catches us looking at him he turns his head, pretends to take a long gaze down the mall corridor. "Shit," Wes seethes. "He was staring at us for a minute solid. Probably half the people here are going to back to some office and rob people blind, but let two teenage brothers sit down and we're the ones under suspicion."

I look around again. Sure, it's mostly white, but there are at least ten other black people in the food-court alone. "Maybe you're reading too much into it," I say.

"Nah. I know what's up. I know that look. Don't tell me you don't."

"I feel you," I say. I can't totally disagree. It was just the other night I felt those looks on me and Lia. But for us it was still kind of a game. Wes just seems so angry about it. And everyone knows how that anger plays out—it sours into wasted rage until you do something to justify the suspicions in the first place. I look across the table at Wes. I wonder if someday, while I'm blowing up on the sports pages, he's going to be one of those mug shots in another section of the paper.

"Check that," he says out of the side of his mouth. He tilts his head toward the escalator, where there's a woman stepping off. She's got the long legs, the tight skirt, the high heels. She's got a model's cheekbones and long blond hair cascading down. There are beautiful women everywhere, but sometimes in a city you'll see one that just kind of pops out of the crowd. "I mean, *damn*, D," Wes says.

"You're not messing around," I say. I've never been one to peep women and talk about them like this, but if it gets Wes' head right, then whatever. What I'm really thinking is that she's got nothing on Lia, but I keep that to myself.

Even now Wes is on edge. He spins in his seat and points at me. "Just promise me this," he says. "You sign your first fat contract, you can mess around with all those groupies. Do your thing. But don't you dare marry a white girl. Don't be one of those guys."

I lean back, exasperated. I mean, *he's* the one who pointed her out and now he's lecturing me? It's tiring trying to keep up. "Wes," I say, "I haven't exactly planned it that far ahead."

"I'm just sayin'," he goes on. "I know we're not supposed to say that kind of stuff, but that's just how it *is*, D. For real. A hookup's one thing, but if JaQuentin catches some guy clocking real time with a white girl, that guy's *out*."

Great. So now I'm getting lectures on sex and race from JaQuentin Peggs, with my boy Wes as a mouthpiece.

He's not done running his mouth. When I don't respond he starts explaining how last night he was making inroads with Norika Winston, some girl that was hanging at JaQuentin's. I know what it means. They talked for about ten minutes and Wes didn't get anywhere. Used to be I'd give him hell for it, but I've had enough. "Let's hit a movie," I say. "Next one starts in five."

Kevin Waltman

I don't care about any flick that's out, but at this point it seems like the only way to hang with Wes without him saying something that will set me on edge.

I'd have better luck going to the rack against Dikembe in his prime than making Mom budge on this one. That doesn't mean I'm not going to try.

"You're acting like he got caught packing weapons or something," I say.

"No. That's not what I'm doing," she says. "I'm acting like you're my son and I know what's best for you. That's final."

I look to Dad, who's said nothing the whole time. He's leaning with his elbows on the table, a glass of ice water beside him, as relaxed as if he were enjoying the Sunday paper all by himself. When Mom asked where I'd been I told her straight up—no sense in lying—and we've been sitting here going round ever since. "Don't look at me," Dad says. "You know I'm with your mother on this." *Maybe*, I think. Or maybe he sees that freight train temper of hers barreling down the tracks and doesn't feel the need to step in on my behalf. Either way, he's no help.

There's no meeting Mom head-on, so I decide to come at it from a different perspective. "Mom, don't you always want me to do the right thing?" I ask.

She narrows her eyes. "Yes," she says, but she anticipates where I'm going. "Just so long as your dad and I determine what the right thing is."

"Fine," I say. "Then explain to me how turning my back on my best friend when he needs me the most is the right thing."

Pull   157

Mom's eyes bulge. She takes a deep breath. Dad purses his lips and squints his eyes, feeling sorry for what's coming my way. Then—*wham!*—Mom's hands smack flat on the table, making Dad's glass shake so hard it sloshes water out. Then she points at me, the tip of her finger about two inches from my nose. "*You* get yourself a high school diploma. *You* finish college when you've got a child. *You* hold down a job and raise two kids. *You* watch the city around you go straight to hell while nobody does a damn thing. *You* watch kid after kid you used to teach grow up and lose their minds. Then—and *only then*—you come back here and sit at my table and tell me what the right thing is."

"Mom, I—"

"Let it go, son." It's Dad now. He just reaches and places his left hand on my arm.

Mom stands and leaves. End of conversation. She thumps her heels down with each step, leaving little aftershocks of her lecture.

Once she's gone, and I hear that bedroom door slam, I turn to Dad again.

"For real," I say, "there are so many worse things guys could be doing. He's not banging. He's not dealing."

He raises his hand to cut me off again. "I know that," he says. "But, Derrick, *He could be doing worse things* isn't a winning argument."

He's got a point. Besides I'm tired of arguing. Out our window, the night has that brittle look, like everything is frozen and could shatter any second. A gust of wind might crack a tree in two. The wrong step might split the sidewalk. I spent all Sunday with Wes, and it was no fun anyway. Every moment with him felt so tense. I found myself thinking all the things Mom does.

Dad and I edge around each other silently. He puts his glass in the dishwasher. I grab an ice pack from the freezer, wrap it in a towel, and head for the couch. He reads in his chair for a minute or two, then picks up the remote. "You mind?" he asks. I just shake my head and he clicks on the T.V. It's the news—all bad, with men furrowing their brows and looking concerned as they rattle off the latest from war-torn countries, from patches of America under deep freeze, of some sordid detail from a triple-murder case in Illinois.

Finally, I can't take it. "You ever think Wes is just getting some bad breaks?" I say. "I mean, there are about a million people in this city doing the same things as he did and they're not getting caught."

For a second, he looks like he's actually considering this. Then he gives me his best "patient Dad" look, smiling slightly and shaking his head. "Derrick, do you really think these are the only two times he's done these things? Do you think that night with you was the only time Wes had drugs on him? Or that the other night was the only time he'd been drunk? He'd have to be unluckiest kid in the whole world for that to be true."

"Whatever," I say. It comes out surly and immature. But if they're going to treat me like I'm Jayson's age, then maybe I'll give them the same attitude he does.

Dad's jaw snaps shut. The muscles in his face tense up. He inhales sharply like he's about to say something, but then he just picks up the remote. He flips around, making stabbing motions at the T.V. When he lands on another news show—same headlines, but different spin—he leans into his chair, pushing back like he's trying to crush something behind him. "Well, you can think what you want," he says. He doesn't even look away from the tube. "But what we say goes. I'm not watching what happened to your uncle happen to you. You're done with Wes. It is what it is."

"What?" I say. My parents hate that phrase—*it is what it is*—chalking it up as one more example that young people have totally forgotten how to communicate any significant meaning to anyone. And now he's laying it on me.

He slowly swivels his head and squints at me. "You heard me, Derrick."

I'm right on the cusp with Dad. It takes him way longer than Mom to hit maximum anger, but Jayson and I have learned the hard way that you do *not* want to push him all the way there. So I drop it at last. It's not fair, but at this point, what is?

18.

I could go. If it were the playoffs, I could go. Monday I did light
jogging during practice. Tuesday I jogged again and shot jumpers.
Wednesday I went half-speed in drills, testing out the calf in basketball
moves. Yesterday more of the same. I never went full-bore, but now and
then I'd test it—plant for a hard cut, push off for a jump. Every time it
responded just fine. I'd go home and do the routine of ice and elevation.
Even that felt like overkill. I never felt a twinge, never an ache, so
tonight when I got to the gym I told Coach I was ready.

"No you're not," he said. "I've been around enough players to
know all of them will tell you he's ready a week before he really is."

So here I sit in street clothes again while my boys get ready to
tangle with Covenant Christian. We've lost two more while I've been
out, but we could maybe take these guys without me. Problem is,
from what Coach said I'm going to be on the pine for Bishop Chatard
tomorrow night too.

I play my part. I clap for the guys, give them a little chatter
as they get loose. As they swing over toward our bench in the lay-up

line, I take a step onto the court and give each guy a quick fist bump. When Fuller comes by, I grab him by the wrist and pull him over to the sideline. He furrows up his brow, worried that something's wrong. I offer a fake jab to his gut to loosen him up. "It's all good, man," I say. Then I pull him in tight and get in his ear. "You know how you wanted to prove you guys could win without me?" Fuller nods. He's breathing a little heavy and has a slight sweat going. It all kind of reinforces how out of place I am in street clothes. This thing I'm trying to do doesn't come natural. But with Fuller still pulled close, I turn both of us and point toward the Covenant Christian end. "These are the guys to do it against. Just attack, man. Go at 'em. They can't handle a bull like you. And, man, even if you don't score, you know Jones and Stanford are gonna eat up their bigs on the glass."

"Got it," Fuller says. It's like he's telling an algebra teacher he understands the problem on the chalkboard. I expected he'd get amped, maybe even crack a smile. Not Fuller. He's going to be a hundred percent serious a hundred percent of the time. Then he jumps back into the layup line to go through his routine. It cracks me up, really. I laugh a little to myself and realize something I didn't think was the case even a month ago—I flat-out like being J.J. Fuller's teammate.

As soon as our talk's over, I feel deflated again. Murphy comes over to me and gives me a pat on the back. "Atta way," he says. "If you can't lace 'em up, then you got to talk up the boys." He launches into a story about how when he was a sophomore in high school, their best player went down for two weeks. He gives me all the details—what kind of player the guy was, who had to step in during the injury, a game-by-game breakdown—but anyone who's ever heard an old player

Kevin Waltman

tell a story knows where it's going. He's going to tell me how the team came together while the guy was out, then really hit the gas when he came back.

I don't want to hear it. Not because I disrespect Murphy or because he doesn't have a point. But when you're a player, you don't want to talk hoops. You want to play. While Murphy keeps on with his story, I look around the gym. Lia's in the bleachers across from us. She catches me looking at her. She gives a quick wink. I look away before I get caught up in thinking about seeing her after the game. I nod at Murphy to make him think I'm still paying attention, then turn and check where my family usually sits, up behind our bench. There's Mom and Dad, as always, even though I won't see any minutes tonight. But Jayson's missing. And so is Kid. That one's a surprise—he's been a fixture in these stands forever. It doesn't matter that Bolden booted him all those years ago. Or that his nephew's not in uniform. Or even if Marion East is struggling to win. The guy's a hoops junkie, and this is his alma mater. So the fact that he's absent makes me a little edgy. For that matter, he's been a ghost for almost a week now.

"You feel me, D?" This is Murphy. He's caught me spacing. I feel like a kid in class who's been called on when he clearly has no idea what the teacher is talking about.

"Yeah," I say. "I get you."

Murphy shakes his head at me. "Man, don't fake it on me. You weren't listening to a word I said."

I protest, acting all indignant. "I'm listening. You're telling about how your team toughed it out your sophomore year."

Murphy rolls his eyes. "Please, D. Don't even." He shakes his head at me, all disappointed. "I was telling you how to attack Howe next weekend when you come back. But you're not listening. You're a hell of a player, but sometimes you just don't listen." Then he heads onto the floor, wanting to talk instead to the guys who are going to play ball tonight.

We won. Or, really, Marion East won. It's hard to say *we* when I was nothing more than a fan with a choice seat. Anyway, it doesn't take much to down Christian Covenant. They hung for a while, then Reynolds got loose for a few threes and Stanford went beast-mode down low. Fuller never really took my advice, but he got his here and there. And even Rider and Jones got in on the act late, tacking on some garbage-time points in a 20-point curb-stomping. And not a one of those guys having as successful a night as I am. Not by a long shot.

Lia's house. Alone. Her room.

She shed her shirt about five minutes ago. It wasn't long after that I got her bra off—didn't even fumble around with the snaps, just undid it smooth like some pro. She was lying back on her bed. I started to climb on top of her—but she put her hand on my stomach for a second.

"Uh uh," she said. "You too." She pointed at my shirt. I ripped that thing off in a heartbeat.

Which puts us here. Both of us on her bed, skin on skin. And every place we meet—her fingers on my stomach, my mouth on her neck—creates a jolt of electricity. In the corner, she's got a lamp on with a shirt draped over it, so it casts us in a dim red glow. My heart is racing so fast I feel a humming in my head, like I'm about to pass out from the tension. Slowly—like any sudden move might break the spell—I let my fingers creep down from her chest to her stomach, then a few more inches to the top of her jeans. As nimble as directing a little touch pass, I undo her button. She gasps. My fingers on her zipper, she grabs my wrist. I wait.

"Oh, Jesus, just do it," she says at last. Then she buries her teeth into my shoulder so hard I bet she draws blood.

She raises her hips off the bed as I peel those jeans off. I stand there above her and just look for a second—Lia Stone, naked in front of me, except for a whisper-thin pair of black panties. I take my jeans off first, then I reach back to her. She hesitates, then raises her hips again.

"Don't stop now," she says. And I don't. Who says I never listen to what I'm told?

We're talking afterward, but our words seem to float away from us and out the window. Nothing stays with us now, not in this afterglow. Her head is on my chest, her leg swung across mine. I pick up bits here and there. She's talking about her dad raising her alone for the most part. Her mom split to Georgia when Lia was six. She sees her in the summers, I think—that part I didn't pay enough attention to. I know this is important—Lia's trying to tell me who she is, what her life's about—but I can't get my head out of the clouds. This isn't my first time. But it's the first time with Lia, and all I know is that I want there to be more times.

The only thing that's bothering me is that I still don't know how to tell if she got hers. I'm afraid to ask, to really say the words. I remember what Wes told me about my lack of swagger. He may be wrong about a million things, but not that one. Even now, I can't just say what I want to say around Lia. I wait a minute and then say, "You good?"

"Very," she says.

But I realize that she'd say that no matter what. If you want a real answer, you've got to ask the real question. I start to work up the words in my head, but she springs off of me. Maybe she sensed what I was going to ask and didn't want to answer. Whatever the reason, she's suddenly bouncing around like her alarm clock just went off. She puts her bra back on, then digs around until she finds her panties. Then, as if she's suddenly embarrassed for me to see her naked, she wriggles around under the covers to put them on. "Come on," she says. She smacks me on the arm. "Get that ass in gear."

When I don't budge, she grabs the sheets and rips them down, exposing me—naked head to toe except for the condom still hanging off me. Now I'm the one who's embarrassed. But when I reach for the covers she beats me to it. She pulls them all the way off the bed, balling them in a pile on the floor. It gives me no choice but to start getting dressed.

"Move it," she says, teasing again. "You don't get to fuck me and then just lay around. I need some quality time before you go."

"That wasn't quality time?" I say, teasing right back.

She pauses. She's got both arms in the sleeves of her sweater, but hasn't pulled it over her head yet. Her jeans are already on, but somehow that pose—her squinting at me over her sweater, her mid-riff still exposed—just floors me. What I'd like to do is pull her right back onto this bed. "You think you're all on point, don't you?" she says. She's still teasing, but there's an edge to it, just enough to let me know I don't get to act on my impulse.

"Well?" I say.

She relents, gives me a wink. "You're okay," she says. "Just never forget I could do that"—she points to the bed, to me—"with any guy I want. So what comes before and after better be good too."

That's when we hear it. The front door. Footsteps. Then a man's voice: "Lia? You home, sweetie?" Her room is at the end of the hallway. It's not a long walk from the front door back here.

We're a blur of hushed obscenities. And while I might have quicks on the court, I've got nothing on Lia here. By the time I've got one leg in my pants, Lia's already smoothing down the covers. She whips her head around to look at me, eyes blazing with sudden anger. "Damnit, Derrick!" she hisses. "What are you standing around for?"

She grabs my shirt and shoes off the floor and shoves them in my arms, then pushes me toward the side door in her room. In the dark, I don't realize where I am at first. But then the door opens again, and Lia's hand slips in to flip on the light. Once that's done, she chirps *I'm in here, Daddy* so innocently it buckles my knees.

So here I stand in her bathroom, surrounded by pink towels and colored soaps and an endless array of lotions and makeup containers. Her shower curtain has a picture of three kittens on it. I feel like I've stepped into the bathroom of a pre-teen. I put my hand to my head and whisper to myself, "What were we thinking?" But then an image of Lia's body flashes through my mind—her neck arching to be kissed, her lips parted. It's not about thinking.

Her bathroom has two doors—one back to her room and the

other to the hallway—and through the second one I can hear a muffled conversation between Lia and her father. His voice rumbles in a low bass for a few seconds. Then hers comes lilting down in high, sing-song tones. Then I hear, plain as day, "Oh, yeah, Derrick's here. I told you he was coming over after the game, Dad."

I know that's my cue, but I've been so caught up in my own drama that I'm still not dressed. My shirt's in my hands, and my pants are sagging down with my belt undone. As I race to finish dressing, footsteps approach from down the hall. I can also hear her Dad responding to the news that I'm here. While I can't make out exactly what he says, there's a shift in his tone—his voice rising in pitch and coming a little faster.

"I swear I told you before I left for the game tonight," Lia sighs. Then there's a light rap on the bathroom door. "You okay in there, Derrick?" she asks. She keeps her voice gentle, but there's just a trace of urgency at the end, like she's saying, *For the love of God get out here and be presentable.*

I get my shirt on, buckle my belt. Then there's my shoes—no socks. I realize that they're still somewhere on her floor, as is my coat—tell-tale signs that we were up to exactly what her dad suspects we were up to. For a second, I consider going in after them, like a criminal returning to the scene to cover up evidence. But what if she didn't close her bedroom door and her dad sees me? There's another knock on the bathroom, a little louder this time, and my decision's made for me. I slip my bare feet into my shoes and pull my pants down an extra inch so he won't catch a glimpse of my ankles and get suspicious. Then I flush the toilet—and somehow this makes me flood with guilt. Somehow it seems like that's the dead giveaway.

The hall light is harsh, far brighter than the bathroom, and I immediately look away.

"Derrick Bowen? I'm Mr. Stone. Good to meet you." When I look again, he's standing halfway down the hall, hand extended. Now, if we met between the lines, I'd take him straight to the rack and bully him all over the place. But there's something in his posture—chest puffed a tad, eyes intense, his hand stiff in the air—that makes him seem like a seven-footer not to be tested.

"Hi," I say. I take those few strides down the hallway and offer my hand. Then I do the thing I told myself I wouldn't—when he pumps my hand, I look away. A sure sign of guilt. I check myself and meet his gaze, but it's too late. He's already peering right into me, still squeezing my hand to death. He's a little pudgy in middle age, but there's some serious tension in his jaw and some real strength in his grip. Behind him, Lia watches us nervously.

Finally, Mr. Stone breaks the standoff. He smiles—a fake, overly cheerful grin—and waves his arm toward their living room like an usher. "Come on and sit down," he says. "Can I get you anything?"

"No," I say, "I'm good."

"Suit yourself."

When we walk into the living room, he points to the couch where Lia's taken a seat. He plops down in what is obviously his chair—a plush recliner that he pushes back in like he doesn't have a care in the world. "Actually, I should be getting home," I say.

"Sit," says Mr. Stone.

"Really?" I say.

"Sit," he says, and it's pretty clear it's no longer a polite request.

Pull

Still, I linger there, standing beside Lia. She reaches up and touches my hand. "Derrick? Just sit, okay?" Her big brown eyes are watery and afraid. *Might as well,* I think. I mean, if any teenagers have ever been busted, it's us. So I sit. I feel my ankles bare against the cool air in the room.

Mr. Stone's eyes go directly to my feet. He puts his chin in his hand and gives a little hmph. He knows.

We make small talk for a while. He asks about the team. About my injury. But his gaze never budges from my feet. I feel sometimes like he's going to whip out a gun and just shoot me right through those ankles. Lia tries to keep the act up, talking cheerily like we're all just hanging out in the middle of the day, not a thing wrong in the world.

At last, I beg out, saying that I'm about to run up against my mom's curfew. Mr. Stone lets me go this time, but he doesn't stand to shake my hand again. Instead, as I pass him on my way to the door he just asks, "Where's your coat, Derrick?"

"I left it in my car," I lie. And then I bumble out into the night. Lia stands in the doorway, probably wishing she could run off with me instead of facing her dad. I glance back at her as I climb in my car. She looks little and scared. But then she does this amazing thing—she straightens up and tilts her head to one side. She gives a mischievous grin. She blows a kiss.

Girl is killer. I start the ignition, my heart racing again. I get those images of her in my head, remember how her body felt under mine. *Who cares?* I think. Her dad isn't going to kill me. For real. If anything was ever worth the trouble that comes with it, then my night with Lia most definitely was.

I thought my night was done. Maybe a shower to slow my racing pulse. Maybe some flipping to find a late game. Then bed.

Nope. Not for this kid. Not with this family.

I get home and Kid's sitting on the front porch steps in fifteen-degree weather. He doesn't have his coat on either. Even in the light of a half-moon, I can tell he's distressed. His head's buried in his hands. He only looks up when he hears my footsteps. Then he tries to act all normal.

"Hey, D, what's the word?" He sniffs big, like he's trying to breathe in the night air, but I can tell he's on the verge of tears.

"You okay, Kid?" I ask.

"Yeah. Yeah. All good." He shrugs, then shivers. "I gotta hit it," he says, then turns and heads across the street to his car.

I stand by our door and watch him go. The taillights pulse at the corner, but he whips into the turn recklessly, like he can't wait to get anywhere but here.

Inside, it's just my dad sitting in his chair and watching T.V. There's a prickliness to the quiet in the house. The heat feels good after being in the cold, but after a second my skin starts to itch. I feel like if I take a wrong step right now, I'll set off a detonator.

Dad shifts in his chair and looks around toward me, his eyes glowing with anger. When he sees it's me, he relaxes and tries to smile—but it's about as convincing as those smiles he gave me when he was in the hospital last year, trying to tell me everything was okay. "You have a good time with Lia?" he asks.

"Yeah," I answer, but I'm not letting this go. "What's up with Kid?"

Dad lifts off his glasses with one hand and rubs the bridge of his nose with the other. Then he draws that hand down over his mouth and neck in frustration. "I'd like to not talk about your uncle right now," he says.

At first it riles me. I mean, what kind of nonsense is that? I'm grown enough to handle whatever's going on. But I'm too beat to tackle more tension.

I hit my room and fall down on the bed, clothes still on. I think I'll never be able to sleep—not with my nerves jangling from my hook-up with Lia, from my frustration over my injury, from Kid's trouble, whatever that might be. Then when I open my eyes again it's three in the morning. I don't even bother undressing—at this point even that can wait until morning.

19.

Fraud. That's the word in the morning. Mom explains it to me and Jayson while Dad scrambles eggs and fries up bacon for breakfast. He's clearly too mad to talk about it so he's focusing on the food instead. Still, he can't help himself from chiming in now and then.

"Your uncle was still collecting unemployment checks all this time," Mom says. "Even though he'd had that new job for a year."

"I *knew* it," Dad snaps. "I *knew* something was going on. New car. New clothes. Acting like some big man."

Mom holds up her hand to tell him that she's got this, that he should just relax. She turns back to us, puts on a patient expression. "He's in real trouble this time. Apparently, he got caught with about six of his friends," she explains. "He'll probably have to pay restitution."

"How much?" I ask. I mean, if he used this coin for his ride, he's in the red something serious.

Mom shakes her head. "Well, when we asked him, he did his Kid thing." She sways her shoulders back and forth like she's dodging something. "He wouldn't answer straight, but we're not talking a few bucks here."

Jayson smirks and rolls his eyes, like he's personally offended by all this. "So, what?" he says. "We're gonna have an uncle in jail?"

"No," Mom says. "That seems really unlikely. Instead, he'll have to go to some classes and do community—"

"He *should*," Dad hollers. He slaps his spatula down on the stovetop and seems to scream directly at the food. "They should send his ass to jail. Keep him in there for a while. Only way he'll ever get his stupid head straightened out."

"Tom, yelling won't help," Mom says, her voice soft as a summer breeze. It's not their usual roles. Mom's typically the one going a hundred miles an hour. Dad's the one who applies the brakes.

So Dad's back stiffens under that little reminder from Mom. He grabs the bacon with some tongs, but grease pops up and burns his wrist. "God*damnit!*" he screams.

"Tom!" Mom seethes. "Language!"

Everyone knows that between my time in the locker room and Jayson's rebelliousness, we're used to language a lot worse than that. But it's a rule in the house and always will be—no cursing. Sure, Mom breaks the rule more than anyone, but she's not letting Dad off the hook.

Problem is, Dad's in no mood. He turns, real slowly, to the table. Without looking, he reaches behind him and snaps the burners off. "You think you know," he says to us all. "Everyone in this family thinks they know everything. So I take it. I get told by"—he points to us one by one—"my son who thinks he's God's gift to the court and my son who thinks he's figured the whole world out at age 13. And, oh, I get told by my wife Kaylene. Even when my brother's in trouble for the seven millionth time, I'm supposed to bite my tongue and be good, dutiful Tom Bowen. Well, listen to me! I can say *goddamnit* in my *goddamn* house whenever I *goddamn* want to!"

And with that he storms out, feet pounding through the living room toward the front door. It's as hot as I've ever seen my Dad. But when Mom gasps and clasps her hand over her mouth—there's hurt all over her face and she's trying not to cry—I see Dad pause mid-stride. He heard that gasp. He knows what he's done. Still, he plows ahead, slamming the door behind him as he goes.

Mom stands, trying to keep some dignity. I recognize that look on her face. It's just how Jasmine used to look when I'd say the worst thing possible to her. Mom's too strong to cry in front of us, but she's trembling. "Food's ready," she rasps. "Fix your own plates." Then she's gone.

Jayson and I do as we're told, moving through the kitchen so quietly you'd think we were thieves. We settle back at the table and start to eat. The food tastes like cardboard to me. The room seems suddenly drab—stains on the table, a small tear in the curtains, scuffs all over the floor.

"So what do you think?" Jayson whispers to me.

I'm about to tell him I think we live in a disaster of a family. We only look normal because all the families around us are even bigger disasters. But that's when the door opens again. Dad steps back inside.

I figure he's headed straight back to beg Mom's forgiveness. But when he sees us, he stops. He hangs his head for a second, then comes to the kitchen—his stride a lot less emphatic than when he stormed out. He pulls up a chair. He folds his hands on the table.

Pull 175

"Boys," he says, "there's nothing that gets me worked up like your uncle. I don't know why exactly. But I think it has a lot to do with the idea that I'm supposed to be watching out for him. That's what big brothers are supposed to do, especially now that our parents are gone. So I take his failures personally. And it also makes me mad because I see all the potential in him. Last year, when I was banged up, he's the one who held us together. I just—"

He trails off, looking away from us for the first time. I wonder if maybe he's going through the long list of Kid's mistakes, a list that just got one item longer. I glance over at Jayson. He's all sulk. I don't think for a second that he was actually hurt by what Dad said, but he's not going to make it easy on him. So I try instead. "It's okay, Dad," I say. "Everyone loses it now and then."

He smiles at me. He takes off his glasses, wipes them with his shirt and then places them on the table. Without them, he looks a few years younger on the spot. I can see a little more resemblance between Dad and Kid—the bright eyes, the high arch of his eyebrows. "No, it's not okay," he says. "Certainly not to you two. You're the best sons I could ever ask for. I should be grateful." Jayson gives a little snort at that, but Dad lets it go. "So I apologize to both of you," Dad continues. "But I also apologize for talking to your mother that way. It's not right. You don't act that way to women. Not any woman. Certainly not to one as good as your mother. If I'm honest with myself, she's all that separates me from being a far bigger mess than your uncle." He looks at me intently, then shifts his gaze to Jayson, who at least has enough sense to straighten up now. "You understand me?" Dad asks. "You're not supposed to act that way. I'm sorry you saw me do it."

"I hear you," I say.

"Yeah," Jayson manages.

That's enough for Dad. He pushes up from the table with a sigh. He takes a long look into the living room, staring at a spot on the wall that separates it and their bedroom. "Now if you'll excuse me," he says. "I need to go apologize to your mother." He gives a mock shudder of fear. "Now I mean it. She's the best woman in the world, but I promise you she's back there storing up some heat that will make my outburst look like nothing." He smiles at us, then gives a quick wink. "Pray for me, guys."

20.

At least I have ball. Enough waiting around. With Bishop Chatard in our gym, it's time to go. And I tell Coach Bolden so.

He sits at the head of the locker room, leaning back in a simple folding chair. He studies me, trying to detect how much he can trust me. I made sure I was the first one in. It's almost like I've caught him unprepared. His shirt isn't tucked in. The laces on one shoe are dangling, about to come undone.

"Give it another week," he says. "Why push it?"

"I'm not pushing it," I say. "I could have gone last night if I needed to."

"But you didn't *need* to," he counters. "And you don't *need* to tonight either. If this were Sectionals then I'd hear some argument, but I want you back at one hundred percent or not at all."

I lift my leg in front of me and hitch up my pants so he can see my calf. Then I flex it a few times. "I *am* a hundred percent," I say. "I swear." It feels like the truth, but I know there's just the slightest discomfort left when I push off of it sometimes, like there's a tiny pebble lodged in the muscle. So maybe 95% would be more honest. But I'm playing tonight. That's just how it is. Enough sitting.

"Okay," Coach says. Even as he concedes, there's a half-frown on his face. It's like he's watching some kid knock in a J but with terrible form. He knows that the short-term success is only setting up a bigger problem down the road. He stands and walks for the door that leads to his office. As he swings the door open, he calls over his shoulder, "Suit on up."

Even in warmups, I heard that buzz ripple through the crowd. When I hit the hardwood in uniform my name passed through the stands in soft waves—*Bowen-Bowen-Bowen's-back-Bowen's-playing*.

Pre-tip, I make the rounds. Chest bump with Stanford. Quick fist bumps with Reynolds and Jones. Then a stop next to Fuller. "We ready to ride now," I shout at him. He tries to stay even as ever, but then I grab both his shoulders and give him a quick shake. "Game time, Fuller! Let's run this." Finally I coax a smile from him, which is a win in its own right.

The ball goes up, and I attack. Chatard's center outleaps Stanford, but I'm quicker to the rock than their guard. I tip it away from him and corral it near the sideline. Fuller's on top of things. He streaks right to the rim. I hit him with a laser right in stride. He doesn't even need to dribble—just catches, rises, and lays one in for a quick 2-0 lead.

Bishop Chatard brings it up. They're too good to get rattled that quick, even on the road. Plus, they've got a solid point guard—a senior named Trey Graves—and he's been through some battles before. He makes sure they take their time. A few reversals. A feed to the post and then back out to Graves. He darts baseline, but I cut him off. So he circles back top, staying patient. When he kicks it to the right wing though, their off-guard tries to muscle through Reynolds. My boy stands his ground, takes the charge. Just like that, all their patience is wasted. Our ball.

I'm not so itchy that I'm going to force. But I didn't wait all this time so I could just run offense for forty seconds at a time. We go through a couple ball reversals, but when I rub off a Jones screen and catch it baseline, I get after it. A power dribble past Graves, and I'm into the lane. There's a tangle of bigs in there, but I don't care. Just rise—that calf muscle firing clean—and bury a mid-range J.

That lets the people know I'm back for real, and they respond. Watching the other guys maul Covenant Christian is nice, but they've got higher hopes than that for the season—and seeing me back in form lets them know those aren't just fantasies.

Bishop Chatard digs. They've got some solid bigs who give Stanford and Jones fits. Plus Graves loses me a couple times for easy buckets. And on our end, it's like my return has sent Fuller and Reynolds into a funk. Every time I drive and kick to them for open looks, they rim it out. After a few of those, they don't even shoot—just pump fake and drive, going nowhere.

So mid-third, as we're nursing a three-point lead, I figure it's *time*. Instead of starting the offense when I cross half-court, I just wave Reynolds down to the baseline. That flattens everyone out so I can solo up Graves. And it's no contest. I give a rhythm dribble left, then freeze him with a cross-over. Into the paint. Quick J from twelve. Bucket.

Next time down, we run the O. But as I'm making my baseline cut, I stop short at the rim. Just turn and seal. Fuller hits me and nobody even contends. An easy rise and throwdown for another deuce.

Then it's time to show off the range. Next possession I fly off a Stanford screen to the wing. Graves—afraid of my burst to the rim—stays back. That leaves me a nice, long look at a three. *Wet.*

Bishop Chatard calls timeout, but I've got the taste now. Bolden talks at us in the huddle, but I've got my eyes on the court the whole time. As soon as the ref comes over to tell us it's almost time to go, I'm up. I pop guys on their shoulders, slap the knees of the guys still sitting—*Let's go!*

Bishop Chatard runs a nice set out of the break. They fake some action to Graves on the wing, but their big bails on the screen for an easy back-door deuce. Lead's back down to six.

Doesn't matter. I race into the frontcourt. I slow up near the top of the circle, but it's just a pause to bait Graves. When he settles onto his heels, I push again. The defense jumps to me. It's an easy bounce pass to Jones at the rack. I put it right in his paws, but he fumbles it for a second. That gives the D a chance to recover. His man gets a piece as he goes up. I have it read the whole way—I move my feet for position and rise to meet the rock just as it skips off the front rim. Not enough momentum on my side for a throwdown, but it's an easy tip. Back to an eight-point spread.

I hound Graves as he brings it up, but he's too good, too experienced, just to rip it from him. He gives it up as soon as he crosses mid-court. They start to cycle through their sets. By this time, I've got a pretty good feel for them. Without the benefit of a timeout, their

Pull

coach can't draw up anything special, so I tag Graves—stay glued on his UCLA cut, stay on top of him when he cuts baseline, then sag to the middle when the ball reverses the other way. And I know what's coming next. They set a cross-screen for him so he can come back to get it at the top of the circle. Since I'm so far off, they can't put a good screen on me, but I let myself get hung up for just a split second. Graves thinks maybe he's got a look, so he doesn't flare way up top. Instead he straight cuts with his hands extended, and that's when I jump. I spring off that screen and into the passing lane. Beat Graves to the spot. Tap the ball away. Scoop it. *Gone.*

The crowd's on their feet before I even hit the lane. So I decide to give them a little sugar. I rise like I'm going for a straight throwdown, but whip my body around at the last second for a filthy reverse.

Place goes bananas. And, yeah, there's a minute left in the third, but this thing's over. Everyone knows the boss is back.

I linger on the baseline for a second, soaking it in while the ref chases down the rock, which rolled all the way to the corner. Then I give a little hop back onto the court to start digging into Graves again. That's when I feel it—it's no tear, nothing serious, just a small little stab in my calf like I was still feeling a week ago. I press on though. No stopping this train now.

The calf held up. Bishop Chatard didn't. Even easing off my leg a bit, I kept it rolling. I finished with 24 and 8 boards as we coasted to a 15-point win over a pretty stout squad.

But in the locker room, things are subdued. Sure, Reynolds is rapping along and bobbing his head to whatever he's got on headphone blast. And Jones and Stanford are talking smack to each other by their lockers, congratulating each other for every block, every bucket, every board. And Bolden and Murphy are huddled at the head of the locker room and cracking their private jokes, maybe convincing each other that we won because they're so much sharper than the brain trust on the Bishop Chatard bench. Still, something's missing. Last year, after a win like that, the locker room would have been bursting with energy.

I lean back in my locker and try not to sweat it. I flex my calf a few times, making sure Bolden's not watching me. It's tender, but there's nothing serious. All good. Fuller walks by, ready to hit the showers. He's got a towel wrapped around his waist. It cuts off a big tattoo of a cross on the right side of his stomach—that ink the only real flavor to Fuller.

Quickly, I rip off my jersey and snap it at him. He just swats at it.

"Come on, big man," I say. "You could at least smile. We *won*, Fuller."

He grins a little, but that's it. "Yeah," he says. "Not bad. I guess we have to get our minds on Howe next weekend. Stay focused, right?"

"Loosen up, Fuller!" I shout. "If you can't enjoy a win, what are you in this for? I mean, you see me break Graves' ankles on that crossover in the third?" I was just saying it to try to get a laugh, but as soon as that question hits him whatever grin he had vanishes.

"I saw it," he says. "Everyone saw the D-Bow Show back in primetime." Then he heads for the shower, his body as tensed up as if he were about to box someone off the glass. Brutal. That interview with Whitfield was a month ago, and I already caught enough grief from it. Calling me out on it now—after a win—is just cold.

Fine, I think. Guys resent me being the star? That's on them. If they'd rather go back to getting thumped by Park Tudor, then they're not in this for the right reasons. But, damn, I really don't want to go down this road—no team ever got far when the star and the supporting cast were pulling in different directions.

21.

There are a million bad things about seeing Wes turn. But maybe
the worst is seeing him in the Marion East hallways—on the days he
decides to show up, that is. He struts like some pimp, this fake hitch
in his stride, his pants sagging just as far as he can let them before
Principal Markey will call him out. He'll give a fist bump to all the guys
people know to avoid—young guns who have the same rumors swirling
around them as JaQuentin—but he ignores everyone else.

It's the only time I see him. And even then, it's not like we hang.
"'Sup, D," he says to me this morning. Then he just keeps slinking
down the hall, on his way to a class he's probably failing.

"Come on, Wes," I say. "I rate more than a *'sup*, don't I?"

He stops mid-step and turns. He smiles and doubles back, then
throws his arms wide. We clasp right hands and pull into each other.
"Sorry, D," he says. "I didn't mean disrespect."

I just laugh it off. There's too much to tell him and no way to
fit it in before the first bell. How do I explain that it has nothing to do
with *respect*? That instead, every time I see him, it feels more and more

like I'm looking at a stranger. Like some alien came down and took over Wes' body. And that half the time I want to cry and the other half I want to jack him in the face just to knock some sense into him. Instead I say, "Aw, it's good. It goes both ways."

We idle in the hallway for a second. I know I've got to split for class, but what I'd rather do is just cut out with Wes. "Heard you been hitting it pretty good," he says.

For a second I think he's talking about me and Lia. I immediately wonder how word got out. It's not like I'm trying to hush things up—most guys hook up with a girl like Lia and it's all they can do not to tweet the details as soon as it's done—but it still surprises me. Then I realize he's talking ball. "On the court?" I ask.

"Yeah," he says. He cocks his head to look at me sideways. "What you think I'm talking about?"

"Nothing," I say.

"Oh," Wes says. He reads it all over me. "You broke yourself off some, didn't you?"

I wince. I don't care about keeping things a secret—back in the day, Wes and I would have told each other first thing if a girl even *looked* at one of us—but it's the way he talks about it. *Broke yourself off some.* That's straight JaQuentin. No way Wes would have talked about a girl that way a year ago. "Just drop it," I say. "It's no big thing. What about you and Norika?"

His whole expression shifts. It's the same look he gets when he talks about yet another way his dad let him down. "Ain't happening," he says. "Using me to get in with JaQuentin." I know that stings. Especially since last year he lost Iesha—a girl he actually cared about—

to JaQuentin too. But maybe this will finally snap him out from JaQuentin's dark spell. "Whatever," Wes says. He throws himself back into his tough pose. "Ex to the next, right?"

The bell sounds. We're late, but that's not what's bothering me. I can handle a disapproving look from a teacher. But when Wes mumbles a *Catch you later* and struts on down the hall, I finally put a finger on what troubles me most about him. That attitude—the sneer, the shrug, the false bravado—is the same thing I see bubbling up in Jayson. Sure, Jayson's a long way from getting in the kind of trouble that Wes is in. With my brother, it's all talk. A pose. Part of the daily game for a young pup. But that's how it started with Wes.

Wes disappears into his classroom. I get my feet shuffling toward mine. I think again about what Dad said the other day. He was supposed to watch after Kid. I've got to watch my brother.

I'm in early, making sure to loosen up my calf. It's not bad, just some tightness. But I want to stretch it out before Bolden gets in so he doesn't think I need more rest. I'm done watching games from the sideline.

Practice gear on, I put my hands on my locker and press back into my calf. I start gently, and then keep working back further as I feel the muscle respond. But when I hear that locker room door swing open, I spring out of my stretch and sit at my locker. To look busy, I re-lace my kicks.

It's Bolden and Murphy both. They're in mid-conversation.

"Haven't had to deal with this in a while," Bolden says. "But you get those big dogs after a kid and it's a mess if you don't handle it."

They see me and stop. It's clear that I was the subject of their conversation. At least they don't try to hide it. "Speak of the devil," Murphy says.

Bolden can tell I'm on high alert, so he slides a chair over in front of me and sits. "Don't worry, Derrick," he says. "This isn't one of those talks where we team up on you. But we've got an issue." He looks at Coach Murphy and then makes a sweeping gesture with his hand as if to say *It's all yours.*

Murphy doesn't waste any time. "I got offered cash from a school to get you to go there," he says. "I'm not going to say which school because the guy who called me was a friend from back in the day. He's a college assistant now."

This kind of stuns me. Schools aren't subtle. When a coach gives me the number of a guy to call if I "need anything at all," I know what it means. But trying to lure me through Coach Murphy? I didn't see that coming. "I swear I haven't taken a thing from anyone," I say. "And I'm not looking for anything. We talked about that already."

Bolden nods. He leans forward, elbows on his knees, and rasps away. "We're not saying that, Derrick. I know where you're coming from. But this is only going to get crazier unless we head it off some."

Crazy talk, I want to say. If there was a way to get schools to stop cheating, then the NCAA would have done it a long time ago. "I don't see how we do that," I admit.

"Give us a list," Murphy says. "Five schools. Hell, you can still change your mind down the road if you want. But right now every school in the country thinks it's open season on you. Hell, a lot of juniors have committed already. You haven't even narrowed it down.

But if you do, maybe there will be a few guys like my old buddy who will spend their energies on other recruits."

"Okay," I say, "but I don't have a list of five. God, I don't have a list of fifteen."

"We don't need it this minute," Bolden says. "And it's not like five is some magic number. Just think about it. Then we'll help you set up some official visits. Let the press know where you're considering. Keep it all organized. Good?"

"Sure," I say. Then Bolden and Murphy stand. They've still got to get ready for practice. It's insane. I've wanted this—to be a prized recruit—since the first time I touched the leather. And everyone knows this is how that plays out. But somehow having that talk with my coaches—so businesslike, so matter-of-fact—makes it seem like I'm getting myself involved in a pretty dirty game, even if I'm not the one cheating. Then again, it makes you wonder. "Hey, Coach Murphy," I say. "Out of curiosity—how much they offer you?"

He smiles. "You really want to know?" he asks. But he doesn't even wait for me to answer. He *wants* to tell, because deep down it's a little bit of a thrill. "Ten grand," he says. "It's enough to make you think," he says. It's a joke, but we all know there's some truth to it.

"So if we win State, you want to call him back and see if you can get twenty?" I say. We all laugh then. But it flashes through my mind—Kid. Money problems and a money solution. I extinguish that as quick as it pops up. We decided a long time ago we weren't playing it that way.

"You know the thing that burns me?" Bolden says. He gestures toward Murphy again. "They called *you* instead of me. They don't think

I could use a little money too? I mean, I'm the head coach, damnit. Historically speaking, I should be first in line on dirty money."

We all laugh again. Then Reynolds comes through the door, followed closely by Stanford and Fuller. Just like that, the conversation's over and we're back to business. Even that amazes me—Coach Joe Bolden, the straightest shooter that's ever been, cracking jokes about guys cheating. I guess he's been around so long it doesn't faze him. Maybe Bolden's like the one honest man at a card table full of cheaters—all he can do is play his hand the best he can and laugh off all the dirty tricks around him.

We rattled off two more after the Bishop Chatard win, bringing us to 11-4. But even with the boost we've got from a four-game win streak, it's still that late January grind. All the shine of the new season is worn off. And we've got more than a month to the excitement of Sectionals. It shows in practice.

Stanford half-asses it in the early drills, then sulks when Bolden calls him out on it. It escalates until Bolden puts us into a set of suicides.

Then we run our sets against full- and half-court traps. It's prep for Cathedral on Friday, since they've been jumping people with their press all year. "They turned Lawrence Central over twenty times last week," Bolden snaps. "You don't get your heads in it, they'll make you look foolish." Only this time it's Fuller and Reynolds who can't get straight. The idea is to always have someone cutting middle so if a trap comes, we can hit the cutter and attack. But the first time Fuller's slow in recognition. Then he mishandles the pass. The next time, Fuller makes the right cut, but the defense takes it away. Jones pops out. I shout for

Reynolds to hit him—an easy pass that would give us numbers—but either he doesn't hear or doesn't care. Instead he tries to lob it all the way across the court to me. It sails a good four feet over my head. I make a leap for it but all that does is tweak my calf. It's minor, but I know I've got to ease off—ratchet it back during practice so I can go full-tilt Friday.

"Get with it now, boys," Murphy shouts. He tries to sound upbeat, but really he's just addressing the situation so Bolden doesn't have to.

We finally get it figured out after a few more tries, so Bolden lets us run five-on-five. It would be a rout under normal circumstances. With the second team pressing—opening up all kinds of space on the floor—we should rip it past them. Not today. The first time we face the press, Stanford inexplicably throws the in-bounds to Jones—he's got no idea what to do with it. Turnover right away. The next time, Fuller forgets his cut again and Reynolds tries to beat the trap on his own. Rider—playing with a chip on his shoulder since he's been exiled back to second team—swipes it from him. And the next time we can't even inbound it cleanly.

It adds up to a lot of frustration. And a lot of extended time on D. I can check Rider, no problem, but the longer I'm in a defensive stance the more I feel that calf flare up. When Reynolds gets beat baseline for an easy deuce, I've had it. Bolden's already putting the whistle to his mouth to stop the drill, but I beat him to it. "Damnit, Reynolds!" I yell. "That's our second team beating you. Get your head out of your ass."

This is what leaders do—call teammates out when they're not giving their best. I guess nobody's explained that to Reynolds, because he gets his back up. "Why don't you just step the hell off," he says.

Pull 191

I roll my eyes. This team. Leading it is like trying to pull a broke-down car up a hill. No way one man can do it. Bolden doesn't offer any help on this one, instead going over to Fuller to instruct him on our press offense again. That's Bolden's way—unless guys are about to come to blows, he lets us settle our own static. Meanwhile Reynolds has sulked off the court to get a swig of water, turning his back on me as if he's too angry to even look. It reminds me of last year when his wiry ass quit on the first day of practice. And who was there to talk him back onto the team? *Me.* And now he's gonna act like this?

"Fine, Reynolds," I say. "I'll just let you get embarrassed against Cathedral."

Reynolds spins around and slams down his water bottle. The water sloshes onto the sideline and the bottle rolls toward the bleachers. From thirty feet away, Reynolds has all kinds of courage. "Someone really needs to knock you on your ass, Bowen," he shouts.

I take a couple steps toward Reynolds, hands out at my sides to say *You wanna go?*

"Easy, easy, easy." This is Murphy, all good cop again. He steps between us even though there's no real chance of us throwing down. Everyone in the gym knows Reynolds isn't going after a guy with twenty pounds on him. He's being a little punk, but he's not dumb.

With Murphy between us, Reynolds gets brave again. "You think you're better than the rest of us," he says. "Like we're just a bunch of scrubs who ought to ask you permission to put on a jersey." He takes a few more steps toward me, but gets stopped abruptly by Murphy's big paw square in his chest.

"That's *enough!*" This is Bolden, finally. The veins in his head pop like they're about to burst. "Grow up! Both of you." He spins to the rest of the players. "All of you, in fact! Grow the hell up." It's been a while since Coach has whipped himself into a top-notch frenzy, but now he lets it loose—stomping his feet, shaking his fists, throwing his head back as he screams. The works. "You show up to practice not ready to go! You loaf through drills! You forget basic sets! And now you start this! You know who does those things? Do you?!" He waits for an answer, but the gym is as silent as a graveyard. "Children do those things! And I am not about to spend my time babysitting a bunch of kids. Grow up or get the hell off my court!"

He storms toward the baseline then. His shoulders heave with his breaths. He veers left, then right, like he's so worked up he doesn't know what to do with himself. Then he finds his target—a stray ball by the baseline. Bolden takes two quick steps, plants his left foot, and boots that thing with a *thwunk*, rocketing it toward the concession area, where it ricochets around like a pinball. Frankly, it's an impressive show from an old man.

He pauses to catch his breath, then turns back to us. The fire's drained from his face and the veins have settled back in. He points to me and Reynolds. "Shake hands. Now. Then let's try to have a practice."

We do as we're told. Reynolds barely grips my hand—just a touch-and-go to satisfy coach. When I shuffle back to the court, I walk past Stanford. He's been silent through the whole ordeal. He's been through these things before. I glance up at him. Of all the guys in the gym, he's the one I can trust. We've seen some battlefields together. "You believe Reynolds talking that nonsense?" I say under my breath.

Stanford snorts. "I believe he might have a point, D," he mutters.

I stop short. We can't get into it now, not after the Bolden tornado that just passed through the gym, but I'm stunned. Stanford is for real taking Reynolds' side? I look around and none of my teammates will make eye contact with me. Meanwhile, Fuller and Rider are both over by Reynolds trying to talk him up a little. Ridiculous.

There's only one thing to do. Show out. Let them be jealous. Let them get their backs up. All they need is a reminder about what I can do. I figure I only need one—a highlight reel play, a monster finish at the rim—to show them what's up. Then I'll spend the rest of the practice just feeding other guys.

My chance comes right away. Since the second team just scored, it's our ball underneath against their full-court pressure. Stanford looks to throw in. I jab cut toward mid-court. I feel another tweak in my calf, but there's no time to worry over that. I sprint back to the baseline, hands extended. An easy pass for Stanford. On the catch, I turn and look. Rider's on me. I know his plan is to force me one side or the other into a trap. I start left, waiting for the D to jump. When the double comes, Fuller empties up the sideline and Reynolds fills middle—but forget that. No need to methodically work it up pass-by-pass. At the last moment, I split the double team.

I push it past mid-court and we've got numbers. Reynolds and Fuller flare to the wings. Stanford steps to the short corner. Jones holds his position low. Every one of them has hands ready and eyes wide, expecting a look. Not this time, boys. Fuller's man peels off and tries to stop my drive, but I leave him reaching with a spin dribble at the top of the key.

Just me and the big now. He's got to choose between stepping to me or checking Jones. He leaves early. Any other time that's an easy assist to Jones at the rim. But I *want* this one. I take another power dribble to get my shoulder past the defender. I take a jump-stop toward the rim, but as I do I feel one more tweak in that calf. At the last instant I think I'll back off, maybe go for the lay-up instead of the dunk. It throws off my rhythm. Instead of springing toward the rim, my weight comes down on my right leg—and so does that defender. He was still going full-tilt while I slowed down—disaster.

I feel the knee give with a series of pops. There's pain, but nothing searing. Not like the calf. In fact, when I crash down all the thump's on my head and elbows. So there's a flicker of hope that I'm okay. Just bruises. But in my heart I know better.

PART III

22.

The doctor was good. He'd seen his share of athletes, you could tell. He knew how to talk to me. I could walk on the leg—had no problem getting to the locker room and into my street clothes and out to the car—but it felt like I might topple on it unless I walked in a perfectly straight line.

"Don't think the worst," he said. "Let's just wait and see."

I stretched back on his table, felt that white paper crinkle up beneath me. My whole body shook, like I was some little kid trembling in the dark. The doctor stopped what he was doing. He put a hand gently on my chest. He took a deep breath. His face went still as I looked up at him, his mouth perfectly even. His face, a shade of honey, was gaunt, but he didn't look unhealthy. More like someone who ran religiously. There wasn't even a hint of a wrinkle, but that hairline— creeping back away from his forehead—showed he was older than his other features suggested. He drummed his slender fingers on my ribcage. "Hey now," he said. "Breathe in there."

While he worked, he kept a monologue going. He seemed to know that if the room went silent, my mind would race to ugly places. He said he knew who I was, that he was a huge hoops fan. He explained he'd gone to Indiana at the same time as Calbert Cheaney—their last real glory years under Bob Knight—and he'd been hooked ever since. As he explained all this, he worked on my leg. First, he pressed gently on the muscles above and below the knee. Then he placed one hand under my knee, the other just below it with his thumb pressed firmly on my shin. He interrupted his little chat to explain what he was doing. "This is the Lachman's test," he said. "Standard. Relax." Then, with more force than I was expecting, he pulled up on my knee while pressing down on my shin. Then again. And again. He let out a small grunt, but I tried not to read too much into it. Then he switched legs, testing my good one—well, good except for that nagging calf injury. Same thing. Same grunt.

Then he lifted my leg slightly, pinning my foot to his side. With his other hand, he grabbed my lower leg and pressed up and in toward my body. I tightened up in resistance, but he patted my kneecap. "Relax. I'm not going to do anything that hurts." So I let him finish the examination. Right leg, then left. A few more grunts along the way.

"Go ahead and sit up," he said.

He drew a rolling chair across the floor. With my legs dangling in front of him, he grabbed my right knee as if to secure it. Somehow it was comforting. He kept his grip up while he spoke. He looked me right in the eyes. "I think it's a torn ACL, Derrick. I know that's not what you want to hear, but—"

I sighed and flopped back again. I covered my eyes with my arm. The whole dream, gone just like that.

The doctor stood up. He didn't make me look at him. Maybe he thought underneath that arm, I was crying and he wanted to save me the embarrassment. Still, he talked me through it. "First of all, Derrick, this isn't a death sentence. There are players all over this city who've gone through this and they're good as new. It's not like it was in the 80s. Or even the 90s. Besides, I could be wrong. These tests have failed before. It could be a bad sprain and not a tear. That would still end your season, but it wouldn't mean surgery. The MRI will tell for certain."

So that brings me to now. Thursday morning. Typically, I'd feel like I was getting away with something, sprung loose in the city while everyone else sweats out tests in the stuffy classrooms of Marion East. But there are tests and there are *tests*. I'd trade place with any of them. Hell, I'd trade place with a guy working on a highway crew or digging ditches or scrubbing toilets.

Anywhere but here. Back in Methodist. The MRI machine in front of me. It's huge, a gigantic gray cylinder. The nurse clamps a little bracket over my knee and hands me some headphones to protect my ears. She talks me through the basics, but it's just sound to me. I'm too nervous. In a way, I wish the doctor wouldn't have held out hope for me. I mean, I know what the test's going to reveal. I've known at some level since the moment my knee gave. But that sliver of hope makes me more nervous somehow. Like if I could just give up hope completely, at least I'd be at ease about it.

Soon enough, I slide into the machine. It makes me think of a body being ushered into the flames at a crematorium. But I only go in to my shoulders, so at least I can stare into the dimly lit room while they run the machine. The nurse is gone. It's just me and the machine.

It starts clicking and clanging and chirping, still loud even through the headphones. It sounds alternately like a motor struggling to turn over, then heat pipes banging, then someone on a clarinet making all the wrong notes.

My knee's torn. My season's over. In spite of what the doctor said, my senior season is in doubt too. Can I be 100% by the time next November rolls around? Can I get my quicks back? Can I ever trust the knee again? Can I?

I stop. I have to. There's no answering those questions, not for a long time. If it's actually torn, there will be surgery. And then rehab. And then? Forget it. One step at a time.

I stare at the shadows on the wall and listen to that machine churn. The whole thing takes twenty minutes, they say, but it feels like a full day. While the machine scans my knee, I scan for something else to think about, something comforting.

Not my teammates.

Not Kid.

Not Jayson.

Certainly not Wes.

Jasmine? No, I tell myself, she's vanished. She's nothing but a text that shows up now and then. I'm supposed to be thinking about Lia. And for a few minutes, I do. She's the best thing I have going right now. But you can't really stop thoughts, can you? Slowly but surely, Lia's face fades and there's Jasmine. Always Jasmine.

Torn. ACL. The call comes from my doctor while I'm between classes. Around me, Marion East is buzzing like any other Friday

Pull

morning. There's a game tonight, so my teammates are rocking some swag—which really is just some cheap sweatshirts with Marion East Basketball printed across the chest. I'm wearing it too, but below that I've got a walking cast over my jeans.

"I'm sorry," the nurse says, but she's not that sorry. She does this every day. She doesn't even wait two seconds before she starts scheduling the surgery for me.

We set the date—three weeks from yesterday's MRI, meaning the last weekend of the regular season. I had an image in my mind for that weekend—the team humming, everything coming together while we ripped into Zionsville and Ben Davis in a tune-up for Sectionals. Now? It'll be me on crutches. Stuck at the end of the bench. Or maybe even behind the bench to shelter me from players diving after loose balls.

I shove the phone back in my pocket. Lockers slam shut. People laugh at jokes. Feet pound the floor on the way to the next class. Everyone else seems to know exactly where they're going. But here I am, lost.

The only thing I do know is that rehab starts now. In fact, it started as soon as that doctor told me what he thought after the physical tests. Coach Bolden has had guys tear ACLs before, so he knows the drill. The more I get my leg stabilized and strengthened before surgery, the better. So the last few nights while the other guys practiced, Coach Murphy monitored me doing light quad sets, put me gingerly through hamstring stretches. Then lots and lots of ice. Ice. God, I've had enough of it already. On my calf and now on my knee. I'm sick of the burning cold, tired already of the swings between numbness and pain.

"Derrick?" It's Lia. She's one of the tallest girls in the school, but right now—her books pinned to her chest, her chin tucked down a little—she seems impossibly small.

I don't even have to say anything. For the last three days, she's been the most positive one. I mean, yeah, my parents have been there every step, but Dad's still bristling about Kid. And Jayson's acted like I've got nothing more than a stubbed toe. Plus, for all the sympathy Bolden and Murphy give me, they've still got a team to coach. Not Lia. She's been there. In person. In encouraging texts each night. In a killer pic she sent me—nothing that would get us arrested, but she knows how to show herself off—the morning before my MRI with the caption *Be better*.

That's something we need catching up on. I mean, that's how bad things have gone—I haven't even had a chance to keep on hooking up with Lia. Even when her dad was gone for a whole day we didn't get together.

But now, as she looks at me, she knows the news. She just drops her book in a pile on the floor and covers the last few feet between us. She throws her arms around me. With only one strong leg to steady us, I sway with her force. "You're gonna be okay, D," she says in my ear.

I hug back, thankful for her. I feel terrible for having thought of Jasmine yesterday. Somehow it seems worse than cheating on Lia. Like I'm determined to torpedo the one good thing I've got left.

23.

The texts stream in again. Really, it started earlier in the week from recruiters who have been in constant contact with me, but now the news is out for real.

Hang in there, Derrick.

Keep your head up, big man. You'll be back.

Sorry to hear about your injury, Derrick. Hang tough.

It's another Who's Who of college hoops—Wisconsin, Louisville, Arizona. I scroll through again, keeping a mental list of who's wished me well. I don't know though. Something seems off. There's a change I can't pinpoint that makes these texts seem empty in a way they didn't after I'd hurt my calf.

In about an hour, we tip against Hamilton Academy. The last two years, this was *the* game. They were the best team in the state, anchored by Vasco Lorbner, who's putting together a killer freshman year for Michigan State these days. Deon Charles is gone too—but without Vasco in the post his flaws have been made evident, and he's seeing a lot of pine at Xavier. But still. For two years, they were the standard in

Indiana basketball. It wasn't that long ago they were recruiting me to transfer so I could keep the ball rolling after Vasco and Deon graduated. This one means something, even if they're just 10-6 coming in.

And here I am in street clothes again, watching the other guys get suited up.

At least now the static between me and my teammates isn't as thick. When they come up, one after another to tell me how sorry they are that I'm not playing, they mean it. Even Reynolds comes over. "You gonna be okay, D," he says. He stands beside me and rests a hand on my shoulder.

The truth is, I want to slap his hand away. I can't take being pitied. Part of me still wants someone to blame—like if Reynolds had just taken my criticism like a man none of this would have happened. Instead, I take a deep breath. He means well. No sense in making things worse. "Thanks, Reynolds," I say. "Just go whip Hamilton Academy, got it?"

"Oh, we about to get after it," he says. It's overly exuberant when just a second ago he was trying to be sympathetic, but this bothers me a lot less than that hand on my shoulder. He's a player. And players are game ready. No matter what.

Coach Murphy comes over. Now, Coach Bolden has been a help, but even with an injury he's all business. He's given me advice on rehab and a clear timeline of what to expect, but he refuses to let me wallow. Murphy, on the other hand, wants to be a pal. He's treated this like when my dad was in the hospital last year, like I need some big emotional outlet or counseling.

"You dealing, Derrick?" he asks. His voice is soft and concerned, like he's talking to a mourner at a funeral.

"I'll be fine, Coach," I say.

He looks up, reaching back for a memory of his playing days. "Man, consider yourself lucky. Used to be a torn ACL meant it was all she wrote. You'll have a chance to come back full strength. Maybe by the opener next year."

"Thanks," I say, but he can tell he's not helping. I mean, why bring up next year? I know exactly how long it takes to rehab an ACL. I know there's a chance it will be mid-season next year before I'm 100%. I don't need somebody else reminding me about it.

"Sorry," he says. Then he makes it worse, trying to joke. "At least the heat from some schools will decrease. Maybe some time away will help you get your head straight about colleges."

I nod, but I don't say anything. I'm tempted to tell him maybe he should have taken his friend up on that offer of ten grand when he had the chance. But I'm not ready to crack jokes yet.

"Murphy!" Bolden shouts. He's at the front of the locker room and he needs his assistant, right this second, to go over the night's game plan. Murphy gives me a weak thumbs up. Then he's off, as obedient as a dog on a short leash.

It's just me again. Everyone else is doing their thing. The closer it gets to tip, the more I'm irrelevant. They might as well cordon my locker off with tape, like a crime scene or a quarantined apartment. No going near the injured body when you've got to get your own ready for battle. And in that bubble of relative silence, it hits me—the thing that was bothering me about all those texts.

I scroll back through my phone to be sure. Back, back, back until I reach the texts that rolled in after my first injury. Sure enough, there's the evidence. Back then, almost everyone who'd made an offer prior to the calf injury made sure to remind me again. Over and over again, they said it: *Our offer still stands.* Or *Soon as you're up for it, let's get you here on an official visit.*

But now? Nothing. Most texts are just by-the-book get-well-soon wishes. Hell, Duke's text is word-for-word like the one they sent a month ago, only without the reminder of an offer. It's like they've got a computer program churning these out. And other schools—Syracuse and Auburn leap to mind—don't even bother this time around.

I suddenly understand that I'm damaged goods. Oh, if I come back next year and ball out, they'll fire up the recruiting machine again. They'll come see me. Send moneymen to buy me out. Send assistants to my house like they never had a doubt I'd return to form. All smiles and handshakes and promises. But if I don't come back like before? They won't think twice. Maybe a few years down the road, when I pop up in the NCAA tournament with a mid-major school, they'll think *Derrick Bowen. Now where I have I heard that name before?* I'll bang out 30 on them, send them home in the first round. Then maybe they'll remember how they backed off on me when I was down.

It's a revenge plan. But that's all down the road. First thing is to make my way across the locker room. Straight line, I'm fine, but I still take it easy. I limp, not trusting my right leg to hold my full weight, even though it probably could.

"Coach, can I borrow a pen and paper?"

Instinctively, Bolden frowns. It's like I'm in a class and didn't bring materials. But then he realizes I'm not doing anything wrong. He motions for me to follow. I walk through the back door of the locker room. This also serves as a side entry to his office, but I realize I've never come through this way. When you're called in to meet him, you always go through the door from the hallway. When you're in the locker room, only Murphy and Bolden can go through this one, like it's some password-encrypted door that keeps the nuclear codes safe. It's silly, I know, but this simple act—Bolden waving me through—makes me feel trusted somehow. It's almost how I felt last year when, at long last, I was given the starting point guard spot.

He reaches into his desk and pulls out a binder. He rips a page out, carefully removes the bits of paper hanging on past the perforation—always the perfectionist. He hands it to me, then plucks a pen from a coffee mug on his desk and gives it to me. "What do you need it for?" he asks. He's not grilling me. Just asking.

"I've got some thoughts on some schools all of a sudden."

Bolden almost smiles. "Good," he says. "Keep yourself looking ahead. That's good." He digs in his pocket and tosses me the keys. "Have some privacy," Bolden says. "Just lock up when you're done and be on the bench a couple minutes before tip."

He heads back into the locker room. I take a second to consider the moment—Coach handing me his keys. Rich kids wait for that day when their father hands over the key to the sports car at last. I'm lucky to get the use of a beater Nova. So for me, this is as big a rite of passage as I'll get.

Right away, I get cracking on what I meant to do. I scroll back through my texts and write down the name of every school that's texted me after my calf injury. I'll check these against the more recent flow of texts. Any school that doesn't send a message now with an assurance of their offer? Dead to me. But I'll keep this list in case I see them between the lines somewhere down the road.

It's clear early we've got a chance. Hamilton Academy hasn't been able to replace Lorbner and Charles—what high school team could?—but my boys have begun to get a feel for things. Rider's super cautious, but at least he's not doing dumb stuff anymore. And if he gets himself in trouble, Reynolds or Fuller sprint to the ball to bail him out. And Stanford? Man, the switch has flipped on for him. By the end of the third, he's got a double-double and when I glance down at the Hamilton Academy bench, their coaches are griping at each other about how to handle Stanford in the post. It's great to see, especially since their head coach, Henry Treat, always looks so smooth and polished.

Hamilton gets a deuce to end the third, cutting our lead to three. As the players come back to the bench, our crowd gives them a well-deserved roar. Sure, it's not for anything I've done, but it gets my blood pumping. The crowd on its feet and Hamilton Academy on the ropes? That's what I like in life.

I hobble onto the floor to bump fists with Reynolds and Fuller. Then I make eye contact with Stanford. "That's what I'm talking about out there," I holler. Gingerly, I hop in his direction and give him a chest bump. Stanford's eases back at the last second, knowing that I've got the bad leg.

"How about you keep it to talking then," Bolden shouts at me. "You want to tear your other ACL acting like an idiot?"

So much for being trusted by Bolden. His comment stings. It also kills the vibe on the bench. It figures Bolden would rip me even

Pull   209

when I'm trying to be a supportive teammate. Even he knows he went too far, because he steps to me and squeezes my shoulder. "I like the enthusiasm," he says, "but you need to use some common sense." That's as close as Bolden will ever get to an apology. I nod and try to laugh it off, but there's no reversing what happened. The guys slump back on the bench, looking exhausted—not from the physical effort, but by controversy surrounding me yet again. And that's the kicker. They blame me for this. I can feel it.

Murphy leaps into the huddle, all chatter and good will. "Come on now. Eight more minutes! We got these guys." Guys nod and clap their hands, but it's hollow. They might as well be saying *Nice try, Coach.*

Bolden crouches in front of the squad and runs them through what to expect in the fourth. When he sees that they've lost focus a little, he cracks his clipboard down on the hardwood. That snaps some chins up. For a second I think maybe he's got them back on track.

Before they break, Stanford gathers the guys around him for a pep talk. When Reynolds wanders off a couple steps, Stanford reaches out and yanks him back in by his jersey. "Get back in here!" he demands. Reynolds obeys, but I can't hear the rest of what Stanford says. When his impromptu huddle splits, the blush on Reynolds' face is evident.

"Crank it up now!" I shout from the bench. Nobody looks my way. So I single out Fuller. "You got this, Fuller," I shout. "Dig in for one more quarter." He nods, but it's like a kid hearing his mother tell him to clean the dishes for the four millionth time. Fuller would just as soon I shut up.

We get it first. Rider walks it into the frontcourt. He takes a deep breath and then starts to attack. He penetrates close to the foul line, but it's just to get the defense jumping. When they squeeze in on him, he kicks it to Fuller on the wing. He offers a shot fake, but his man doesn't bite, so Fuller looks to the post. Stanford's there, hand raised for the rock. "Ball!" he shouts, but Fuller just pump fakes. It's the right decision—Stanford was a good four feet off the block and a second defender was already hedging down. But Stanford's not having it. He pauses for a second before re-posting on the other side. He gives Fuller a long glare, like he's personally offended by not having got the orange.

Finally, Stanford cuts to the other side. Since he's late on the cut, his man beats him to the spot. That doesn't matter to Stanford. I can hear him call *Ball!* again even from the other side of the floor. Only this time Reynolds has the rock. He doesn't even look Stanford's way. Maybe it's a little payback for that show coming out of the break. Or maybe he actually thinks he's got a look. Either way, Reynolds puts it on the deck. Two dribbles right, then a snap-back move to free himself. It's a nice shake, but Reynolds doesn't really have that kind of shot in his repertoire—it's a deep fade-away and, predictably, it scrapes front iron. Frustrated, Stanford barrels through his man in pursuit of the rebound. It's an easy whistle. Foul on Stanford. Hamilton Academy ball.

At least they don't snipe at each other on the way back down. Fuller, Stanford, and Reynolds all just stare at the floor. But their body language—hands clenching, heads shaking—makes it evident they're all angry. Whether that's at me or Bolden or each other or themselves, it doesn't matter. The feel on that floor is not one that comes off a winning team. Rider and Jones clap their hands, try to rally guys for a

Pull 211

defensive stand, but nobody's taking orders from them. You'd think we were down a dozen.

It's all the life Hamilton Academy needs. They come down, click out a few reversals, get Reynolds hung up on a cross-screen and locate their best shooter for a golden look from deep. Even before he releases, you can hear our crowd groan. And he delivers, of course. Tie game.

This time Fuller and Reynolds get into it. As they come into the frontcourt, I hear Reynolds shouting "Switch that!" at Fuller, who swats his hand at Reynolds like he's batting away a gnat. Behind them, Rider looks nervous. He's kept his cool most of the game, but now that the other guys are starting to wilt, he comes unwound. Hamilton Academy pressures him. Rather than making the easy pass, he just bolts. Buries his head and goes screaming toward the lane. A defender slides over, flicks the ball away, and it's a run-out.

They finish with an uncontested jam on the other end, putting them up two.

Time out.

It's clear what's happening. Sure, they all resented my status—and maybe I could have done a better job as a leader. But now that I'm out, they're all fighting to be the man in charge. It's like one of those mob movies when the boss goes down and the rest of the family starts offing each other.

When guys come back to the huddle, Bolden gives them his best evil staredown. Once everyone's seated, he leans in, thudding his heel on the court with every word. "What. The. Holy. Hell?!" That gets their attention and he crouches down. "What's going on out there?"

Another mistake by Bolden—he actually asked it as if he were expecting an answer. And he gets five at once. All the starters start shouting. They point at each other in blame. They act insulted when someone else calls them out.

It takes some screaming, but Bolden gets them settled back down. He explains, very methodically, that we are still right in the game with Hamilton Academy, and if we would have the sense to pull our heads out of our rear ends, then we could pick up a nice win. The guys nod, but the shout of *Team!* when they exit the huddle is so lacking in enthusiasm you'd think they were heading into a math quiz instead of a basketball game.

And that's how it goes. The bickering is done. But whatever zip they played with earlier is gone, and Hamilton Academy slowly pulls away, cruising to a nine-point victory.

Afterward, the locker room is silent. Like a funeral. And it's our season that's getting buried.

I'm first one out, since I don't have to shower off. Before I can make it five steps, there's Whitfield, his phone already out.

"Derrick, a comment on tonight's game?"

Frankly, I'm surprised to see him here. It's not like our showdown with Hamilton Academy has the same allure as last year. Maybe he just wants to irritate. Regardless, I try not to act shocked. I shrug. "It was a tough one," I say. "We were right there, but it just kind of got away from us." It's a lame answer, all sports cliché, but I figure that's best at this point.

"About that," he says. He leans in and lowers his voice, like maybe he can trick me into thinking that this is all just between us,

Pull

secrets between good friends. "Does this team miss your leadership more, or is it just a question of talent?"

"I don't know about that," I say. "It's not that simple."

I take a few steps down the hallway, an obvious hint that I don't want to answer any more questions. Standing at the edge of the court is Kid, waiting on me—and there's a whole lot of mess there too. It's the first I've seen him since all the news crashed down. I'm not sure I'm quite ready for him. So I pause and let Whitfield do his thing. "What's it like for you having to watch, knowing you can't help your team?"

I sigh. Nothing to do but answer truthfully. "It's hard. Not being able to get out there is hard. And having to think about next year even though it's just February is hard." Then I remember how I've screwed things up in past interviews. Maybe it's time to say the right thing. "But there are more ways to help the team. I need to be another set of eyes for the coaches. I need to help some of the younger players get up to speed."

Whitfield nods. He liked that, so maybe it'll make the paper—or at least his blog. He stays after me though. "But that's not the same as scoring 20 a game is it? At the end of the day, isn't there too big a drop-off in talent for this team to have real success?"

"I don't think so," I say. I mean, he's right. Any fool can see that. But it's one thing for me to think that. Teams are family. Whitfield? He's got family somewhere, but it's not in our locker room.

He laughs a little, thinking I'm just feeding him a line. "Wasn't it evident tonight?" he asks. "Where does this team go now when they need a big bucket?"

I take a deep breath. Nothing good ever came from losing your

Kevin Waltman

temper with the media, even if it's just someone like Whitfield—a far cry from someone reporting for *Outside the Lines*. I look down the hall, see Kid still waiting. He's got his arms hugged to his chest and he can't stand still.

"Man, you don't know," I say. I point to the locker room. "There's talent in there. There's size. There's skill. There's shooters. But most of all there's a will to win." As I speak my voice keeps getting louder, but I don't care. I've just had enough—of everything. "The guys in there bust their tails, and they're not about to just let all that work be for nothing. Not because they lost to Hamilton tonight. Not because I'm hurt. And not because people from outside the locker room think they're finished. They'll pull together. You watch." Then I'm done. I just turn my back on Whitfield and head toward Kid.

"Any decisions on schools?" he calls after me.

I whip my head around. "No!" I shout. And then I act like there's not a thing in the world behind me. Just Kid out in front. I take the last few strides to him. He's turned away now, lost in nervous thought. When I grab him by the elbow, he practically leaps out of his shoes. "Just me, Kid," I say.

He gathers himself, gives a half-laugh at his own jumpiness. "Your family already went home," he says.

"You're here," I say. "What's up?"

He looks away. He's so tense it's like there's an electric current running through him. I feel like every time he gazes out at this gym he's really searching for some alternate version of his past. One where he stayed out of trouble. Stayed in the game. "Aw, Derrick," he says. "I screwed up again."

"I heard," I say. It sounds harsh, way more than I intended. "Want to hash it out?" I ask.

He looks down at the hardwood. He's got old shoes on, their different shades faded to a blur of brown. "Not really," he says. "But I owe you. Let's take a ride."

Then we walk in silence toward his car. Around us, we see Hamilton Academy families waiting on their players. They're chirping with excitement over the win. I hate it, the way these bright and shiny families from Hamilton County seem to have taken over our gym. But what's really bugging me as Kid and I trudge along is how he said he owes me. I know what he means, I think. He's the adult, and I'm still the kid. So it shouldn't be me worrying over him. Kid shouldn't feel that way. He's been there for me. Every step of the way. My freshman season when Hamilton Academy cranked up the pressure on me, he was on my side in the end. Last season when Dad was laid up, Kid stepped in and kept our family together. And every time—from when I was a runt up to right now—that things have gone wrong on the court, Kid's been there. I know I should be telling him this, but I also know that it would just embarrass him—that somehow telling him all the good things he's done would just make him feel worse tonight.

We exit those Marion East doors and get hit by a burst of wind. Normally, I'd bound down the steps to get to the car, but these days I've got to take them one at a time with a hand on the railing. Kid, not held back by anything, hustles out ahead of me until he remembers. Then he turns, comes back, and offers a hand to help me down the steps.

"I got it," I say.

"Just go easy," Kid says. Pretty interesting advice coming from him.

Maybe it's just knowing what I know about Kid, but his Chrysler 300 already looks beat up. Mud and slush are splattered across the body. The tires look a little flat. There's a tiny chip in the windshield on the passenger side.

Kid unlocks it, and we climb in. That new car smell is long gone, replaced by something foul—that old cologne and fast food combination that his Nova had when he handed it down to me. There are boxes stacked in the back seat, and Kid notices me looking.

"Packing up," he says as he starts the car.

"Where you going?"

He whips out into traffic and heads south. "I don't know," he admits. "But I'm getting booted from my place. Can't make the rent."

Kid's place was never nice. It was one of those old, generic apartments that had promise once upon a time. But now the carpet's stained in a million spots. The paint has gone from a bright cream to a depressing beige. There were always Coke cans and beer bottles thrown on the floor. Old pizza boxes out on the counter. Usually some piece of electronic equipment he'd opened up to fix, only to quit halfway through. And his walls were bare except for frayed posters of old school rappers—N.W.A., Boogie Down Productions, Eric B. and Rakim—guys I would never have heard if it weren't for Kid shoving them down my throat. I bet he got it tightened up over the last few months, for when April came over. But to think that he's getting kicked out of that just makes me sad.

We get hung up at a light on Central. There's still some chill hanging on us, so Kid cranks up the heater. It rattles a little with the effort. He pats the dashboard like he's comforting an old dog. "This baby's probably next," he says.

Pull   217

"What?"

"Next to go." He sighs. "I can make the payment this month, but I'm looking at what I have to pay back, and—"

He trails off. The light turns green. We ride again in silence. Kid turns off Central, only to head south again after a couple blocks. We're just meandering. As we approach downtown in our roundabout way, I want to ask questions. How much does he have to pay back? How did he get caught? And, damn, what was he thinking? But each time those things form in my head I hear my mom's voice, the way she sounded when I got picked up at the end of the summer. I don't want to do that to Kid.

Finally, Kid pulls over. He's in front of a diner I've never even noticed before. The rest of the block is dark. Through the diner's window you can see a few men—all sitting alone, all looking as brokedown as Kid—slowly crushing burgers and fries. Kid kills the engine and puts his hand on the door. I figure this is my signal to get out too, but at the last minute Kid just flops back in his seat. "I knew I'd get caught," he says. He can't look at me while he explains, staring instead at a spot on the ceiling of the car. "I mean, if I kept doing it. Early on, I thought I'd just take a freebie, then get out before it got too big and people noticed. So the plan was just get a few extra unemployment checks while I started that new job. And, D, it's not like those checks were breaking someone's budget. But for me? That little extra bump? For once—just once in my life—I got to live a little fat. It's not like I was flying first-class to Rio or living in some mansion in Meridian Hills. I just got to enjoy myself the way a man my age—" He breaks off his train of thought again. Maybe he realized he was making excuses, listing out all those rationalizations that he must have been telling himself for a year. He lowers his head and stares down at his hands in his lap. He speaks softly now. "Listen, D. I knew it was wrong. I'm not stupid. But I did it anyway. And I kept doing it. And I swaggered all around with my chest out while inside I was churning, just waiting for the hammer to come down. Story of my life. I just can't stop myself sometimes." Then he looks up at me. His eyes are on the verge of tears. I fight the impulse to look away. "I just wanted to explain that to you. And to tell you that things aren't gonna be that way for you. D, you're a different breed. You got all the fire I had, but you know how to keep yourself in check."

I don't know if he's right about that last part. Either way, there's no chance to get into it more. He just says *Awwwww* to shake it all off and then yanks his door open. I climb out and we head toward the diner.

"Figure you can still throw down some post-game grub even if you didn't suit up," Kid says.

Then I realize something. "Hey, I've only got a few bucks, Kid," I say.

He smiles. He points to the diner. "Derrick, take a look. This ain't St. Elmo's. Even your broke-ass uncle can spot you here."

We both laugh a little, but it's tinged with something. Regret? Sadness? I don't know. But as Kid places his hand on the diner door, I have to ask just one question. "Kid," I say, "what about April? How's she handling this?"

Kid's back stiffens and he looks away. Then he swivels his head back my way and cocks it, a smirk on his face. "For real, D?" he says. "You need that answered?"

I shake my head no and we go on in. My man Kid. Busted.

Evicted. Dropped by his girl. You get off the straight and narrow and it never stops being a hard road.

"It's not going to hurt your leg, is it?" Lia asks.

She's serious, but so am I when I say, "Right now I don't care if they have to amputate."

We're getting to be pretty regular at this. It's like the moment her Dad steps out the door, she's mashing out a text to me. And I don't waste time getting here. The only thought that runs through my head— other than getting the condom out of its wrapper—is that I better get my knee better soon, because if Kid needs his old Nova back I'll have to be sprinting the two miles to her apartment. Then again, torn ACL or not, I get that message from her and I could probably cover those miles faster than I can cover the court on a run-out.

"I don't want to hurt you," she says, but now she's just teasing. She says it like a challenge. Like I'm not man enough.

Then we're going. And it's all I can do to clear my head enough to say, "Nothing hurts now." Everything else in the world fades into namelessness. It's just us. Just this.

After a while she takes control. Suddenly not caring about my knee, she pushes me off and slings me down so she can get on top. After that, it's not long. She just eases her body down on mine, and her head nestles onto my shoulder. I feel her hot breaths—still coming fast—on my neck.

Even without checking I know I'm bumping up against curfew. It's been a long night. This has been the best part, by far, but if I'm late getting home all that other noise will seem like play compared to what my mom does to me. Lia must sense it too, because she nestles close to my ear and says, "It's okay. I know you've got to get home."

"I'm sorry," I say. But even as that's out of my mouth I start reaching for my clothes.

"Just hit it and quit it, I guess," she says. She's teasing, I know, but it stops me. I turn to look at her, see her eyes playful in the dark of her room. I can't help it—I dive in for one more long kiss. And then it's all I can do to stop. She has to put her hand on my chest. "You know I'm just playing," she says. "And you know you better be gone before my dad gets back. His card game won't last forever."

I stand then, gingerly hitch my pants up. Now that the process of leaving has started, I hurry. I throw on my sweater and snatch up my keys. There's probably still some time before her dad gets home, but I don't want to risk it. It's not like the guy trusts me that much to begin with. But before I hit the road I turn to her one last time. "Lia, I'd stay all night if I could," I say. And to my own surprise, I realize I truly mean it.

24.

Saturday's a new day. I wake up early. The first thing on my mind is Lia.
All those images from last night rushing back. I pound out a quick text,
but then delete it. She's into me, but any girl gets a 7:00 a.m. text from a
guy and they'll think he's creeping pretty hard.

I slip on an old hand-me-down sweatshirt from Uncle Kid,
some vintage Pacers gear from those Reggie Miller teams in the 90s.
It's frayed at the wrists and has a hole in the belly—it's about the most
comfortable Saturday morning gear that's ever existed.

Dad's already up. As soon as he sees me, he offers to sling
together some breakfast. I tell him I got it and fix myself some cereal
and toast. We talk softly to each other—Jayson and Mom are still
asleep. It's nothing—the team, the weather, school. I don't dare bring
up Uncle Kid.

Then there's shouting from the street. I can't make out the exact
words, but it pierces the Saturday morning calm. If it was a weekend

night, maybe shouting would be expected. But this time of day? Dad and I are drawn to the window.

Standing next to an idling SUV, their breath making puffs in the air as they shout, stand JaQuentin Peggs and his tatted up partner. Despite the cold, they're only in sweatshirts and jeans.

Now that I'm next to the window, I can make out they're yelling.

"I know you can hear me, you little bitch!" JaQuentin shouts. "You best come out here and face me like a man!"

Then it's his boy shouting. "You gonna get fucked up either way. Might as well deal with it."

I turn my head just a sliver toward Dad. His eyebrows are pinched down in concern. Like I said, noise like this isn't news, but if it's happening this early in the morning then they must be seriously worked up. When I look again though, I see JaQuentin stagger as he hollers, like the very force of his anger has him off balance. Then his boy whispers something to him and they both nearly double over laughing. They're lit up. And it's clear now that they're not up early—they're still out from last night.

Now it's Dad who turns to me. "They're shouting at Wes' house, aren't they?" he asks.

I just nod.

"Don't take this the wrong way, Derrick, but that"—he jabs his index finger at the window pane—"is precisely why we stopped you from hanging with Wes."

"I understand," I say. That scene out the window isn't exactly encouraging. Then again, maybe it means Wes needs someone in his corner more than ever. Maybe JaQuentin is just messing around, or maybe he's so wasted he thinks he's somewhere else. But I doubt it. And the truth is I doubt I could do much to help Wes if it came to it. My bare hands against what Peggs and his boy are probably packing in his ride? That's not exactly a fair fight.

A police car rolls up to the corner, and that's that. The officer isn't going to make a thing about it, but he pauses at the intersection just to let JaQuentin and his friend know they have eyes on them. JaQuentin whistles and then shouts one last unintelligible thing, and the two retreat to the S.U.V. The officer idles until they pull out all nice and easy.

Before I even ask, Dad answers. "You can go check on him if you want," he says. "But that's it. Don't get involved in that mess."

I sling on my puffy coat and head down the street. Maybe it's that ache in my leg and the way it seems to just be hanging there from the knee down, but the whole street seems charged with danger. It's not even half a block to Wes' house, but I keep checking over my shoulder like maybe Peggs will come screeching back, all business. When I finally knock on Wes' door, the sound seems to echo like a gunshot.

There's motion behind the door, but it doesn't open. "Wes, it's me!" I shout. "Open up!"

The front curtain moves. I see Wes peeking out. Then the bolt flips and he opens the door. He waves me in like I should hurry, then slams the door behind me and turns the bolt again.

As soon as my eyes adjust to the darkness inside, I realize things have gone all kinds of haywire. There's no sign of his mom, though the door to her room is closed. It looks like Wes has been fending for himself for a while. The living room is all fast food wrappers and pizza boxes, the mess knee deep in some spots. The television is busted, a crack jagging like a lightning bolt down the screen. The kitchen table has become a depository for dirty laundry. That's a real bad sign for someone like Wes, who—no matter what else is going down—has always taken pride in looking fresh. The air's thick with the stink of alcohol. When I take a few steps toward the kitchen, I can see why. The counters are lined with brown bottles, with more piled in the sink.

I hang my head. It's been clear since we were little that Wes' mom was just hanging on, especially after his dad split. And now, obviously, she's let go. No way Wes drained those bottles on his own. Even for a grown woman, it's evidence of a months-long binge.

It settles on me like all that winter snow gathering on the branches of a tree. I clear a spot between pizza boxes on the couch and sit. All this time, Wes needed me.

"'Sup, D?" Wes asks. Now that we're safely inside he's resumed his tough posturing. He stands while I sit, hands on his hips like he's impatient to be getting somewhere.

"Wes," I say, but then just trail off. I gesture toward the chaos around us.

"What?" he says. Then he laughs. "Yeah, I should clean a little. But what's got you knocking on a brother's door so early?"

I push myself from the couch and stand. Even that makes him take a step back. For all his bad-ass act, any sudden move throws him. But I'm not trying to intimidate him. I just want him to know it's time to stop fooling. "Come on, Wes. Don't act like that. You don't think I could hear JaQuentin and what's-his-name from all the way down the street?"

Wes shrugs it off. "Q and Flake? They just messin'."

Q and Flake? He talks about them like they're just any old guys from Marion East. And *Flake?* I know a crew name when I hear one.

"Don't," I say. "Just don't. If they're just fooling around, then how come you're hiding in here like there's a S.W.A.T. team outside?"

"Who's hiding?" Wes says, his voice rising. "It's early and I didn't want to get up. It's not like it's any of your business anyway."

"Wes, you need some help, man."

"Oh, and you're here to save me?" he snaps. "You gonna play hero? Shit. You don't know what you're talking about." He almost shouts this, but he's looking away now.

"Where's your mom?" I ask. It's a cruel shot, but I've got to push the issue.

"Sleeping." He speaks in a raspy whisper now instead of a shout.

"Things aren't right, Wes."

"It's no big thing," he says. He tries to laugh it off again. "At least I don't have her all up in my business like your folks are with you. Being able to do what you want isn't so bad, y'know?"

"Wes," I say, "it's okay to tell me what's going on."

I try to keep my voice as even as possible. I want to push, but I don't want to set him off. He stares at his living room, toward that mountain of laundry on the table, then at all those bottles. *Come on, Wes*, I think, trying to will him to bend, *just admit you need some help.*

But it's no good. He wrinkles up his face like he smells something bad. His eyes are wild with anger and fear. Then he points to the door. "Get the fuck out, D," he says.

"Wes, man—"

"Get out!" he screams. "Get the fuck back to your house. You think you're so much better than me. You and your parents always got your noses in the air. Nobody needs your help, D."

His fists are clenched like he might punch me. But behind that menacing expression all I see is fear. And sadness. And those quivering eyes he had when we were ten, and he was worried we'd get caught rifling through an abandoned apartment.

So I just limp on home. You can't go back to how things were. You have to move forward.

It's like that tension in Wes' house is a virus, and I've carried it with me down the street. As soon as I walk in the door, I hear it—Dad and Jayson going full tilt.

"You do not take that tone with me or your mother," Dad shouts.

"What?! It's just okay for you to yell, but not me?"

Rage fills Dad's face. I don't know what set this off. But when I look at Jayson, it's clear he's in no mood to back down. His face is flushed from screaming. Mom is standing behind them. She's not usually one to stand on the sidelines in a dispute, but she looks more worried than angry.

Dad takes a deep breath and tries to calm things. "Jayson, I understand why you feel that way, but that's no excuse. We've been walking on egg-shells around you for months now, but this I-don't-care attitude has got to go."

Jayson huffs. "It's not an attitude," he spits. "I really don't care what you two think about me."

For the first time ever, Dad rears back his hand. He doesn't do it—he doesn't even come close to following through. But it's still

Pull 227

enough. Mom shouts, "Thomas, no!" And Jayson spins and huffs to his room, as indignant as if he actually got a smack—which, to be honest, he would have deserved.

Once Jayson storms past, their eyes settle on me. Both Mom and Dad look suddenly ashamed to have had me see this display. They start to mutter out apologies, but I shrug it off. I tell them I've got a lot more to worry about than this latest drama with Jayson. Which is true. Then again, as I head back to my room I remember how the noise with Wes began when he started to sneer at the world the way Jayson does these days. I take a long look at a stack of homework I should tackle before tonight's game. But I know what's more important. I walk gingerly to Jayson's door and knock.

No answer. I knock again.

"Go. A. Way."

I test the handle. Unlocked. I'm not going to just barge in and be disrespectful, but I crack the door enough to whisper into his room. "Just me, Jayson."

He grunts. But he doesn't tell me to back off. Finally, I hear him sigh and he says, "Come on, then."

He's lying on his bed, turned to face the wall. It's the pose of someone who's been crying over a fresh heartbreak, but that's not Jayson's style. He's just trying to be difficult. I close the door behind me and stand in the middle of his room. It hasn't been cleaned in forever. It's like a miniature version of Wes' place, minus the empty bottles.

"What's up?" I ask, trying to be casual.

Jayson rolls over, stares at me, then shakes his head in disbelief that I asked that question. "Forget it," he says.

Fine. I'm sick of trying to help people that don't want help. So I change the subject. I gesture toward his X-Box. "Want to hit up the sticks?"

He sneers and rolls his eyes. "No offense, but it's not really fun playing with someone who can't hang."

It's another snide answer, but I let it go. After all, it's true—I'm about as close to Jayson's talent level on the Box as he is to mine on the deck. It's pretty clear Jayson's not going to let me break through this wall, so I turn to go. I knock a Coke can out of my way and head for the door.

"Don't be knocking stuff around in my room," Jayson snaps.

I turn back around. Truth is, I know right where my dad was coming from when he raised his hand a few minutes ago. I don't do it though. Jayson might not want to talk, but he needs it. So I calm myself down. Take a deep breath. Tell myself that no matter what Jayson says, I'm going to meet this one head on without flinching. "Jayson," I say, "you gotta talk to me, man."

"I don't gotta do a damn thing," he says.

"It's me," I say. I spread my arms out like someone about to get a pat-down. He huffs and looks away. He mutters something under his breath, but I can't make it out. "I know Mom and Dad can get uptight," I say. "I mean, I *know* it. So I feel what's going on with you. But, man, you've got to admit that you've been going at them pretty good for a while."

"Yeah," he admits. He still won't look at me.

"So?"

"So, I'm just—" He stops himself. He picks at a thread on his blanket for a second. Then he looks at me at last. "Why you even care, D? Don't you have bigger things to worry about?"

That's not cool, but I don't let it show. "Jayson, there's no bigger thing than this."

"Coulda fooled me," he says. Then, maybe knowing he's laying it on too thick, he looks down again. He swings his feet out from his bed and then leaps off. He picks a few sweatshirts off the floor and wads them together. He carries them to his closet and dumps them in his hamper. Then he starts picking up more off the floor, stacking the trash in the can and piling books and magazines on his already cluttered dresser. This goes on for a full minute before he looks at me again. "You still here? Can't you see I'm busy?"

"I'm not going anywhere," I say.

He throws a pair of jeans right back on the floor. They land with a thump, like maybe his phone was in there. He shakes his head and looks at the ceiling, like a man who just can't believe his luck. "Fine," he says. "You really want to know?"

"Damn straight," I say.

Jayson clears some school papers off an old beanbag that's held together with masking tape, then he flops down on it. I clear some floor space and sit, my bad leg stretched out in front of me. He looks me square in the eye and starts. "You know how hard it is to get the time of day when your older brother's an all-state baller?" It's not a question he wants me to answer, so he just plunges ahead. "I mean, it was cool for a while. Still is, I guess. Like, there's times I still get into it. The games. The hype. And, D, don't get me wrong. I want to see it happen for you. But, man, sometimes I just want it to be about me, you know? Just once."

I start to stammer out an apology. It's a hard thing to hear. Because this isn't just a teammate who's sour because he's not getting enough touches. This is my brother. And he's got a legit gripe. I want to protest, but deep down I know we've all ignored him. As soon as I start to speak, he shakes his head. He doesn't want to hear it. He's not rude about it, but it's pretty clear that this is his time to talk—he's been walking around with all this bottled up, so it's best not to try and slow him down now.

He lets it all out. He explains to me that it was bad enough when it was all about hoops, but when I started having problems—my trouble at the end of the summer, my injuries—and I was still the center of everything, it just hit him wrong. "Even when you're bad news, you're the only news there is," he says. "Besides Kid," he adds, then offers a disgusted little laugh. "I'm sorry I feel that way, D. I know I'm not supposed to."

Now I realize it's my turn to talk. I reach out to him—we're across the room from each other, so it's not to touch him, but I open my palm like I'm offering him a hand up. "Jayson, you can feel any way you want to. For real. You got every right. And I'm sorry, man."

"You don't have to apologize," he says. "That's not what I'm asking for."

"I think I do have to," I say. "But okay. Tell me what you do want." He looks away again. Somehow, I've hit a nerve again. "Just say it, Jayson."

He offers a half-smile. He kicks at an old t-shirt on the floor. "I've been doing this thing," he says. "I haven't told anybody." He looks mortified to say it. That scares me.

"What?" I ask. My throat is dry with anxiety. I can't take one more person in real trouble. Most of all, not Jayson.

He mutters the answer, speaking down to his lap. I have to ask him to repeat it. He doesn't really want to, but he knows I'm not going anywhere. And deep down he wants to talk. Otherwise, he wouldn't have said everything that's already come out. "I'm in the school play," he says. He sounds ashamed.

"That's cool," I say. Then, with more enthusiasm, I add, "You ought to be proud of that, Jayson."

"Proud?" he says. "I mean, being in a play? It's not, like, manly, is it? It's not like balling out on the hardwood." He looks dejected and shrugs again. "Anyway, I'm only doing it because the drama teacher says I've got talent."

Jayson talented at drama? Man, how could we have not seen this coming? I stifle a laugh, because the truth is Jayson's clearly conflicted on this. "I don't know what to tell you about what makes you a man. I mean, I can roll up a triple-double when I'm healthy. And last night I hooked up with the most bangin' girl in the history of Marion East. But I don't think that stuff makes me a man." I think about my failures with Wes, about how for all my eye-popping stats, I never really led the team like I should have this year. "I kind of think I've got a long way to go for that."

"Yeah, but plays?" Jayson whines. "It's not how I want to see myself."

I nod, because I get it. It's hard to prove you're a man. If a guy's not a star athlete, then where does he go? It's not cool to be good at math, at music, at history. So guys have to act tough. For someone like

Wes, that's a dead end. In some ways, that happened to me last year. I got my head all mixed up with Daniella—and I did her wrong—mostly because I wanted to see myself as some player. "But you're good at it?" I ask Jayson.

"That's what the teacher says."

"Then do it, man."

"I guess," Jayson says. He squints and looks away, but he doesn't reject the advice outright. In fact, after a second he tilts his head and purses his lips in consideration. "Thanks, D," he says. It's sincere, almost happy, but he also stands as he says it. That's a signal that this conversation has gone as far as he'll let it. Cool with me. It was progress. Better than I got with Wes.

I stand too, wobbling for a second on my bad leg. "Hey, what set you and Dad off anyway?" I ask.

Jayson stops cold, like he'd forgotten all about it. Then he smiles sheepishly. "Aw, he just told me not to check my phone at the breakfast table, and we kind of went crazy from there."

I know there's more to it than that. "Come on, man. You said something, didn't you?"

He hangs his head. "I said Dad was being stupid."

"Oh, Jayson!" I say. We both know that word—*stupid*—is straight-up off-limits to say about someone in this house. Especially for Dad. "For someone who's worried about being a man, you sure got a pair."

That cracks him up. For the first time in too long, he's like the old Jayson. When he's done laughing, he points to his X-Box. "Come on, D," he says. "If you really want a whippin' on there, I'll give you one."

To try making it fair, Jayson takes the Sixers and gives me LeBron and the Cavs. But he's right. On here, I'm no match. He's up double-digits almost immediately. He's mastered the game so much that he turns and looks straight at me sometimes. "Three from the corner," he says, then—for emphasis—raises his right hand like he's actually the one shooting. And, of course, he's right. Then he eases back on me, letting me keep it close for a while. But it's quickly clear what he really wants out of this trip on the sticks. "So," he says, "Lia?"

"Yeah. What about it?"

He sets his controller down and crosses his arms. "D, you gotta spill."

I take the opportunity to get an easy jam with King James. "I don't gotta do a thing."

He hits pause. "Uh uh," he says. He points back to his bean bag. "I sat there and answered everything you wanted. And, man, I'm your little brother. You owe it to me to give the deets."

"No details to tell," I lie, but he sees the smirk on my face.

"For starters," he says, "let's get real clear about what hook up means. You—"

"Don't get crude, man," I say, cutting him off before he can finish his sentence. "Don't talk about Lia like that."

"I get it," Jayson says. "You two got it going on. You wouldn't get your back up if you weren't."

"Shut up," I say. I reach over to his controller to un-pause the game. "You don't know."

"Oh, I know."

"No, you don't."

"D, I know," he says, starting to laugh. "I know it sure as I know I'm about to drop another three on you here."

He's right, of course. On all counts.

25.

If we struggled with Hamilton Academy, then a trip to Pike might just turn into a beatdown.

Still, even on the bus ride the team's energy has changed. It's like a deep freeze broke. I hit my standard spot—the seat behind Coach Bolden, across from Coach Murphy—but as players file on, almost every one of them stops for a second. Jones gives a fist bump. Fuller gives me a *Whatup* and asks how my knee's feeling. Even Reynolds and Stanford—who at points have been about as likely to shoot me as talk to me—at least say *Hey, D* as they pass by. And then there's Rider. He slides right into the seat behind me and leans over so his elbows rest on my seatback. The pose makes him look like some fourth-grader who's all excited about a field trip. He just looks at me.

"What?" I ask, a little puzzled. He hesitates—it's like we're riding back from a bad loss and he doesn't want to be the one to break Bolden's command for silence. I relax my pose. "Just talk, Rider. It's all good."

"I was thinking," he starts. Then he looks across at Murphy, who's eyeing him. "Well, okay, Coach Murphy told me. He said I'd do a lot better to spend the ride to Pike picking your brain instead of buried in my headphones."

I can feel Murphy watching me now. But after wrestling things out with Jayson and Wes, handling Rider's request is easy. I straighten up and turn so my back's against the side of the bus. That way I can make better eye contact with Rider.

"Here's the deal on Pike," I say. And I just start unloading the scouting report on him. First, he needs to know the history. We swept them last year, including a killer in the Sectional Championship. Plus, they lost their best player, Major Newsome, who's dropping about a dozen a game for Dayton this year. So you'd think it would be a down year for them. But they've stepped up—nobody more than Devin Drew, the point guard Rider will need to check. With Newsome gone, he's flourished. Their bigs have gotten more involved too. And that's why they're sitting at 17-3, ranked #10 in the state. And we're in their gym to boot.

I lay it on pretty thick. By the time I'm done, Rider looks intimidated. So I backhand him on his elbow. "Now here's the good news," I say. "Drew's no better than you've seen before. He can bury a spot-up and he's a demon on the drive, but if you make him settle for pull-ups, he's uncomfortable. So here's what you do." I explain false pressure to Rider. Granted, Bolden's explained the concept only about five hundred times, but sometimes players only listen to other players. So I walk him through it—every time Drew catches, Rider needs to come at him hard, hands out, like he wants to pressure him. "Then right when you arrive, you want to jump back and give yourself some space." I hop in my seat as demonstration. "He'll see you running at him and pass on the J, because he's dying for a reason to put it on the deck. But if you time it right, he won't be able to blow by. He'll only have that pull-up he hates."

Rider nods, soaking it in. I walk him through a few more things—where our advantages are on the other end, mainly. But before he goes, I remind him about how to play Drew. That's the key thing, so he gets that first and last.

Then he thanks me and heads toward the back of the bus. We careen into a turn and Rider about tumbles into Stanford's lap, but they both laugh it off. If someone didn't know any better, you'd think this team was riding a ten-game winning streak.

Pike gives us a wake-up call pretty quick. Drew flat turns Rider inside-out. First time down Rider—forgetting everything I told him—comes at him too hot, and Drew blows past for a quick deuce. The next time Rider gets pinned on a screen and Drew drops a trey. And then it just gets worse. Rider remembers my false pressure lesson, but Drew freezes him with a head fake and rips past for a drive-and-dish. To top it off, Rider finally plays it right and gets Drew to settle for a tough pull-up—and of course it banks home.

On that last one, Rider finally turns toward our bench, a pleading look on his face. "That's okay," I shout. "We can live with him taking that—he can't keep knocking it down."

Rider nods. From the other end of the court, I hear Drew shout in my direction. I can't make it out, but I know the basic message—he's gently informing me that he very much can drop that pull-up all night, and that I best mind my own business. The ref gives him a stern look, like one more word will earn a T. But all that matters is that as Rider brings the ball up, he takes a deep breath and nods a couple times—just trying to get his head straight. The kid's going to be okay. And not just because he's sticking with it—but because everyone else on the floor is fighting for their basketball lives. Despite the Devin Drew highlight reel, we're only down four.

As Rider crosses the mid-court stripe, Reynolds sprints the hash to get the ball. When Rider gives it up, Reynolds barks a few things at Rider. It's not mean, but it's forceful. And it's crazy to see Reynolds get that baby face all squinched up—but maybe he's actually been waiting for a chance to lead a little.

Whatever Reynolds said, it works. He takes a few rhythm dribbles right, then hits Fuller at the top of the key. A quick look to Stanford low, but when he can't find position, Fuller rips it back to Reynolds on the wing. He drives middle, then kicks to Jones on the left baseline. Nothing there. But Jones power dribbles toward the middle and gets the D to sag. Fuller pins Drew on a screen, leaving Rider wide open back on the right wing. Jones finds him and Rider steps into it like a vet—bang!

Our bench explodes. So does our crowd. But what's more important is Rider. He pounds his own chest, but he doesn't get carried away. Instead, he jumps right onto Drew's hip, pressuring him the whole way up. Drew's way too good to let Rider rip it from him, but he gets himself in too much of a rush to prove it. Instead of setting the offense, Drew tries to take Rider all the way to the rack. He gets there, but it's so long in coming that Coach Murphy would have had time to bolt from the bench to challenge. He doesn't have to, because Jones is

Pull   239

already there—and he slaps that thing back out to mid-court. Reynolds beats his man to the loose ball, then cruises ahead for a deuce.

And just like that, we're up one at Pike. It's early, but when Pike calls time our whole bench practically pours onto the floor to meet the team. I keep it reasonable—no chest bumps this time. But I get right in Rider's ear to tell him to keep up the good work. Then, once Bolden's had his say in the huddle, I get to Rider one more time before the ball goes live again. "It's a marathon, man," I say. "Don't get too low. Don't get too high. Just keep fighting and let the guys around you make plays." I point to Drew, who's staring right back at us. He's clearly re-focused, his eyes narrowed and angry. "He's gonna get his. You don't have to outscore him. Just help Marion East outscore Pike, you feel me?"

Rider smiles. For real. Like for the first time all year things make sense for him. "Most def," he says. "Straight, straight, straight."

Then he's gone, practically sprinting to go check Drew.

Rider's been good, hanging with Drew play for play. Reynolds has been the fire, getting guys revved back up every time we start to fall behind. And Jones and Stanford have been warriors down low, pushing us to an advantage on the boards through sheer will.

But Fuller's been the revelation tonight. It started slow—a put-back in the first, plus a couple freebies. Then he knocked in a mid-range in the second, followed by a rare triple. But in this second half, he's gone off. A couple short corner Js. A hoop-and-harm on a stick-back. A sweet drive past his man and then around a challenging big. Plus another three—and on that one he didn't even hesitate, just caught it on the move and let fly. On top of that, he's still doing his typical Fuller thing—challenging drivers, helping Jones and Stanford on the glass, tracking down loose balls. All hustle, all the time. The thing is, except for his last couple buckets, there's been no real flash. The casual observer might be thinking, *Well, that kid's putting together a decent game, but he's not making eyes pop.* But he's the reason we're tied with Pike with three minutes to go. When Pike calls time and their players slog back to the bench—a little frustrated because they can't put us away—their head coach meets them at the hash mark. "For the love of God," he shouts, "can somebody figure out how to check number thirty?"

We're not quite in the huddle yet, so everyone hears it. Murphy's the first to react. He starts looking at guys' jerseys, making a big production of it. He even lifts up my sweater like he's checking to see if I've got a number on my T-shirt underneath. "Thirty?" he asks. "Who's this number thirty they're sweating?" Guys are already laughing, so Murphy looks at Fuller and rears back like he's in shock. "You're thirty? J.J. Fuller?" Then he quits fooling and pounds Fuller on the chest. "Way to get after it, big man."

The only guy not laughing is Fuller. He's got concentration etched on his face. He mouths an inaudible *Thanks* to Murphy, but judging by Fuller's expression you'd think we were down a dozen. Of course, that's right up Bolden's alley. "Are we done clowning?" he growls. Everyone sits and listens but this time it's different. Instead of being disgusted that Bolden killed the buzz, everyone's focused. "You know they want to isolate Drew on this next touch," he says. He points at Rider. "That means you're in the cross-hairs. But just stay with him. False pressure and then make him settle. The rest of you be ready to help, but don't leave your man too early. Make Drew earn it."

Then we break the huddle with a resounding *Team!* Before he gets away, I grab Fuller's jersey real quick. I get right in his ear. Fuller's sweating in streams, still breathing heavy despite the timeout. And here I am in khakis, my heart rate barely raised. Still, if this is the only way I can help, this is what I've got to do. "You don't have to get all hype and pound your chest about it," I say. "Just be you. But, Fuller, you're in the zone. And I can tell you nights like this don't come around that often. So ride it. You get a look to bury these guys, pull the damn trigger."

"On it," he says. We bump fists, then he's off to the hardwood, and I'm back to the pine. But Fuller calls to me. I turn around. "Is it okay if I do pound my chest a little?" Then he gives a sheepish grin, like he's not sure he's allowed to crack jokes.

"Go on with yourself," I call.

Pike in-bounds to Drew. They flatten out right away, just like Bolden said. The good news for Rider is that he doesn't have to fight through any screens to find his man. The bad news is he's on an island with one of the better point guards in the state. Drew sizes Rider up. He gives a few bounces left, then crouches down and crosses right. He jabs right a few times, trying to get Rider to bite. Then he gives a hesitation, like he's about to pull from range. Rider plays it perfectly—he hops, hands up, at Drew, but he keeps his balance. Drew sees those hands flash and lowers his shoulder. But Rider's there. He cuts him off. Drew has no choice but to pick up his dribble. He extends his elbow a little to push Rider off-balance—the kind of move a senior gets away with on a freshman—but he's still stuck in that mid-range area he hates. And this time his shot comes up flat. Tired legs.

Stanford rips it and turns. He hits Rider at the near hash. I can see what Rider sees—lots of open space with just Drew back. My instinct is to yell *Push!* But I rein myself in. That's what I'd do, but Rider needs to take it easy.

When I see him turn up court with a head full of steam, I stand. "Wait for trailers!" I yell.

Rider eases back on his speed, then centers the ball. Reynolds fills on one wing, but he's blanketed. So Rider keeps pushing it up. He's no real threat, but Fuller's man reacts out of habit. He pinches down on the drive, and Rider does the right thing—he lasers one out to Fuller, who's standing all alone behind the arc.

The whole Pike crowd groans when they see him catch it. And sure enough, Fuller rings up his third triple of the night. Our lead. At Pike. Late.

Then they come unglued. Drew takes the in-bounds and gets a crazed look in his eyes. It's like he's taking this game as a personal insult. Everyone watching knows he's headed rack-to-rack. Rider stays on him the whole way, funneling him right into Jones, who stands his ground. Charge.

The Pike coach throws up his arms in protest, then stomps a few times begging for a blocking call instead. But even he knows. For a senior to get whistled for a charge at that point, at home no less, it had to be a no-brainer. The ref just holds his hand up to the Pike bench as if to say *Save it*, and they all simmer down.

When we inbound the ball, we're in no hurry. Bolden shouts at them to work for a good one. We reverse and reverse. A look in to Stanford. A kick out to Reynolds. A pass to Rider out top to re-set.

The longer we hold it, the jumpier Pike gets. Drew jumps so hard

Pull 243

at the pass to Rider that his momentum carries him almost to mid-court. Then, when he recovers, he keeps reaching on Rider, hoping to poke one free. He's desperate.

After one more reach, Rider backs away for some space and then looks to the bench. Right at me. Maybe it's my emotions getting the better of me. Maybe it's just the force of my wanting to be out of these street shoes and into D Rose 5s. Whatever it is, I nod urgently. *Take him*, I mouth.

Rider looks back at Drew. Then he dribbles the ball away from his body, just daring Drew. And, of course, Drew lunges. Quick as a rabbit, Rider crosses it back to his left. He knifes into the lane, head up. The bigs both jump at him, and he's got his pick. He goes with the sure thing: Stanford, who muscles in a nasty jam. Plus, a late whistle on a wing player trying to help.

Lord, we're up five. With Stanford headed to the line. Even against Pike, that's just about ballgame. And whatever doubt was left vanishes when Drew completes his meltdown. He punches the air and screams at the ref, totally out of control. He wants a carry call on Rider. Instead, he gets a big fat T.

The ride home is *loud*. Stanford cranks some Gucci Mane on a portable speaker. Bolden doesn't even blink about it. Everybody's swarming all over the bus, high fiving each other and talking trash. I can't exactly join in with my leg the way it is, but it's good enough to just chill and enjoy my boys having a good time. They deserve it.

Even Murphy gets into it. As we roll across the Kessler intersection, he stands and hollers. "That's Marion East ball at its finest, boys. Hang in there, and then when it's crunch time"—he makes a stabbing motion in front of him—"go for the kill."

That gets everyone howling again. But it's also too much for Bolden. The players talking nonsense is one thing, but he grabs Murphy by the sleeve and gives him a severe frown. Murphy slumps back in his seat, defeated by Bolden's discipline once again.

By the time we cross 38th, the party's died down. Guys start gathering up their stuff. Some of them mash out a few texts to see what the word is for Saturday night. Me? I'm heading home. It's not sulking or anything, but Kid caught me after the game and said he was coming over. So we'll see what's up with that.

We hit the Marion East lot and everyone files off. When Fuller goes past, I stop him. I want him to know just how good he was tonight. Everyone yaps during a game, and everyone strokes ego in the aftermath—but now that things are calmed down, he needs to hear some real talk. "What you did out there tonight was straight kill it," I tell him.

There's no shrugging it off now. I can tell this means something to Fuller. "Thanks, D, I'm just sorry you couldn't be out there with us."

We head off the bus, then walk together to the gym. The wind whips around the corner, and we both pull our coats tight against it. Then, in the warm, low-lit gym, I figure I might as well tell Fuller what's really been on my mind. "Man, you know I'd like nothing more than to be balling out with you guys," I say. "But even when my leg was right, my head wasn't. I'm sorry I wasn't a better teammate this year."

Fuller stops. He extends his arm, then gives me a real formal handshake. "I appreciate that," he says. "But I've been thinking too. All that stuff goes two ways."

"True," a voice says. It's Stanford. He'd been standing off to the side, checking a text, but now he steps to us. "And, D, the season ain't over. I saw how you coached Rider up tonight. Man, you been there for us more than you think."

"I don't know," I say. "None of this played out the way I wanted." Even as we talk, I wonder what's changed. Only yesterday, these guys were sick to death of me. Winning cures everything, I guess.

Then Fuller smiles. He elbows Stanford. "He doesn't know," he says. Stanford laughs.

"Know what?" I ask. They just stand there, pleased with some secret. "What?" I plead.

Stanford's the one who caves. "Aww, man, we heard you."

"Heard what?"

"Last night when you cracked on that reporter. Hell, everyone heard. You snapped him up pretty good." Then he reaches and gives my shoulder a shake. He smiles, relaxing all that practiced scowl out of his face. "But you were sticking up for us, D. You had our backs. That kind of pulls people together, y'know?"

At home, it's family meeting time. Mom and Dad are at the kitchen table, one sitting on either side of Uncle Kid. He just stares down at his hands like he's cuffed there.

There are two chairs opposite Kid—one for me and one for Jayson. But it's clear Jayson is opting out of this sit-down. He's kicked back in Dad's recliner, a blanket over him. He's flipping through channels with the volume low.

Thing is, I was all set to come home and talk colleges. I've been carrying around that list I made in Coach Bolden's office, but I haven't shared it with anyone.

Dad motions to the open chairs. "Sit," he says. I obey.

Mom calls to Jayson to come over, but he barely stirs. "I'm good," he says. Mom inhales sharply like she's about to rip into him, but then she catches herself. She holds her breath for a second, shakes her head, then shifts her attention back to the people at her kitchen table.

Once I sit, Dad motions toward Kid to speak. When he hesitates, Dad says, "Go ahead. This is on you."

Kid's jaw flexes a few times in anger. At the same time, I see his eyes fill with shame. He wants to smash something or break down and cry all at the same time.

Finally, he starts talking. At first, he tells me all the stuff I already know. He's neck-deep in debt. He's getting booted from his place. He's about to lose his wheels. I get a little impatient, tired from always being on this end of other people's problems. But if this season's taught me anything, it's that once in a while you've got to think about what things are like for other people—and right now, it's pretty clear that Kid's humiliated. At last he gets to the point. "I need a place to stay until I get back on my feet," he says. He looks at me just for a second and then, like he's nervous, he looks away again. Maybe I'm supposed to say something, but I don't know what it is. So Kid's forced to continue. "That means I need to crash here for a while." He takes one more deep breath. He rubs his neck in frustration. "That means you and Jayson got to make room for me, and it's only right that I ask you if that's okay."

So there it is. Truth is, I hate the notion of taking on a roommate. But Kid's family. And he's also a grown man who's being forced to ask permission from a high schooler. I can see in his eyes that he needs this, but he's also angry—furious, really—at that need.

"Anything, Kid," I say. "You know that."

He nods at me, a silent thank you. Dad glares at him because Kid doesn't actually say it, but even Dad knows maybe it's time to back off. Instead, he springs into action mode. He claps his hands, just like Bolden does sometimes to get our attention. "So," he shouts, "ground rules. First, no more Kid. In this house, you're Sidney. Okay?" He looks around, daring anyone to challenge him. "For tonight, you can crash on the couch. Tomorrow, the first order of business will be to start moving Jayson in to share Derrick's room. Depending on—"

"Wait, what?!" Jayson's up now. He stands in the living room, arms wide in protest. "How come I've got to move my stuff? This is bull—" He almost finishes off that last word, his lips pursing into a *sh*. But he knows better.

Dad doesn't raise his voice. He's not going to get baited into another go-round with Jayson. "You had a chance to come to the table, but you said you were good."

Mom stifles a smile, but I know she's loving it. She so wanted to jump him earlier, but this is a better way for Jayson to get his. Jayson just storms to his room. Drama? You bet. When his door slams, the whole house shakes. If it weren't for having to wrestle with Kid's problems, Mom and Dad would both be up after that kind of display. "When we're done with your brother, we're going to need to talk about your son," Mom tells Dad.

"My son?" Dad protests. "You know he didn't get that temper from my side."

"Oh, like you don't have a temper. You just don't let it out, Thomas. You just pack it all in and sulk." She points toward the hallway. "Sound familiar?"

They're not really fighting, just kind of needling each other. You can tell they both like it. They've been down this road way too many times for there to be any landmines left. Kid—I don't think I'll ever be able to think of him as Sidney—sinks back in his chair. Maybe he's happy to have the focus off him, but his face is unreadable.

"I can tell you what my dad would have done with Jayson," Mom says. Then she breaks into her imitation of her father, adding some rasp and southern drawl to her voice. "That boy's got nothin' a good whoopin' won't fix."

Everyone laughs then. I'm old enough to remember that kind of fire from my grandpa before the last few years when it was all sickness and pain for him. So I know Mom's impersonation was spot on.

Then I shock everyone. "Can I just say something in defense of Jayson?"

Dad bites. "Well, he's about to become your roommate, so let's hear this so we can remind you about it a week from now when you're ready to kill him."

He's got a point. Inwardly, I cringe at the prospect of cramped quarters with Jayson. He'll be all up in my stuff. I realize I need to change the pass-code on my phone, or before I know it he'll be sending fake texts to Lia. But that's for another time. "He's got a fair gripe with us," I say. "And I think we can probably do better by him."

26.

Jayson can't see an upside. For him, Kid moving in just makes it seem like he's the one who got evicted. I've done my best to make my room partly his—stacked some clothes on the floor so he could have half the closet, re-arranged so we could squeeze a cot in for him, even set up some crates so he'd have a place to stack his books and videos.

"Still not mine," he says. "It's not like I can really kick back when you're here."

I point out that between my time at practices and with Lia, he's got the room to himself more often than I do. That draws a *whatever* from him, so I head out to the living room, closing the door—my door, if I want to get technical about it—behind me so Jayson can have his space.

"I'm sorry," I hear. It's Kid, waiting on me in the living room. He must have heard the whole argument. He blames himself for it, a habit of his these days. Jayson's grumpy, Mom's car is low on oil, the internet is out—Kid apologizes like he made it happen.

"Don't sweat it, Kid," I say. I double check for my dad's

presence, since we're only following his "call him Sidney" rule if he's here to correct us. Besides, all I really want is for Kid to start acting like himself.

Since we're the only two around, I decide to hit him up for some advice. I've still got that list folded in my pocket, but I haven't talked about it to anyone yet. Kid's watching the *30 for 30* about an old player from Chicago. While it drones on, I head to the kitchen to fix myself an ice bag. Then, when the show hits a commercial, I settle onto the couch. "Kid," I say, "I need some advice."

He leans forward, all attention. But then he catches himself and turns his palms up in apology again. "I don't know I'm the one you should be asking," he says.

"Stop it, man," I say. But even that sends Kid further into himself. He sinks back in the chair and shrugs. He's sitting in what is usually Dad's chair, and he can't get comfortable. He keeps shifting and re-shifting like he's sitting on pins. "Kid," I say, more patient this time. "For real. I need to run some things by you."

Kid stands. That settles him. From the couch, I look up and take stock of him. That height that made him a force in the post is bent a little now. His shoulders slump and the new weight makes him seem shorter. There are hints of gray at his temples, wrinkles up and down his clothes. His shoelaces are untied. Maybe if he helps me, it'll end up helping him pull himself back together too.

"Some schools backed off me when I went down this time," I say.

He lowers his head and shakes it mournfully back and forth. "That's cold," he says. Then he looks toward the window, remembering. "I remember when they did that to me. It's a mean business, man." He shoves his hands in his pockets. "Of course, that was all my fault. Yours is just bad luck."

"It is what it is," I say. I want to get past that talk, get to the thing I really could use help on. "But I've got a list of schools that stood by me." I reach into my pocket and pull out that paper. Hand it to Kid. He looks at it for a second and purses his lips. I know exactly what he's thinking—other than Indiana, the schools on there aren't exactly elites. It's not like I'm down to offers from the Stony Brook and Youngstown States, but gone are the Kentuckys, the Dukes, the Louisvilles. "What do you think?" I ask.

He starts to talk, then pauses. The documentary comes back from commercial, and he turns to look at it while he's thinking. I watch too. Kid points to the tube. "You too much of a young pup to remember this guy," he says. "But he was the one. The golden child. He got hyped as Magic Johnson with Larry Bird's jumpshot. Best Chicago product ever. I mean, *ever*, D."

I pay attention for a few minutes, check some highlights of the kid. I don't know about best ever, but it doesn't take long for me to recognize some serious skills in him. "What was his name?" I ask.

"Ben Wilson," Kid says.

"So how come I never heard of him?"

Kid looks at me square in the eye now. This isn't that fake bravado he put on all winter. He's serious as can be. "He got shot and killed the night before his senior season started," Kid says. I think this is part of another lecture about me steering clear of Wes, but that part doesn't come. Instead, Kid shakes his head again. "Maybe I should remember that, for all I got myself into when I was young, I'm still one of the lucky ones."

That hangs between us for a second or two, both of us unsure of what to say next. Kid comes back to the point though. He holds that paper in front of him and backhands it with his other hand. "I know what you're asking," he says. "You want to know if you should stick with these schools even when you get better and start dominating again. Right?"

"That's about it," I say.

He hands the paper back to me. "I always lived by this," he says. "You got to get what's best for you whenever you can. So the old me would say take the best offer that comes around. And all the stuff anyone wants to throw at you." Then he smiles, more to himself than to me. "But that way of thinking got me nowhere. Still gets me nowhere. So I'll tell you what I really think, even if I never lived by it—you have to honor people that stand by you in tough times." Almost against his own will, his gaze returns to Dad's chair. He nods, again to himself. I realize that Dad and Kid are as different as two people can be, but they're still brothers.

I thank Kid for his advice, then get up, ice bag and all, to go check on my brother. So what if he feels crowded? Another couple years and I won't be around at all. So I'm going to hang with Jayson while I can. When I get to that closed door, I stop. I hear noise from the other side. At first, I think it's just the commentary on his NBA game, but then I realize it's his voice. I lean in, ear to the door. This is more of an intrusion on his privacy than anything he's complained about, but I can't help myself. Jayson speaks, then waits, then speaks again. His voice rises in anger. Then it backs down, suddenly apologetic. I think for a second that he's just on the phone, but then it clicks—lines. My boy's working on his lines for the play. He'd lose his mind if he knew I was eavesdropping on him doing this, so after a couple more seconds I limp back to the couch again.

But I feel proud of him. Most definitely. He's in there putting his sweat in. And that's all anyone can ever really do.

If April thought she got the third degree when she visited, she should see the treatment Lia's getting. The thing is, my parents don't even mean to do it. When I told them I wanted to bring Lia over for dinner they were straight up excited. They got sick of seeing me moping around all heart-hurt from Jasmine. And this is a good signal to Dad that I'm not just using Lia like I did Daniella last year.

But Lia walks in the door and the questions come out. What do you like in school? Do you think you'll go on to college? What does your father do?

"Stop!" I shout. It's a little too forceful. Mom gives me a look like she's a ref about to jack me up with a T. "Sorry," I say. "I know you two don't even mean to do it, but you're on Lia so hard I'm surprised she can breathe. Give her a break. Please."

"I can handle myself, Derrick," Lia says. "A few questions don't scare me." That's all show for my parents. And it works too, as Mom and Dad both kind of lean back with their mouths curled up, impressed at Lia's confidence. Then Lia gives me a quick wink to let me know she appreciates me having her back.

That wink sets me racing in a way I don't want to show in front of my parents. So I'm thrilled, for once, when Jayson comes in and hijacks everything.

"What's this?" he says, pointing to the table. He makes it sound like he's asking about dinner, but we all know he's thrown by Lia's presence.

Mom plays it straight. "Just dinner," she says. "Roasted carrots, fried potatoes, flank steak. Don't worry, Jayson. Even we can fancy it up now and then."

Jayson acts hurt. He yanks his chair so hard the seat bangs on the underside of the table. Then he reaches across the table and stabs at a piece of steak. He won't even look at Lia.

Dad coughs. I told them all about Jayson's deal—even though he swore me to secrecy—but there's only so much rude behavior they'll stand. "Jayson," he says, "some manners would be nice. Perhaps you noticed we have a guest."

"I saw," he snips. "Hey, Lia."

Mom opens her mouth to crack on Jayson, but she's too slow. "I thought you were a little player," Lia says. "Smooth. That was the word at Marion East, you know—watch out for Jayson Bowen when he gets here. He'll have all the girls lining up. But I guess I'll have to report back that you're just another eighth-grader who doesn't know how to talk to girls yet."

Out of the corner of my eye, I see Mom and Dad smile. They love it. And, immediately, they love Lia. Jayson? Not so much. He turns red. His eyes dart around. He wants to pop, I can tell. But he knows he's met his match. "You tell the girls at Marion East—" he starts. He trails off, not knowing how to finish. He gazes around for help. Nobody steps up.

"Tell them what?" Lia says.

Jayson looks at Dad. "Where's Kid?" he asks, trying to change the subject.

Dad answers, his voice flat as blacktop. "At work."

"What was I supposed to tell everyone?" Lia asks again, staying after Jayson.

"Awww," he drawls, "come on. I'm sorry. Let's just eat."

Everyone laughs a little. We settle in and eat for a while. I peep on Lia a little. Even dressed conservatively—she's in a plain white sweater and blue jeans—she looks incredible. And when I take a quick look at Jayson, I see him checking her pretty hard. So I decide to pile on just a little. "You know, Lia," I say, "you could tell everyone that Jayson Bowen is a big talker until someone talks back a little."

"Come on, D," he says. "Cut me some slack."

I laugh. "Man, nobody in this world has been cut more slack than you have."

I expect Jayson to pop back at me, but it's Lia who knees me. "I don't know, Derrick. I've cut you plenty of slack already."

Now, there's nothing behind this. I've been on my best behavior with Lia from the jump. But that's one of those lines a girl can throw down on a guy and there's nothing you can say. Protest at all and you just look like a chump. I just look at her and shake my head. She grins and gives one of those lightning-quick winks again.

"So let me keep score here," Mom says to Lia. "Lia two, Jayson zero, and Derrick zero. You know how to snap a man up." Then she points at me with her fork. "Treat this one right," she tells me.

Mom and Lia share a laugh between them, while the rest of us sit back and take it. I'm cool with it though. Lia's the first girl since Jasmine that I've introduced to my parents, so all in all I'm calling this one a win.

27.

Without me, the team went up to Zionsville and nabbed a nice win. But they came home and got walloped by Ben Davis. There's no shame in that, but it put a fizzle on the momentum they had built up. Tomorrow night's the last game of the regular season, against Roncalli. But there's a lot more to the day than that.

This morning, it means surgery. First thing. Nothing like going to Methodist Hospital at sunrise on a Friday. The people all seem happy enough. The nurses crack jokes to each other and laugh softly. The doctors clip by, a lot of zip in their stride for such an early morning. But none of them are getting their knees cut open today. Mom and Dad sit on either side of me, trying to keep me calm. Mom even reaches over and gives my hand a squeeze, telling me that everything's all right, just like she would if I were five and scared of the dark.

Jayson's at school, of course. But it turns out, tonight is his play. And it's not just that he's *in* it. He let it slip to me that he's the lead. I swore to him again that I'd tell nobody. But when he realized that I had surgery the same day as his performance, his face fell. He wouldn't admit it, but he was hoping he'd get at least some audience. I apologized, even told him that I could still make it—under the knife first thing, basic rehab in the hospital, then a discharge by late afternoon. He didn't buy it for a second. And, truth is, if I get out early, it's not like I'll want to go straight from the hospital to a middle school play. So I finally had to spill it to Mom and Dad—Jayson will be mad at me, but he needs to have some people there.

"You two don't have to stay," I tell my parents. "And I don't need you tonight. Go see Jayson."

"Hush," Mom says.

"For real," I say. "Kid'll be here after a while. Lia said she'd come straight from school. There's no sense in you two just sitting around while I'm knocked out."

"Stop," Dad says. "We're not letting our son go through this without his parents."

I know what I'm suggesting seems ridiculous to them, but I wouldn't mind having some alone time to clear my head.

"I think being in this hospital is making me ill," Mom says. We spent a lot of time in the hospital beside Dad last year, so I don't blame her. But when I look at her she really *does* look sick, her skin a few shades lighter than normal.

"Hospitals will do that," Dad says. He fetches her a bottle of water and she pops a couple Tylenol from her purse. "After this," Dad says, "let's all make a deal not to spend any more time in hospitals."

"Fair enough," I say. We both smile, but I can't muster a laugh.

Soon enough, I'm called back. They go ahead and put me in a bed with two chairs beside it for my parents. The nurse draws the curtain to give us some sense of privacy, but nobody says a word until the surgeon comes. He looks reasonably young. Has some color to his face, like he took a winter trip to Florida or something. And his hair is like a sculpture, a thick sea of black parted neatly on the right. He's a bit too polished, but I don't know what I expected. But all that fades away as soon as he starts talking. He walks us all through each step—the small incisions for the arthroscope, the drilled holes in the bones, the graft from below the kneecap, then some screws and stitches to keep everything in place. "It sounds more complicated than it is," he says. "You'll be in recovery for a few hours and then we'll run some tests. But you can be home by dinner."

Mom frowns like she thinks he's being flippant. But his confidence is good for me. He makes an exit, telling us we'll get started in about twenty minutes, that we can just breathe easy until then.

I wait a few minutes, but then I press Mom and Dad again. "Go to Jayson's play tonight," I say. "You can see me after surgery and then still have time to make it. I'll hang at home with Kid."

They talk over each other in explanation, saying that one child's surgery wins over another's play, and that Jayson doesn't even want them there anyway.

"Please go," I say. "Jayson thinks it's all about me anyway. And if nobody's at his play, he'll be right." I pause, then hit them with the clincher. "Besides, since when did you base your parenting decisions on what Jayson wanted?"

They both lean back in their chairs. Mom in particular, still pale, looks too tired to put up a fight. "Fine," she says. "Dad will go to the play. I'll stay with you."

That's a decent compromise, so I let it go. Then, soon enough, they come to wheel me back. I say my good-byes to Mom and Dad. There's a sudden urge to cling to them, like I'm some little kid getting on the school bus for the first time. But I fight it. Chin up.

When I get to the surgery room, I see they've put a poster up above me so I have something to focus on. It's of Derrick Rose, slicing through the lane. At first I smile. He's had the game I've most admired since I was a kid. He's why I rock the D Rose 5s. Then again, maybe he's not the player they should be showing me. Truth is, he's never been quite the same since he went under the knife.

The surgeon said it went well. Full recovery expected, though he insisted the timetable is different for every athlete. Then he stressed the importance of the rehab exercises and he was gone.

Then it was a few hours of check-ins by nurses. They made sure my leg was properly elevated. Kept checking that the knee wasn't bent at all. Through it all, Mom and Dad stood watch. They'd try to distract me with some chatter about any old thing—politics, old family stories, the weather. But I wasn't having it. I just wanted out of there. Finally, Kid showed up to relieve my parents. Then Lia as soon as she could race over from school. She looked good, but stressed. I appreciated her being there, but I silently seethed at how she worried over me. It made me feel less like her boyfriend and more like her problem child.

At last, they got me out of bed for some quad sets. Standard stuff. They liked what they saw enough to check me out. Like the surgeon said—in time for dinner.

I could walk on my crutches, but the hospital insists on Kid wheeling me to the car. No more fancy ride for him now—just that old Nova that was supposed to become mine. So we get to the parking lot, Kid behind me and Lia walking by my side. "You want me to take you?" Lia asks. She points to her ride a few spaces away.

"Nah. Kid's got it," I say.

She pulls her coat tighter around her, even though the weather's given us a break at last—spots of sunshine coming through the gray, the temp climbing toward 50. "Well, I'll just follow you to your place," she says.

"You don't have to do that," I say.

Now she frowns, all that beauty tightening down into a hurt expression. "I know I don't have to. I want to."

The more she presses, the more I'm desperate to be free of her. At the same time, I'd like to just go to her place and curl up with her, pretend the rest of the world doesn't even exist. I don't know how to explain it. My own heart is a lot harder to solve than any math problem I've ever stressed. "Lia," I say. "I'm just gonna go home and sleep. There's really no point."

"No point?" she says, getting heated up. But then she checks herself. She's not going to stand here and beg. "Just text me later if you want," she says. Then she turns to her car, climbs in and speeds away. As soon as she's gone, I feel her absence like a wound.

Kid slides my crutches into the backseat, then helps me into the front. He climbs in and shakes his head at me. "Real well played with the honey," he says. Surgery or not, he's not passing up a chance to needle me over girls.

"Man, you know how it is," I say, trying to play it off.

We drive a couple blocks in silence. Then Kid, suddenly serious, says, "Yeah, I do know how it is, D. Sometimes you just have to be with family."

All's quiet until Jayson bursts home from the play. I'm on the couch, leg elevated, and he comes straight at me. "How could you?!" he hollers. If he put as much emotion into the play as he's putting on in our living room, then he must have killed.

"Jayson," Mom snaps. She's been reclined in Dad's chair for the past hour, still trying to chase away the nausea that popped up at the hospital. Now she sits up straight. "Did you forget that your brother just got out of *surgery?*"

"Come on," Jayson says. "It's not like they were replacing a lung. He's already out." Then he wheels back to me. "But, D, what part of 'secret' do you not get? Why do I have to look out in the audience and see Dad there with his camera like some idiot?"

Mom about leaps out of her chair when she hears *idiot*. But it's Kid, who's been sitting over at the table combing through the newspaper, who changes the vibe in the room. He just starts cracking up. He leans back and howls at the ceiling. We all stare. Then, once he's settled, he shakes his head at Jayson. "Young pup, you've got an uncle who's got a debt he can't pay. You've got a brother who can't walk and who still screws things up with girls even when he's the best point guard in the state. We *need* you Jayson. These days you're our only damn hope. So step up."

Jayson's too mad to just give it up, but I see him soften at Kid's little speech. The tension drains out of his shoulders and his hands drop from his hips.

About that time Dad finally comes through the door. I can see it on his face—the way his eyes are narrowed and his lips are still a little tight like there's something sour in his mouth. He and Jayson went round and round on the short ride home. He was probably hanging in the car for a second, taking deep breaths and counting to twenty. As he walks in, I can feel the room tense back up. He turns to me. "How's the leg?"

"Okay, I—"

He just keeps walking past. He gives a little wave to Mom and acts like Jayson isn't even there. He finally stops when he gets to the kitchen table, where Kid's still sitting.

"You ready, Sidney?" he asks. "I'll give you a lift."

Kid grabs his wallet off the table and stands. Nods at Dad. They start for the door, but this time Jayson pipes up. "Where are you guys going?"

"We've both got late shifts," Dad deadpans. "We work, you know?" He starts for the door again.

All Mom has to do is cough. Dad stops. He exhales. All the anger drains from his face. "You okay, dear?" he asks.

She smiles. For years it was so rare that Dad would get worked up, but Jayson's got his buttons pushed 24-7. I think Mom likes that she can be the chill one for a while. "I'm fine," she says, smooth as butter. "But I was hoping to get a report on our young actor."

Even in the dim light of the living room, I can see Jayson blush at that. He shakes his head like he's disgusted.

Dad takes another deep breath and answers. "He was incredible," he says. All the edge is gone from his voice. He's clearly sincere. As he talks, I see Jayson's embarrassment deepen. "The other kids were lucky to remember their lines, but Jayson was actually *acting*. He's on another level already." Then Dad adds a little punch line, his edge back—"Now if he could just act his age off the stage, we'd be in business."

Then Dad turns to Kid, and the two older Bowen brothers head out the door wordlessly. The two younger ones are left speechless in the living room, their mother watching them. Jayson stares at the front door. It's like he's trying to figure out if he should be angry at Dad's final words or proud for all the words that preceded it. Finally, I reach my hand out from the couch. "You really tear it up?" I ask.

"Yeah, I kinda did," Jayson says. He smiles for real now. Then he bends down to slap me five.

That's it. Except for one more thing. I check my phone and there's a missed text from Wes: *You still think you can help me? I might need it to be soon.*

28.

They beat Roncalli in the closer to end on a good note and push our record to 14-6. But tonight it gets real for my boys. First round of Sectionals. Pike's the host school, but we've got Lawrence North up first. My freshman year, they were the big dogs of the Sectional we had to knock off, but they've dipped some since then. They're just barely above .500 this year.

As we bus up I-65 toward Pike, I get surrounded by Fuller, Stanford, and Reynolds. I already gave Rider the breakdown for the game before we hit the road, so now I'm just chatting with the vets. Thing is, since they've been in a playoff atmosphere before, they really don't need my advice. We talk some basics of the game plan. Check their shooter, Mike Bell, anywhere 25 and in. Double hard on their power forward, Martavis Richardson, but let any of the chumps they rotate at center solo if they want it. That barely gets us past the 38th Street exit.

"So talk, D," Fuller says. "I know everyone's asking you, but you got to tell your boys. Where you heading next year?"

I shake my head. Try to wave them off. They're not having it though. They all start ragging on me to spill, throw some information their way.

"Look, D," Reynolds says at last. "I might have been a pain for you, but I need this. You know the only looks I'll get when I'm a senior are D-II if I'm lucky."

I've got no choice but to cave. At this point, I feel like I owe something to these guys. Between our in-fighting and my injuries, this season's been a struggle. But here we are, at the end of the line, together. "Fine," I say. They all lean in. "But for real, you can't tell anyone. I haven't even mentioned schools to my folks yet. I'm waiting until the season's done to talk it over with them and Coach, then we'll spill a list to Whitfield. Before then, it'll just distract from your season."

"Okay, okay, okay," Stanford says. "Just tell it."

So I tell them my list—making them the first people to hear it aside from Kid. I rattle off my five, and they have the same reaction as Kid—a little puzzled at some of the inclusions. So I add, like I'm trying to justify my decisions for them, "It's not like I've ruled everyone else out. But those were the best schools that kept offers out for me after the ACL tear." Like I have to remind them of it, I hold my crutches up as evidence.

"Can't be," Fuller says. "No way everyone backed off after an injury." He seems truly troubled by the notion, like up until this point he thought college basketball was filled with only the most ethical and steadfast coaches.

"Not everyone did," I say. "But most of the real elites did. I think maybe it's more than the ACL. With that plus the calf injury, they might think I'm injury prone."

They soak it in. They lean back in their seats. They shouldn't be pinning hopes on me, but everyone that's ever walked the halls at Marion East—much less pulled on a jersey—wants to see a local baller bang it on the biggest stages. Hop to a powerhouse like Kentucky. Bring home some hardware. Leap to the L after a year or two. But I know a couple things now. The first is that you can't make much of a leap when you're worried too much about what other people want. And the second is that if you get caught up in what's down the road, you lose sight of what's in front of you.

So when Stanford tells me I still have a chance to show out next year, I don't hesitate. "Forget next year," I say. "Forget all that. You three just show out tonight, you feel me?"

Show out is the truth, sure enough. We were worried about Martavis Richardson in the post, but we forgot something—Richardson has to check Stanford. First time down Stanford swims past him for a board and a bucket. Later in the first, Stanford steps to the shallow corner for a look off a Reynolds drive. When that one falls, Stanford gets his scowl on. He thumps his chest a few times as he races back on D. Coach tells him to just take it easy. But I know Stanford. He gets a little swole up. He's determined to try to take over. When I was running point, I'd try to rein in his emotions—maybe even skip him on a touch just so he'd cool down—but now I just urge him on.

"Richardson ain't nothin'," I holler at him. "Just wear him out, Stanford."

He looks my way and gives me a few emphatic nods, then bodies up on D. I get a look from Coach Bolden too, but it's not nearly as enthusiastic. He just points to my spot behind the bench. "Sit," he seethes.

I obey, hobbling back on my crutches, but Bolden's not truly mad at me. Next dead ball, he comes all the way down to me. "I love the energy, D," he says. "But put it into teaching Rider. Be more a coach than a cheerleader, right?"

"Got it," I say. But as I do, Fuller pokes the ball free and we get a fast break. Lawrence North cuts off the first wave, but Stanford's trailing the play with a clean run at the rim. Fuller slides a dime to him right in time and Stanford gangstas one home on top of a guard. Our crowd explodes. I do too. "That's what I'm talking about, Stanford," I scream. There's no way he can hear me from the other end, but Bolden sure does. He just looks at me in exasperation, like *What did I just say?* "Okay, Coach, okay," I say. "But that thing was nasty."

Even Bolden has to smile at that.

By the time we get to the end of the first, the rout is on. Stanford's already in double digits. Reynolds is getting loose too. He's buried a couple threes from deep. Then, when the second quarter starts, Fuller decides to get in on the act. An awkward runner that gets a roll. A mid-range J from the wing. A baseline drive that ends with him muscling one home.

Our lead swells to ten. To thirteen. And by the end of the half—with Jones and Rider starting to chip in some timely buckets too—we're up 44-25.

As Lawrence North slouches toward their locker room, it's clear they're finished. They're not talking. Not even the coaches. And the players don't even look angry at the whipping they're taking. Nope—they just want to get the rest of it over with so they can be done with their deflated season.

Stanford hosts.

Pike's on tap tomorrow night, so none of the players are drinking a thing stronger than Coke. But this isn't exactly like Fuller's party from earlier in the year. At Stanford's, people are getting loose. He's swiped a whiskey bottle from his mom's cabinet—how he'll explain it later is his problem, I guess. And people keep showing up with plastic bags filled with sixers and bottles of cheap booze they've scored, either on fake I.D.s or from generous older siblings. Judging from the glaze on some eyes, some people have been living it up before they made it here.

A good chunk of Marion East is at Stanford's. Dancing, talking game to each other, sneaking off to get busy in the back bedroom or the back alley or their cars. Good for them, I guess. But nobody's got it made like I do. Even when Stanford drops some old school Jay-Z, I can't dance a step with my knee—but who cares? Lia's curled up on the couch beside me. She's warmed by a few drinks of her own, but it's just enough to make her extra flirty. "Too bad you can't dance with me," she purrs. "I wanted to show you some new moves."

"I bet," I say.

"Then again, there are moves and there are moves." She traces a fingernail down my chest until it rests on the button of my jeans.

I laugh at her and bat her hand away.

"Aww, you never want to have any fun," she says, all mock hurt.

"I'm up for fun," I say. "Later." My hesitancy is all show. Truth is I'd like nothing more than to find the first unoccupied room. She gets like this and my whole world feels electrified. But teasing her just makes it more intense—especially since it's usually the other way around. Plus, I'm enjoying watching everyone have fun. It's not exactly the way I want a post-game celebration—watching the game with screws in my knee was never part of the dream—but it sure beats losing.

Fuller comes over and sits on the other side of Lia. Crowding again. This time I don't mind, because I don't know how much longer I could have held out on Lia. "How you kids doing?" he asks. We both laugh. Fuller's face falls into a worried expression. "What? What'd I say?"

"Kids?" I repeat. "Fuller, you my boy and all, but sometimes you talk like a thirty-year-old. You have got to loosen up."

"I'm not that bad," he protests.

Now Lia jumps in on him. "You dance yet? Even one song?" When Fuller doesn't respond, she just gives him a deep, knowing *Mmm-hmmm*. Then she points across the room. "See that girl?" Fuller turns with his whole body, leaning forward like a dog on a scent. Lia backhands his shoulder. "Look at me. God, don't be so obvious."

Fuller turns back to her, but he's still practically panting. "What about her?" he asks.

"Her name's Erica Cotton. And she keeps asking me about you." As Lia talks, Fuller's eyes grow as wide as they do when he's got a free run at the rim. "But she has one rule. She won't hook up with any guy who won't dance."

Fuller's eyes narrow again. His eyebrows pinch together. "You for real?"

"I swear it," Lia says. "Get out there and dance, and I'll introduce you to her."

Fuller takes a deep breath. Then another. It's like he's steeling himself for a clutch free throw. "Okay," he says, more to himself than anyone else. "I got this."

He walks hesitantly to where people are dancing. As the music thumps along, the bass so high that glasses and beer cans rattle on tables, Fuller glances back. Lia motions for him to go on. Then she pulls herself tighter to me and leans her head on my shoulder.

"How you know that girl?" I ask.

"Who?"

"Erica. The one all into Fuller."

Lia laughs. "I've never talked to her before in my life," she says. "But you're right. Fuller's got to lighten up. I figured dancing would be a good first step for him."

I look down at her. "You're evil," I tease.

"A little."

Then we watch Fuller. He just bobs his head at first, feeling out the rhythm. And then—bless him—he goes for it. He crouches down and jumps back and forth. He twitches his body to the beat. And the whole time his face is as creased in concentration as ever. He even dances serious. And not very well—all elbows and knees. But that's not the point. The boy's trying, and everyone picks up on it. Practically the whole team hollers in approval, the name Fuller swelling across the room. Then they start chanting his name, laughing and clapping in approval. The girl looks a little surprised by the whole scene, but she doesn't seem to mind. And after a little bit she starts getting into it too. She doesn't quite grind up on him, but she's encouraging him plenty.

When the song's done, Fuller comes back. He's breathing hard, a light sweat on his forehead, but he's here to demand his reward. "Well?" he says to Lia. Then he nods to the girl she pointed out earlier.

Lia stands. "Let's go." She takes Fuller by the hand and leads him across the room. She glances back at me, smiles and shrugs. The girl's winging it. But something tells me she's got this. Not surprisingly, in about ten seconds she's coaxed a broad smile from the girl, and the three of them are chatting it up. At one point, Fuller looks at Lia—his face aghast and his palms turned up—then nearly doubles over laughing. The truth is out, I guess.

I check my phone. Five missed texts. All from Wes. Each one is him asking me where I'm at with increasing urgency. I hit him back to let him know I'm at Stanford's and in, like, two seconds he responds. *On my way D.*

I try not to think anything about it. I ease back into the couch again. I flex my knee gently. Can't help it. It's like I have to check it every two minutes to see if it feels stronger, even though I know it's going to feel the same way it did the last time—sore, basically. I'm not allowed to take a step without crutches for at least another week, but I still have workouts. Quad sets, hamstring curls, sitting knee flexions four times a day. Hamstring stretches every waking hour. It's not like I get a sweat up, but I can feel the work in my knee. It's a good pain, a sign that the recovery has begun. I know I have a long way. Months. Close to a year maybe. But it's just like getting better at your game—it doesn't happen overnight, but day by day by day. My first goal is to get totally free of crutches in two weeks, because that means no more limp. Then the next goal will be adding resistance to a stationary bike or to hamstring curls.

I have to stop myself from thinking that far ahead. Right here. Right now.

Lia comes back to me, laughing, but Fuller stays put. He's in his groove now, chatting up that girl a mile a minute. All good.

Lia sits beside me, but then leans across. She lets her body press against my lap as she does, but she's reaching to my end of the couch. She grabs my crutches and then sets them in front of me. "Please tell me you're ready to bolt," she says. She surveys the room. "It's a nice party and all, but you probably need to go lie down." She drawls those last two words out. She's had enough waiting.

"Let's split," I say. I swear the way she gets me racing I could spring off this couch and unleash a forty-inch vertical on one leg.

But just as I start to situate my crutches under my arms, there's a commotion at the door. A wave of people swell back from the entrance. Everyone else turns to see what the deal is. Even at my height, there are too many bodies between me and the disturbance to tell. Doesn't matter—there's a bad vibe rippling through the room. As Pusha T starts dropping rhymes on the sound system, I get the sudden feeling that things are about take a bad turn. Not a person in here is looking for trouble, but it doesn't mean trouble won't find kids on a Friday night in the city.

I point to the back door through the kitchen. "Come on, Lia," I say. I can't move fast enough on my crutches though. As I lumber across the linoleum, I feel a tug on my sleeve, pulling me down and back.

"D," a voice says. "D, you swore, man."

Even before I turn around, I know it's Wes. And when I do spin to see him, his face is creased with worry. Stanford's behind him,

Pull   273

frowning away. "I told him we didn't need his noise here," Stanford says, "but he said you told him to come, D. That true?"

I've got no time to worry about trying to soothe feelings. I get right to the heart of it. "Look, Stanford. He's my boy. He asked me where I was and I told him. I didn't mean anything by it."

Stanford frowns again, but then his shoulders relax. "Fine," he says. Then he turns to Wes. "But don't come in my house shoving people out of the way. I don't care what kind of hurry you're in."

Behind them, the party starts to lurch back into action though people keep checking over their shoulders now and then to make sure everything's okay. Which it's not. I can tell that just by looking at Wes. Lia can sense it too. "Come on," she says, her breath hot on my neck.

I'm pulled in two directions. I have no doubt which one would be better for me. Alone time with Lia or a step into the static of Wes' life? That's a no-brainer. Problem is, Wes is right. I did tell him I'd be there for him.

"Talk," I tell him. "Tell me what the deal is." I hear Lia sigh behind me. This is going to cost me with her.

"It's no biggie," Wes says, but he's lying. He wouldn't be this out of sorts if it wasn't something big. "I just need you to hang on to something for me. Just, like, keep it in your car for a day or two."

And there it is. The same kind of noise that brought down Kid. "I don't have a car anymore," I say. "It had to go back to my uncle." I'm hoping that excuse will do, but I know better.

"Then just stash it somewhere," Wes says. He looks around frantically. Lia's listening in, tapping her foot on the kitchen floor impatiently. Stanford's still hanging there too, standing guard to make sure nothing bad goes down in his house. Wes fidgets under their stares, then points to the back door. We head that direction, but we don't go out into the cold. He just wants some separation so he can talk to me without the others hearing. "Look, D, I messed up. Big. Okay? Just tell me you can help."

I take a deep breath. I can still feel the stares from Lia and Stanford, plus half the rest of the party. "Fine," I say, "but you have to be straight with me. Tell me what's going on."

Now it's Wes' turn to take a deep breath. His eyes are glassy with weed or the beginning of tears or both. He doesn't even try to meet my gaze. When he talks, he looks right down at the floor. But he spills it. All of it. He swears that JaQuentin isn't truly part of a set, but that he's been dealing pretty heavy between 34th and 38th—"just weed," Wes says, like that makes it all okay. Wes was just hanging, not really messing with anything serious, until JaQuentin stole Norika Wheaton from him. This just a year after Wes lost Iesha to JaQuentin in the same way. And on top of it, JaQuentin was still hooking up with Iesha. "I just lost it, D," he says. "I just tweaked." So what did my boy do? He boosted some weed from JaQuentin to try and sell it on his own. That's what drew JaQuentin to our street that morning a while back. And if that wasn't enough, Wes got back in with him and did it again. "Once for Iesha," he says. "And once for Norika."

"Lord, Wes," I say. "What were you thinking?"

Now he looks back up at me. "I'm thinking I need your help," he pleads. "I tried to unload it to some guy in the GangstaVille Crew, but that went all kinds of wrong." I wait him out, let him keep spilling. "I showed up with half, and he jacked it. So now the rest is in my trunk.

And if JaQuentin catches me with it, he'll know it was me again. Last time it was just a few ounces, but now?"

"How much are we talking?" I ask. In a way, it doesn't matter. I'm not holding a single ounce for Wes no matter what. But I want to know just how deep a hole he's dug himself.

Wes hangs his head again. "It had to be like five pounds."

I deflate. Five minutes ago everyone was having a good time. People were laughing. Hell, Fuller was making it with a girl he'd just met. Now? I'm staring at a dead man. And I can't help him. Not the way he wants. I gather up the will to tell him, but then there's another disturbance at the door. And this time the people coming in aren't messing around. Instead of people rolling back in waves, they're pinballing off the walls.

"Step the fuck back!" someone yells.

And when people do as they're told—even Stanford, who briefly had his chest puffed out again—I see who that someone is. JaQuentin Peggs. With his inked up friend, the one Wes referred to as Flake.

For a second, it's just the two of them standing in the middle of Stanford's living room, everyone else pressing back toward the walls. The music still thumps away, but not a soul is moving. JaQuentin and Flake look from one person to the next, their eyes bloodshot but bent on destruction. Wes and I are tucked back into the kitchen far enough that they don't see us right away. "Wes!" JaQuentin hollers. "Don't play. I know you're here. Your ride's right outside!"

Nobody says a word in response, but one by one heads turn—all pointed back to the kitchen. JaQuentin and Flake march toward us side by side. When they reach the kitchen, Wes steps out to meet them. He holds his hands out like he's completely baffled.

JaQuentin's not having it. "Do not fuck with me, boy," he sneers. "You think you can play me? Where is it?"

"Where's wha—" Wes starts.

"Do not!" JaQuentin screams. He takes two big strides into the kitchen, stopping just inches from Wes. Stanford makes a motion to stop him, but Flake just puts a mitt in Stanford's chest, stopping him cold. "The stash or the cash," JaQuentin says to Wes.

Wes' jaw starts to move, but no words come out. JaQuentin's so livid I figure the only thing stopping him from acing Wes right here right now is all the witnesses. But this is going to end badly.

Lia steps to me and grabs my hand. She leans into me as if she needs my crutches as much as I do. And then I do something I wasn't even planning on. I don't even think. I just break free from Lia and lurch forward on my crutches. I position myself right between JaQuentin and Wes. Around me, I can feel everyone inhale, the way a crowd does just before I rise for a throwdown. Only now, they're anticipating something else entirely. "He's good for it," I say.

Slowly, JaQuentin raises his gaze from Wes and swivels his head to look at me. "Who the fuck asked you, Bowen?" he says. "Why don't you just limp back to your bitch over there and let me handle this."

I let my crutches drop to the floor with a clatter. I stand up as tall as I can, lording my inches over JaQuentin. *Stupid, stupid, stupid,* I think, even as I'm doing it. "He's good for it," I repeat. "Give him time, and he's good for it. And if you talk shit about Lia again I'll whip your ass right here, even on one leg."

JaQuentin squares his body to me. He leans forward and pulls

Pull   277

back one side of his coat. There, at his hip, I see the butt of a gun.
"Fuck you say?" he says.

It's all over, I think. In my head I hear all those warnings people
have been giving me all year, I hear the wail of sirens, I hear my
mother's sobs.

"He told you to step back," a voice says. I stop reeling and look to
locate the voice. It's Stanford. He swats Flake's hand away from him and
steps into the showdown. He gets between me and JaQuentin just like I
did for Wes a minute ago. "So you best listen up."

A body comes into the kitchen. Fuller—charging ahead like he's
been launched from a cannon. True to form, he doesn't have anything
smooth to say—just "Yeah!"—but it's emphatic enough as he positions
himself right next to Stanford.

Fuller looks back toward Reynolds, Jones, and Rider. They're
hovering by the edge of the kitchen and Fuller gestures toward them.
He's thinking that it's their turn to step in now. The whole team as one.
But they don't budge. Some would say they're worse teammates, but the
truth is they probably just have more sense than the rest of us.

There's an agonizing few seconds where nobody backs down.
And then, finally, JaQuentin blinks, his bluff called. He shakes his
head in disbelief. "Fine," he says. "You people are crazy." He nods to
Flake, and they both start to retreat. But then he re-thinks something
and turns around. He points a finger back at Wes, his thumb cocked
behind it. "It's worth three grand," he says. "Plus another grand for the
trouble. You better not make a liar out of your boy." And on that he
aims the finger at me. He steps my way. The wall of players between us
stiffens again. But, still pointing, he leans between Jones and Stanford

to whisper to me. "You get a pass on this one. Because, you know, ain't nobody want to see someone with your skills come crashing down. But, Bowen, you step to me again—ever—and you're just another body on the street."

Then they're gone. As soon as that door shuts behind JaQuentin and Flake, the chatter starts up. Everyone's all hyped to spin their take on it, texting and tweeting to friends. In the kitchen I bend down and pick up my crutches. Then I hug it out with Fuller and Stanford, offering them a thank you that can't even begin to get across what I owe them. Then I turn back to Lia—she's fuming, I can tell. But when I say we should hit it, she just nods.

Then there's Wes. He steps up to me, hand extended. "Thanks, D. You my boy," he says. Like I just did him solid by helping him on an algebra test or something.

"Don't give me that shit," I say. "You and I are sitting down tomorrow to figure this out. You're gonna be good on that money. And you ever put me in that kind of position again, I'll pull the trigger myself."

29.

We picked Sure Burger. Seemed neutral enough. And Kid suggested that people think a little clearer when they've got full bellies. Later tonight, it's Sectional finals. Normally that would have me hyped into the red, but right now I'm trying to keep my head straight. After last night, I know I put myself on the hook for Wes. I suppose if it all goes haywire, JaQuentin's going to be after Wes instead of me, but now this is partly my problem.

"Chill," Kid says. "Eat." He points to my fries.

I do as instructed, but I check my phone. Quarter after twelve. "Can you believe this? He's showing up late after last night?"

"This is gonna be okay, D," Kid says. I didn't dare tell Mom or Dad about any of this, but I wanted Kid by my side. He's been through enough messes like this to have a nose for them. He starts in on his bacon cheeseburger like there's nothing more important in the world.

Finally, Wes slumps through the door. He gives me a sheepish look. "Traffic," he says.

I inhale sharply at his ridiculous excuse. Kid and I took the same streets here, and it's not like this is rush hour. I'm in no mood for more nonsense.

Kid jumps in first. "It's cool, Wes," he says. "Just sit."

I turn to Kid, incredulous that he's going so soft on a guy that about got me killed. But Kid holds up his hand, a signal to take it easy. Plus, without even bothering to order food, Wes pulls up a chair. He's a tad more relaxed now. Maybe Kid knows what he's doing. Maybe he's been in Wes' position so often he knows that if you come at a brother too hard it'll just make him jet.

Kid already knows the story—Wes gave the weed that was left back to JaQuentin, but he's still on the hook for almost three grand— but he makes Wes tell it, just so we're all clear. When Wes finishes, Kid leans across the table. He's serious, but he's not trying to intimidate him. "That it? That's the whole thing?"

Wes starts to nod, then catches himself. "I also snatched a chain from his apartment one night."

Kid puts his hand to his forehead with a little smack. "For real? Does he know?"

"I figure he's got some suspicions," Wes admits.

This time I can't stop myself. "What the hell you thinking, Wes?"

Wes shakes his head, like I've asked the stupidest question ever. Then he looks straight at me. "Man, you don't get it. You hop from Jasmine to Lia. Two choicest girls in the city. And that's just how you get to roll. But me? I don't get a chance very often, and the guy nabbed two girls from me. Two!" He holds his fingers up in the air for emphasis.

"Wes, I get you were hurt, but—" Again, Kid holds his hand up for me to stop.

"Easy, people," Kid says. He gets this expression on his face like he's about to lay down some truth for us. I've had about enough of that. But when he starts in, I realize he knows what he's about on this topic. "You know, I'm not one to be lecturing anyone about doing stupid things. Hell, Wes might owe a few grand to a local thug, but I owe a lot more than that to the federal government. But one thing I recognize is that our basic problem is the same thing. We're both trying to be a man. Trying to be tough. Act big. Story of my life." He shakes his head, like he's thinking back on the long line of mistakes he's made. Then he plunges ahead. "You know who never acted all swole and tried to seem like a big man?"

Wes and I just stare at him, clueless as to the answer. Then Kid jerks his thumb at me. "Derrick's dad. My brother. He just buckled down and did his work. And, you know, a long time ago when I was around the age of you two, he tried to tell me. He told me that anyone who was trying to *act* like a man wasn't *being* a man." Then he points his finger at Wes. "Here's the other thing I've learned. When the cost comes due for acting that way, you've got to step up and pay it."

Wes nods in understanding, but then he puts his hands out palms up. "Yeah, but that's the thing. I can't pay what I owe. I gave JaQuentin back the weed I still had, and I can give him back the chain. But still. I don't have the dough."

Kid's got the answers this time too. He clicks them off one by one. First, he says to just mail the chain back to JaQuentin and never let on about it. Then he hits the money situation. He explains that JaQuentin's like anyone else—he may want people to think he's thugged out, but what he wants even more is his money. "You show him a little bit of the cash," Kid says, "you'll be surprised how patient he is for the rest."

Wes gets it, but points out that he still doesn't have any source of income.

Kid smiles a little. "Funny enough, getting a job is the best way to generate some cash flow. And I might be able to help." He explains that the bar where he works, Faces, could always use an extra set of hands cleaning up. When Wes points out that he's too young to work at a bar, Kid smiles again. "That's the beauty of a place like Faces. They really don't give a shit, and they'll pay you in cash to keep it off the books."

There, with the hiss of patties on the grill and the sound of the Coke machine churning ice, Wes looks like he's about to weep in gratitude. He practically lunges across the table to shake Kid's hand. "I can't thank you enough," he says. "You're saving me." Then he looks at you. "Both of you are saving me."

Now Kid's smile turns into a laugh. "Before you start hugging it out, let me be straight. This job is for lousy pay to come in at dawn and clean up puke and piss in the seediest bar in Indianapolis. It's not like I'm putting you in a corner office at Eli Lilly."

"I don't care, man," Wes says. "It's a chance." Then he looks at me. "Anything else?"

"That about covers it," I say. I want Wes to make it. I do. But I don't ever want to be put in last night's position again. And I want Wes to know it. So all I give him is a cold stare.

Wes stands to make his exit. I at least give him the courtesy of a handshake, but then he turns to go. The whole thing didn't even take long enough for Kid and me to finish our food. As I watch him leave, I wonder if Wes will ever be the same. If we can patch our friendship at some point. But I realize that at this point I barely even recognize the person walking out the door.

"Think he's going to make it?" I ask Kid.

"There's never a sure thing for young pups around here," he says. "Old dogs too, I guess. And, man, some income can help his situation, but let's not kid ourselves about the kind of people he'll run into working at Faces. If he wants to find more trouble, he'll find it there."

Outside, Wes pauses on the sidewalk to check his phone. He tucks it back in his pocket, then gazes around like he's not sure which way he wants to go. Then he moves on, heading south.

"If he wants to find more trouble," I tell Kid, "he's not going to have to wait for Faces. It's on any block he walks."

"True enough," Kid says. Then he starts polishing off the rest of his meal, looking away like he's deep in thought.

This time the family meeting's on my terms. Well, family plus Coach Bolden and Coach Murphy. When Kid and I get back, the others are already squeezed around the kitchen table. Kid ends up sitting next to Bolden. He looks about as comfortable as a prostitute forced to sit next to a preacher. But he toughs it out. He knows this is my time.

Kid knows what's coming. I've already told the guys on the team too. Still, as I reach into my back pocket for my list, I'm nervous. Telling Coach? Telling Mom and Dad? That feels as official as signing a letter of intent. So instead of just laying it out there for them, I feel the need to explain myself. "The schools on this list," I say, "are the ones that didn't waver when I tore up my leg. And they've done it all by the book like we asked. No crazy stuff." I take a deep breath. "So I want to take official visits to these places as soon as I can." And with that, I let the page flutter down on the kitchen table.

Jayson grabs it first, despite my parents' telling him to wait his turn. Kid just leans back. Dad notices and jabs a thumb in his brother's direction. "He already knows?" he asks me.

I just nod yes.

At first I think Dad's going to get mad, but he just nods. "Fair enough," he says. "Kid probably has as much insight on this as any of us." Dad sees us all react to his calling him Kid. "What?" he says. "You think I actually thought Sidney would stick? I know you all call him Kid when you think I can't hear you. So just go ahead. He's Kid." It's permission for the rest of us, but I realize that in a way this is Dad's way of forgiving his brother.

About that time, Jayson finally holds up the paper. "Hey!" he shouts. "Let's focus on Derrick, okay. You want to hear these schools or not?" I see his plan. He wants to be the one to break the news to everyone. And he clearly digs the chance. He flattens the paper out on the table and clears his throat, like he's about to launch into a monologue on stage. "First, Indiana," he says. Nods all around. No surprise.

"Michigan," Jayson says. More nods. I see Coach Murphy wrinkle his nose a little—for whatever reason, he's always bad-mouthing the Wolverines—but he sees me checking him and erases that sneer right away.

"Marquette." This draws a *Huh* from Dad, plus a quizzical look from Coach Bolden. It's not like Marquette is a nothing school. After all, it's in the Big East and it's where D-Wade went—but his stint there was a lifetime ago. And it's not like the Big East now is what the Big East was back in the day.

"Clemson."

Now I get the raised eyebrows all around. It's not like Clemson should be a shock. It's an ACC school, after all. Still, Mom's the first to ask. "Really? Why Clemson?" She's trying not to sound skeptical, but it shows through.

"It's an ACC school. Plus, their coach is from Indiana." Mom nods, but she's unconvinced. So I explain a little more. "I kind of like the idea of trying to knock off the Dukes and Carolinas and Louisvilles. I figure a Marion East player needs to be an underdog." That passes judgment for my mom. Then all eyes are on Jayson again.

"Alabama," he says. Even Jayson looks surprised on that one. It's an SEC school. I'd have the chance to knock off Kentucky and Florida each year. But it's football first there, and everyone knows basketball's an afterthought. Still, I realize that's not why people are so surprised. No. It's because of the geography.

This time Mom slaps her hand on the table. "Oh come on, Derrick," she says. "My dad didn't break his back to make it up here so his grandson could move to Alabama!"

I start to protest, but she's not having it. In fact, she clasps her hand over her mouth like she's going to be ill—the very thought of Alabama a noxious gas. She pauses a second, then stands and leaves the table. She mutters an apology to everyone else, then hurries off to the bathroom. I look back toward everyone else—every single eyebrow is raised in worry and surprise. I mean, I expected some resistance, but not like this.

Dad stands to get people drinks, doing his best to make extra noise in the kitchen so we can't hear if Mom's actually getting sick in the bathroom. When she comes back into the kitchen, smoothing her shirt as she walks, Dad just pauses and looks at her. "I'm fine," she says flatly. Then she sits at the table again like nothing happened. Jayson's the only one who dares to ask, but she cuts him off too. "I said I'm fine." Then she stares at me. "I was just a little surprised to find my son thought going to college in Alabama was a good idea."

"And don't forget that Clemson's in South Carolina," Jayson chimes in. That draws a withering look from Dad, but it shouldn't surprise anyone that Jayson's going to say the one thing that could make the room more tense.

Kid, Bolden, and Murphy all keep their mouths shut. They know they're here to lend support to me, but they don't dare cross Mom. So it's up to Dad. "Kaylene," he says.

"Oh, don't start talking to me with your *It's-all-gonna-be-okay* voice," she snaps. Then she looks at me again. "You know I'll support what you want. And it's sure not like racism ends once you get north of the Ohio River. But if you bring those coaches here for a home visit, you better believe they're getting some questions about what life is like for a young black man in the"—she breaks off, searching for the right word, her eyes bulging— "in the dirty South," she finishes.

Jayson can't help it. He snorts a few times, trying to choke back a laugh. But then he just loses it.

"What!?" our parents scream in unison.

He finally regains his composure and politely informs my mom that people her age are not supposed to use the phrase *Dirty South*. "I think it means something else than what you think," he says.

That loosens everyone up. It gives me a chance to explain that Alabama might be the heart of Dixie, but they've got a black coach who has NBA hardware. So if it's good enough for him, then I'm interested. Then everyone daydreams out loud about where I might end up. It's obvious that they're all pulling—in some small way, at least—for the Big Ten schools. But who cares? It's fun to just lose myself for a while, dream up back-to-back titles at Marquette. An undefeated run at Indiana. A Bowen-led Clemson squad dumping Duke on Coach K's court.

Finally Coach Bolden brings us back to earth. He explains our next step should be to contact the schools and to leak our list to the *Star* reporter, Whitfield. I hate the idea of giving him some scoop, but then I check myself. If the season's taught me anything, it's that most people are scrambling as best they can. It's not like Whitfield's getting rich off his gig, so maybe the guy could use a little inside information.

Then Bolden stands. He grabs his coat and reminds us that he's actually got a real game to prep for tonight. He looks at my parents. "I don't know the head coaches at those schools personally," he says, "but what I do know about them is all good. They seem to be the kind of guys that will help Derrick improve on the court. But they'll run his ass to class too. I know that's important to you both."

Mom looks like she could hug him. Kid slinks to the fridge, still not ready to engage with Bolden in any direct way. I decide it right then and there—when I take my official visits, Kid's coming with if he wants. Maybe it will be bittersweet for him, but these are the trips he should have been taking back in the day. I want him in this mix—as much for him as for me.

Kevin Waltman

30.

Pike's not messing around. As soon as they step out for warmups, their whole demeanor is different. Last time they were jacking up twenty-five footers, probably thinking they could beat us in their sleep. This time, they're pushing it. Devin Drew sprints through their lay-up line like he's been lit on fire. It only takes a couple minutes before he's got a full sweat up. When he sees one of their back-up bigs try a step-back—out of the guy's range, I guess—he lights right into him. And it's not like any teammates jump to step in. No. They just keep warming up with a military focus. These guys are out for blood.

So is their crowd. People are in their seats early, clapping and stomping. It feels like their energy raises the temperature in the gym by a few extra degrees. The past two years, we've stolen what they thought belonged to them—title of Sectional champs—and they want it back.

As the clock ticks toward zeroes, a swell of sound rises. Their band drives the crowd into a bigger frenzy. At first, they just play bass and drums in a slow, pulsing beat. Then the horns come in and the beat

Pull

gets faster. It's not so much a song as a methodic noise—louder and faster with each tick. And by the time the lineups are announced, the whole place is chanting on the insistent beat—*Pike! Pike! Pike! Pike!* When I was in uniform, scenes like this would have just got me more amped. Nothing better than hitting the mute button on a wild crowd. Now it just makes me anxious. I silently worry that my boys can't hang.

It doesn't take long to find out. Pike controls the tip and sets up. Their crowd hums in anticipation. Drew tries getting right to the rim, but Rider does a good job keeping leverage. So Drew kicks it to the wing, and they go to work. A look to the post. A reversal to the left wing. Then Drew comes flying off a down-screen and catches up top. Rider plays it right—comes at him with false pressure, but keeps his balance. Drew's not waiting around though. He dips that shoulder and goes. This time Rider can't contain him, and Drew knifes into the lane. The Pike crowd rises, expecting a finish at the rim. Then, *whap!* Stanford arrives at the last moment and deposits Drew's shot into the third row.

I guess we are ready to hang.

Our crowd thinks so too. As Stanford swaggers, chest puffed, our section of the crowd makes some serious noise. We don't match the Pike crowd in numbers, but we meet their volume and then some. Most of the energy from the crowd is for the same reason Pike's crowd is hyped—Sectional championship. But I know people have fallen in love with our team a little more this year. Everyone loves an underdog, and my boys have shown they still have plenty of bite without me. A couple weeks ago, maybe I'd have resented that—like they're getting special props just because I'm not around to save them—but not anymore. Not after watching these guys pull together. Not after last night.

"Keep after 'em," I shout. Only Reynolds is close enough to hear me over the roar of the crowd, but he nods in enthusiastic agreement. And he responds too. He recognizes Pike's inbounds play, cuts off the entry to his man, then peels off at the last second. They try to just lob it out top to Drew, but Reynolds jumps it. He beats Drew to the spot, leaps, taps the rock away. Rider scoops and pushes. Fuller trails, sprinting for all he's worth. Rider takes it all the way to the rim, draws Drew to him, then drops the rock off for Fuller, who rips down an easy finish. 2-0, but it feels like a statement.

And we're not done. Even before Fuller scored, Bolden was on his feet. He stomps his heel on the floor three times and screams. "Full! Full!" He waves with both arms, telling everyone to pick Pike up in a press. Everyone plasters to their man. Even Jones, who's still down on the defensive end, a good 70 feet from the action, bodies up. It catches Pike on their heels. Drew retrieves the ball to in-bound it. Their two-guard tries to shake free. He creates a little space from Reynolds, but Drew's pass comes low. It ricochets off their two's shin right into Reynolds' hands. His momentum takes him away from the bucket, but it gives him a second to gather. When he does, he spots Rider baseline, wide open. Reynolds rifles it to him. Rider catches, squares, rises. Wet.

This one prompts a quick timeout from the Pike bench. We're not even a minute in, and they can feel things coming loose. While their players hustle to the bench, their coaches gather in a tight circle on the court. From this distance, I can't hear what they're saying, but the head coach's head is bobbing up and down with such ferocity that the assistants lean back in fear.

On our end, Bolden's just coaching the boys up. "Remember," he

Pull   291

says, "their whole team is drive-happy. Even the bigs. That means help is important." He jabs his marker at Stanford. "Just like you helped on the first possession. That's got to happen for us again and again and again." Then he runs through some reminders about our offensive sets. When it's time to break, he just smiles. "Remember, this is what you practice for. This. You owe it to yourselves to lay it all out there tonight."

I swear Bolden still can get to me. Right now, I'm ready to hit the boards, crutches and all.

They give everything Coach could ask and more. Fuller's knees look rubbed raw from floor burns. Rider's sporting a welt on his cheek from a stray elbow. Stanford looks like he's lost twenty pounds in water weight from sweating it out in the paint. And Reynolds and Jones have done everything but gouge eyes and pull hair fighting for loose balls. Even Coach has given it everything, screaming himself hoarse at the refs.

But all the effort's taken its toll. The Pike coaches aren't dummies. Except for Drew, they keep a steady rotation going, exploiting our lack of depth. Coach Bolden has always hated going to the bench—he picks five or six players he trusts. He tells us if a healthy 18-year-old can't play 32 minutes of basketball a night, he might as well just retire. But I look out at the court now and see some wobbly legs on our squad. I peep at the scoreboard. We're nursing a four-point lead with 1:30 to go in the third. Pike ball. *Hang tight here*, I think. *Get a breather between quarters. Then let adrenaline take us home.*

Drew brings it up slowly. He checks the Pike bench for a signal from their coaches, then relays it to the team. Standing near the top of the circle, Rider's bent at the waist, his hands tugging down on his shorts. He takes a deep breath, like a boxer getting called out for one last round. Seeing that, I expect Drew to just attack, but he kicks it to the wing. They run a series of ball-screens—drive middle and look for the screener rolling to the bucket. When it's not there, they reverse to the other side and basically run it right back to the middle. It's nothing complex, but I can see it wearing us down.

We defend it cleanly through three straight reversals. Then finally Fuller gets hung up on a screen. Jones jumps to stop the driver, but that leaves Jones' man rolling free. Pike gets him the rock—but there's Stanford again, challenging. He doesn't get another rejection, but he alters the shot. It banks off toward the baseline. Reynolds crashes down to clean it up, but he can't get a clean handle. The Pike players pounce in a pack. Their center ends up with it, gets a decent look from twelve. Long. Stanford has it for a second, but can't squeeze the orange. Pike scrapes it away, and then it's Drew with it for a leaner in the lane. Short. This one drops to the floor and it's another scrum.

Our entire bench, every voice in our crowd, urges—*Dig it out!* Even as it unfolds, I know this—we get this stop, we can hold for the last shot of the quarter, go to the break up six or even seven. But Pike simply has more fresh bodies. They get a fourth shot, then a fifth. Then, finally, with Jones, Stanford, and Fuller all standing there flat-footed, Pike gets a tip-in to fall. Two-point game.

While the Pike fans rise in unison, everyone wearing a Marion East jersey slumps down a little. Bolden sees it. "Come on," he shouts to the other end. "Let's go! Bring it up! Keep digging!"

As Rider obeys, Bolden turns for a long look down the bench. I've seen this for three years now. He'll look toward the bench with hope, as if—in some great season-long secret—we've been storing James Harden there, just waiting for the right time. And, of course, it's always the same old bench. Guys he didn't trust enough to give minutes to back in November, let alone Sectionals. And me. On crutches.

It's a good thing he's turned this way. He doesn't even see it go down. At mid-court, Rider gets jumped pretty good by Drew. Rider is about to back up, but he's straddling the mid-court stripe. Confused as to whether he can go back or not, he looks at the ref. That's all the opening Drew needs. He pokes the ball free, then has a clean run-out.

Bolden hears the crowd react, then turns just in time to see Rider hack at Drew on the shot. It still falls, of course. Plus the whistle.

It wasn't for a lack of fight. Just a lack of depth. And talent. And maybe luck.

Pike 62—Marion East 53. Final.

No tears. We know that rule. But it stings enough for tears, that's for sure. I feel for the guys that put so much into tonight, who fought so hard. And I know that now my junior year is officially over. Sure, my minutes were done the second my knee buckled in practice. But this is different. The book's closed on three-fourths of my high school career. Just one shot left.

I make sure to go from player to player, telling them how proud they should be. It's met with nods and fist bumps from Reynolds, Rider, and Jones. They mumble a thanks, but that's all I'm going to get from them. Not a problem. They're beat down, and players have a right to sulk out a rough loss in their own way.

When I tell Fuller the same thing, he reaches up for a handshake.

Then he pulls himself up—I've got to pinch down on my crutches to help support him. Then Fuller just hugs me. "We gonna get it right next year, D," he says. "You and me, man."

We pull away from each other. I don't know what to tell him. But he knows where we stand with each other. And right now my goals aren't about rehabbing my knee or setting up campus visits or showing up recruiters who ditched me. It's getting back to Sectional finals with Fuller. Taking back the title. And more.

That just leaves Stanford. It's not like we've always been tight, but he showed me what he was made of last night. Thing is, that's that with Stanford. He's a senior. Fuller and I can comfort ourselves with talk of next year, about how we'll do this and that and everything. Stanford can't.

"I'm sorry," I say.

"For what?" he sneers. If he can't retreat into fantasies about future seasons, then Stanford's going to return to his tough-guy mode.

"For not telling you sooner that your thug face makes you look stupid," I say. Anger flashes across his face, but he knows I'm just messing. "Naw, man," I say. "I'm sorry for not being a better teammate when I had a chance. For real."

"Funny," Stanford says. There's a little mischief left in him, and it's his turn to mess with me. "I kind of figured you were going to apologize for almost setting off a shootout in my kitchen."

"Shiiit," I say. "I had that under control."

We laugh at each other's nonsense. Then it's a quick fist bump, and we're out. I head for the locker room door, but Stanford's got one last message for me. "D," he calls. I turn around. "Bring the truth on every damn body next year. No more messing around, you feel me?"

"I feel you," I say, and then I push on the locker room door.

There, in the half-light of the emptying gym, are my people. They could have waited at home like most families, but it's how they are. They want to see me before I climb on that bus. Mom and Dad give me quick hugs and shower me with all the clichés that are supposed to make players feel better. Then Kid just gets in my ear about schools. "I've been thinking it's got to be Indiana," he starts, and he just keeps right on rattling while we walk. All noise and rhythm, the old Kid again.

Then Jayson, who was hanging back a few feet, backhands me on the elbow. "'Bout time this season's over," he says. "Now maybe I can get some attention in this family."

I know he's joking, but I stiffen up on my crutches like I'm offended. "Listen, Jayson, because this is important," I say. I lean down to look him in the eye. "I always got your back, little brother."

He huffs and looks away. Then he speaks up to the darkened rafters, but still plain as day. "I know you do. I got yours, too."

31.

April in the city. Mid 70s. The streets shining in the sun.

And here I am, chilling with the finest girl in Marion East. No crutches. No setbacks. Just me and Lia on a Saturday afternoon, sipping Cokes on a restaurant patio on North College. Yeah, we get buses rumbling by and cars backfiring and the low thump-thump of bass in passing stereos, but this is as close as it gets to paradise. Until I make it to the L, that is, and sign a rookie contract fat enough to buy my own island.

We're solid, Lia and me. Sure, it took some smoothing after that showdown with JaQuentin, but with basketball over—and with no major work to get in until my knee heals—I've had plenty of time to make it up to her. No more over-the-top stuff either. With Kid still pinching pennies, nobody's throwing Pacers tix in my lap. And I'm not trying to wow her at fancy places downtown. We just chill on our blocks, go to movies, sneak in whatever action we can when the parents are gone. Just how people do.

"You do your exercises today?" she asks.

"First thing every day," I say.

"Good." She smiles. "I'm not into wasting time on scrubs. You best own the court next year."

"Oh, so you wouldn't hang with me if I weren't a baller?" I ask.

She smiles again. Drops her shades to conceal her eyes. "Well, maybe," she teases. "I mean, I'm kind of getting used to you at this point." She swirls her straw in her Coke, then sips from it.

"Good," I say. "I won't be able to play AAU this summer. I'll need someone to keep me entertained."

She laughs then, tells me I'm straight up crazy. Then, with her heel, she jabs my good knee under the table.

What's straight up crazy is being seventeen. Some moments, it feels like I could own this city. Got a girl. Got ball. Got a knee that's getting better and a whole future in front of me. And then I think about how flimsy it all is. One wrong step and that future comes crashing down. Or one wrong word at the wrong time and some guy like JaQuentin can blow out your match.

At home, things are holding together. But what happens the next time Dad's hours get cut? Or the next time Kid gets off the tracks? Or the next time Jayson decides he needs to act the fool? What separates us from the families that go under? I want to say it's because we're a little too tough, a little too smart. Maybe we are. Or maybe we're just stepping on the right spots of very thin ice.

I try not to think about it too much. Instead, I do those knee exercises like a religious ritual. Instead, I call Lia and feel good about life.

"Hey, Jasmine!" Lia squeals. "Where you been?"

I almost spill my drink turning to see. And there she is—Jasmine Winters. First time I've seen her in months. She looks good, as always.

Kevin Waltman

But there's also something off—some anxious tension in her face, a nervous twitchiness in her stance. She and Lia start chatting straight away, but their words merge into the sound of passing traffic. While they talk, Jasmine keeps glancing nervously at me.

I stare. My heart races. I feel guilty, like I'm cheating on my girlfriend.

And then it hits me, a cold dagger that cuts through the warmth of the day. As long as Jasmine was just some name on my phone, chiming in with a text now and then, I could ignore her. Hell, sometimes I hit delete and just doubled down on time with Lia. But now that she's here, flesh and blood, it all comes rushing back. I can feel the realization stretch forward into the summer, casting a shadow over all that lies ahead. Maybe I'm in love with Lia, or still falling in love with her—but Jasmine still moves me like nobody else can.

Jasmine won't look at me. In a way, I'm glad. If we locked eyes, I'm sure Lia would be able to read my expression. But it tells me that maybe Jasmine is thinking the same thing. Like maybe she's not peeping at me because she's all on fire too.

Forget it, I tell myself. Forget Jasmine. There's no going back in this life. You can't change the results of previous games, but you sure can derail the present by clinging to the past. I look at Lia, study her as she talks to Jasmine. She's the one who stuck with me through everything. And you know what? When I'm with her, things feel right. Like I'm not trying to be anyone special for her or play out some baller role. I can just be me. I never quite felt that way with Jasmine.

I scoot over closer to Lia, put my hand on her knee. Just that touch gives me the power to look up at Jasmine. "Long time," I say.

"Hey, Derrick," she says. "I know. Things have been crazy."

"Tell me about it," I say.

Then there's a long pause where nobody says anything. Finally, Jasmine sighs. "Well," she says, "I better get going. I've got to crack the books again."

We say our goodbyes, and everything's good. I just relax in the sun with Lia.

Only later do I see Jasmine's text on my phone, sent just a minute after she took off. *It has been a long time*, it says. *Too long. Let's hang sometime.*

I move to delete it, but I can't quite pull the trigger.

Kevin Waltman